I didn't like being the one hiding. The one sweating. When you're a cop you can almost pick up the scent of that sweat and the fear. You're usually on the trail of a stupid kid who's botched a job that seemed easy enough when all the factors weren't weighed.

Now I knew how it felt.

Icicles were melting in my arm pits and spilling down my torso. I'd acted on impulse, thinking I could pull it off with bravado and will power. I was starting to feel like I'd knocked over a liquor store and found my car blocked in...

A Gordian Knot Books Production — Gordian Knot is an imprint of Crossroad Press.

Copyright © 2020 by Sidney Williams
ISBN 978-1-952979-82-8
For information address Crossroad Press at 141 Brayden Dr., Hertford, NC 27944
www.crossroadpress.com

First edition

FOOL'S RUN

A SI REARDON NOVEL

SIDNEY WILLIAMS

Life's a fool's run on a crooked road. You have to find the best route you can.

—Richard Jasso
Prison Inmate

THE GIRLS

"**W**as most disappointing."
     Adam Holst flexed his fingers around his cell, his gaze falling on his wife, Grace. She sat at the end of a sofa, attention focused on a tablet computer propped against her curled legs. She looked comfortable and content in lounging pajamas. She didn't realize who he was talking to.

"Look, Val," Holst said. "I really want to apologize. Sometimes with politicians, you have things all wrapped up, then they get a better offer."

Alexeeva gave only a mild grunt.

"They think something will get them more votes, they're gonna chase that," Holst went on, improvising. "We'll get the next one."

"The contract, I was uh, counting it. Counting on it. That's it."

"Yeah, yeah, I hear you. There'll be other deals. We'll do business."

Grace looked his way now. Holst's tone and the mention of Val's name, Valentine Alexeeva actually, had not escaped notice.

A call from Val was serious. It indicated he wasn't taking bad news well. The deal he'd been hoping for had involved a vehicle maintenance contract with the city of New Orleans. Adam had worked with a couple of members of the city-parish council to help assure things went Alexeeva's way, but some details had soured. Holst had worried it wouldn't sit well in the Ukrainian's brain.

Something like a tire iron or wrench dropping on concrete sounded behind Alexeeva now. He must be in the flagship garage where he tended to spend much of his time. He'd be sitting in a swivel chair at a battered metal desk amid the oil and fumes wearing a Brookes Brother's suit fit for a corporate board room. He was working to become a polished American businessman, so he'd dropped the leather jackets and gold chains a good while back.

"You know, I don't like when my partners drop ball. Is important, someone keeps word."

"I warned you nothing's a hundred percent guaranteed."

Holst had risen, and he paced now, waving a gesture of reassurance at Grace as she pulled blonde tresses away from her face. With the mention of Alexeeva's name, everyone's temperature rose. He'd known going in working with Alexeeva put him in questionable territory, but he'd thought the deal was almost a sure thing, and making deals was his business.

"I hear you on that, too, Val. I thought the council members could be trusted."

"Lesson must be learned."

"Look, I know you want to expand into government contracts. We'll get there. We'll find…"

"You've checked the children's rooms lately?"

Holst froze, mid-step with more apologies still forming in his throat. His jaw wouldn't move, and his eyes stared into his wife's. He couldn't hide his terror even as he saw the exploding fear in her expression.

"What?"

"The children. You see them?"

"Grace, check on the girls, now."

Her expression mingled quizzical with horror.

"Now."

She sprang from the sofa. Bare feet fluttered across the carpet to the staircase, pajamas fluttering wing-like around her lithe form as she ascended.

"Look, Val," Holst said into the phone, "it's one fucking contract."

"But, to me, an important one."

Grace disappeared into the upstairs hallway as Alexeeva made him wait in silence. Holst's heart slammed his ribcage as the seconds ticked. Then Grace fluttered back to the second-floor railing, hair askew, eyes flaring with terror as she looked down at him.

"They're not in their rooms."

Alexeeva had heard. He chuckled. "No, no, I am scared they are not."

Damn him and his broken English. Why was he afraid they weren't? Holst didn't like the answer or the games. This was business, not something his family should be involved in. He was just a guy who connected people, greased wheels, turned a buck to assure that they had a nice house, he had great suits, and Grace had expensive lounging pajamas. He sailed through life on the self-image that he was a polished, smooth businessman. How had that turned into a mess with this guy?

He forced down anger. He had to reason.

"Look, look, look, Val. This isn't necessary. There are other deals. What do we need to do?"

He touched his forehead and pulled his hand back over his hair, dragging back locks that were wet and oily with perspiration.

"What does he want?" Grace screamed from upstairs.

"It is difficult to perform the act, how is it? Retroactively?"

"Right, we can't go back, but we can look forward. We're businessmen. There has to be something we can work out."

"What are names?" Alexeeva asked.

"What do you...? Dagney is the youngest. She's seven. Dahlia is thirteen."

They had blond hair like Grace's, and they were slender like her, Dahlia gangly at the moment, Dagney still cute with baby fat on her cheeks and dimples, destined to be the beauty. They must be sitting across from Alexeeva now.

How could it be that a half hour ago Holst and Grace had stood over each and touched lips to foreheads before leaving their rooms with only nightlights?

How had they not heard something?

Alexeeva kept a filthy old sofa across from his desk and liked making people in suits sit on it for meetings. They must be terrified, sitting there, clutching each other but Holst couldn't hear any whimpers over the phone. Alexeeva would have them flanked by henchmen. Flanking the girls, wearing suits less elegant than Alexeeva's, he probably had Taras Seleznyov and Nestor Zhirov on hand. Taras, the brainy one, probably looked over nervously at the man-mountain that was Nestor. Taras might feel a little more empathy. Nestor would follow any order without question.

Holst had to talk, to reason.

"Val, there's another possible deal coming up. It involves an ambulance fleet. You know those are expensive. They like to re-do the guts of those, save the body and chassis."

"Confusion, Mr. Holst, has set in. This is not the negotiation. This is the retribution. I wanted to give you the opportunity for your, um…." He covered the phone for a moment, consulting with someone. "Your goodbyes."

"Jesus, Val. Come on. City contracts are up for renewal all the time. We'll get it the next time. Big picture. I'm going to Baton Rouge next week."

"Concerns me why?"

"I'm going to be talking to some…state House members… You know, the Legislature. State contracts."

The son of a bitch was sitting there checking his nails. He kept them perfectly manicured these days. He sat with a manicurist buffing and filing where another assistant had his dick in her mouth because he was lusting after respectability. With the nails.

Holst flushed that thought. It didn't need to be with him while he was talking about the girls. What would Alexeeva have in mind for them?

Holst couldn't threaten as well as Liam Neeson could.

"House? Not as good as Senate, right?"

"There are going to be some opportunities…"

"Daddy."

Dagney's voice.

It sounded far away and hollow. Alexeeva had lifted the phone toward the girls.

"Sweetheart? We'll get this worked out."

"Youngest cries. Older one, very quiet."

"Put them on, let me talk to them. These opportunities, Val.

They're north. You don't have much north. It's new territory for you. Very good business."

"Long drive, sorry."

"We have to be able to work out something. Please, don't send them to anywhere, you know. Don't let them...."

"You worry they will go to work in sex world?" He just chuckled.

Grace had floated down the stairs in a near daze. She dropped beside Holst on the sofa, gripping his shoulder as she leaned toward the phone.

"Val, please. Whatever you're planning. Let me talk to them."

"I hold up phone again. Might be wise, not promise, just speak."

Holst tilted the phone toward Grace.

"Dahlia, Dagney. It's Mommy. I'm sorry, babies, we're going to try...."

"Enough," Alexeeva said. "No promise, I said."

Holst pressed the phone back to his ear. His palm had covered it in sweat, but he gripped it tight.

"Come on, Val. Val, talk to me. I can find other opportunities. I have lots of connections."

Nothing.

"Val?"

"Is important to live up to commitments. Mr. Holst, Mrs. Holst, very sorry. Enjoyed dinner the last time I was there."

The sound that followed was unmistakable. A gunshot. From Nestor's weapon—some big, black sidearm of the Russian manufacture he preferred? He called it the Strike One.

Jesus.

"Val, please...."

A weapon roared again.

Then Holst sat listening to silence. Alexeeva had disconnected the call, and Grace sat beside him.

Weeping.

PART 1
THREE YEARS LATER
REARDON

CHAPTER 1

I wouldn't have agreed to meet with the woman at all under normal circumstances, but my circumstances hadn't been normal in quite a while. When she called on my new, disposable cell, I was wandering the French Quarter and, amid all of the tourists and ongoing sense of festivities, wondering where my ex-wife had taken our daughter. I'd just bought a bottle and was thinking I might, for expediency, employ someone to help drink it. I scanned the crowd for the right candidate.

I'd just been turned down for a job. Guy thought I'd been served a raw deal, but still the name Silas Reardon had been in too many headlines. The fact my conviction had been overturned was a technicality he didn't really want to debate. Didn't change the media coverage. No crooks nor perceived crooks on the payroll. He was an old friend named Gilbert Lombardi, and he hadn't been my first stop. Nobody wanted to dance with me.

It was on that thought that the phone jibbered, the cell I'd purchased to have a call back number was seeming like a waste of my cash, even though it had felt like an expression of freedom in the moment. I hadn't been allowed to own one while I sweated out my time inside David Wade Correctional's cinder block walls.

I answered, hoping someone had had a change of heart, decided I was at least worthy of following an errant husband around and fished my resume out of the trash.

"Mr. Reardon?"

A crisp, professional and efficient voice. A little deep and a little sultry. Almost as interesting as the brunette I'd noticed leaning against a corner near Pirate's Alley.

"Yeah?"

"My name is Rose Cantor," came the voice from the phone. "I've followed your case in the news."

She sounded nice, but the brunette across the way was slender with graceful, almost feline movements, about 20 with a cultivated college girl look. Maybe she took some courses at UNO. Subtle touches for a girlfriend experience.

"Fame's not all it looks like in the tabloids," I said.

"I thought we might talk."

So, Rose Cantor had the number. She knew somebody. Somebody I'd talked to recently. She couldn't be just a random groupie who'd fixated on a cop in the news, but I couldn't rule her out as a representative of one special interest group or another. I'd had letters from lots of them when I'd been doing time, marking off calendar days in the protective unit in North Louisiana.

"What's this about?" I asked.

"A possibility."

I'd turned down various fringe group offers during the appeal. The offers hadn't come with any big payouts. My new attorney, Clinton Laroque, hadn't turned his meter off, but he had advised against aligning myself with anything high profile or even anything sketchy. Since the possibility of re-trial rested in the prosecutor's hands, that recommendation still held.

I said: "What's the offer?"

"This would just be a conversation."

My potential employee walked away on a fifty-something tourist's arm, getting lost in the crowd.

I said: "Why not?"

Rose exceeded expectations by parsecs.

As I walked into the restaurant bar, she slid off a stool, but I almost passed, thinking she wasn't even a possibility. Then she extended her hand.

"I'm Rose."

I had to force myself not to hold on too long as I took her in. Five-six, tight black suit, open enough at the throat to be interesting. Long brown hair, grey-green eyes, full lips and sculpted cheekbones. The hair was swept mostly to her right side with curls resting on her shoulder. She'd passed forty, but she didn't give the years much opportunity to show. Toned arms and trim legs were obvious beneath the fabric. She worked out though not to an excess that made her look all muscle and bone. I took my hand back, and looked into her professional smile as a bit of flowery perfume caught my nostrils.

"What brings me to this little corner of heaven?" I asked.

"I have some clients who'd like a word with you."

"You're an attorney?"

"The shingle formally reads special counsel."

"That's suitably ambiguous."

"Would you like a drink?"

Her glass of white wine sat on the bar showing beads of condensation.

"I'm fine."

"Nothing at all?"

If she was going to twist my arm: "Bourbon. Little ice."

Perhaps ironically, the bartender poured Four Roses, and we settled onto barstools. I looked over at the mirror in the dim light.

I wore the charcoal suit bought for the most recent round of hearings. On the street earlier, I'd tugged my tie away from my throat as the humidity gnawed at me but I looked okay. I'd had a haircut before I'd left N-5 Special Management Unit where I'd done my time alongside other convicted law enforcement officers and child molesters. The rooms there hadn't been air conditioned so I'd spent enough time outside to avoid the pallor that often comes with incarceration.

"Who gave you my number?"

"Not who you think. Don't spend too much time analyzing that."

"Jerry really seemed to feel sorry for me."

"Wasn't him. Would you be willing to have a conversation with some people?"

"Do I have to appear at gun shows or any political rallies?"

"I don't think it would be that public."

Something started to tingle. Maybe this wasn't quite the offer I'd first assumed.

"You're not up on the details?"

"I'm not really into the minutia," she said.

She turned on her stool and I eyed the soft, smooth flesh of her throat as I took in more of her smell. I pushed away thoughts of what would've been said by Richard Jasso, the con who'd come close to being a friend in N-5. Let's just say it would have been crude.

She didn't deserve crude. She wasn't suggesting anything with the turn, just trying for a better view of my expression, but I felt a deep burn. Her tan was better than mine, glistening with just a hint of the humidity. I tried to hide the effect she was having, to keep it noncommittal, but she could tell I was at least intrigued.

"You'll get a meal in a nice place. Hear some people out. You decide to walk away, it never happened."

I looked into her eyes, at her full lips and took another whiff of her, and fought to keep my head clear. Wasn't easy. I'd been inside a long time and my wife had been gone longer than that.

"What the hell?" I said.

CHAPTER 2

"I think we may be a little crowded tonight."

The maître d' scanned a sheet on his podium.

Rose had deposited me at the corner near a pastel orange building with black ironwork a few blocks off Bourbon. Inside, lighting was low, supplemented by a few aquariums set into the walls, glowing with brightly colored fish and coral. It all looked a little nicer and featured a better atmosphere than the communal dining I'd grown used to.

"Would you mind sharing a table? We have a spot in one of our private rooms." If he was putting on a show, it was a good performance.

When I said that was not a problem, he ushered me back to a little area with just a few candlelit tables off the main dining room. Only one was occupied: a couple in their early forties, sitting, stiff and not quite shoulder to shoulder. A suit and a black dress. The man had well-tended, greying curls and looked lean with long arms. The woman: blonde, slender and angular but possessing rounded cheeks. The brown eyes harbored a soft innocence though it lingered beneath a hazy, haunted veil.

"So nice to have company," she said, as I settled into a chair.

"Can I start you off with a glass of wine?" the waiter asked.

"Bourbon. Whatever brand's open. A little ice."

The man extended his hand. "Adam," he said. "My wife, Grace."

I shook the man's hand. The woman gave mine a quick squeeze.

"I guess you know who I am, or else the guy up front really is expecting a bus."

"We know, Mr. Reardon." The wife smiled a faint smile. Grace, it was easy to think of her by that name.

A heavy crystal glass with a splash of amber-gold in it landed in front of me, and I picked it up for a sip and a burn.

"I guess you can solve the mystery I've been living with for the last few hours."

I'd had time for only a little checking on Rose Cantor. Her shingle really did say special counsel, and it hung from a prestigious firm. They'd reached some sort of arrangement that was mutually beneficial.

Grace smiled again. That seemed to be the affirmative. Then she reached for a clutch purse that hung on the back of her chair, producing a small black folder. It looked like something that would hold the invite for an elegant cocktail party. She drew out a heavy paper photo card with other pictures tucked inside it.

I flipped it open to find a family portrait, a vertical of the couple across from me, younger by a few years and looking a bit warmer in general. In front of them, blond children smiled for the camera. More pictures were loose in the folder, the girls aged slightly if you flipped through them.

In one, the older of the two had been caught at play on a sunny day, a huge bubble with traces of rainbow forming behind her from the tennis racket-sized wand she held. Her smile was wide, her face aglow.

"Dahlia," the woman said.

The younger smiled with an effervescent glow from a studio shot, wearing overalls, sitting on a bale of hay with appropriate props scattered around her including a wash tub and a cowboy hat discarded to avoid hiding her wavy tresses.

"And Dagney."

"They're beautiful children." It was the kind of thing you were supposed to say. It was true, and of course they reminded me of Juliana. Was that by design?

"They're gone," the woman said.

The solemn finality made it clear they weren't visiting a grandmother in Seattle.

"What happened?"

"They were murdered."

I tossed back a swallow of the bourbon and looked at the photos on the table again. A chill gripped me. It was one of the fears that stalks the imagination of every parent.

"How?"

"It was part of a lesson," Adam said. "For me."

Tears came to Grace's eyes.

"What were you involved in?"

"I was involved with a man," he said. "In business. I didn't realize quite what he was tangled with. Or had been"

"Which was?"

"Previously the Vory. Do you know what that is?"

"I know what the justice department says it is or used to. It's a matter of some debate, but's it's supposed to be an affiliation of criminal organizations in the Russian vicinity."

"There's no doubt about his activities in Southeast Europe. Name the crime. Even when he rose, he liked to do some of his own dirty work. He worked to establish himself with a little more legitimacy in the U.S. after a couple of Europol operations broke things up for him back home."

They didn't look like people who'd even know what Europol was. I barely did. It wasn't the kind of crime you encountered in day-to-day police work.

"His activities being...?"

"The usual early on. They call it transitional crime when it crosses borders. Blackmail. Extortion. Human trafficking. He's cleaned up his act a little, but his hands are dirty."

"Bloody," Grace Holst said. "Even though he's gained even more respectability in the last few years, polished himself a little more."

Adam looked at her then nodded affirmation.

"You wanted to work with Keyser Söze anyway?"

Grace shot a hard look at her husband with that question, and any lingering innocence was replaced with a black, stone-cold hatred that made apparent why they were still shoulder to shoulder.

"A lot's become clearer in the interim," he said. "He seemed a little rough around the edges, but I didn't know all of that then.

Like I said, he wanted some legitimacy. I was trying to help him get some city contracts for mutual benefit. Not my best decision, but he'd ditched the gold chains by then, and he didn't have a lot of tattoos and everything like the bad guys do in movies."

"Contracts didn't work out?"

"Palms were greased. Promises were made. This is New Orleans. You know how things go."

"Somebody else had more grease?"

"I didn't have people on tight enough leashes. He was unhappy."

"The girls disappeared from our house one night, and we got a call," Grace said. "A call that couldn't be verified as to its source, of course."

She had to grab for a napkin and dab her eyes before makeup was affected.

"Nothing could be proved," she said.

"Cops?"

"They made an effort. You got a sense they were being careful, but they tried. We had private investigators. They tried too. There was nothing that would stick to him. No proof we'd talked to the girls on a phone call, no proof he'd been near them."

"I don't see what I might turn up that the authorities missed. I'm sure they took this seriously, and I wasn't Sherlock Holmes when I was on the job. It's not like the movies."

"We didn't come to you for more investigation," Adam said. "If we ever had any illusions, they're long gone."

"I know there's a lot of pain," I said. "I can imagine anyway. I have a child."

"The best imagination couldn't capture it," Grace said.

"I'll stipulate to that."

"You'd probably acknowledge too there's nothing we could do to bring the girls back. We know that. We know anything you accomplish wouldn't bring closure, but it would be something. It would keep it from happening to someone else."

"It would do that. I'm just not the man to handle that."

She leaned forward, resting her arms on the table as she looked at me.

"The other day, I read about an abduction that was stopped

in Gretna. A man tried to snatch a girl away from her mother in broad daylight. While they walked along in their neighborhood. The mother fought the man, but he dragged the girl into a car anyway and almost got away. Some neighbors were near and helped stop him and save the girl. When the police arrested the man and ran a check on who he was, they found there'd been a similar incident. A girl who wasn't so lucky."

I closed my eyes and bowed my head. You didn't have to look far for bad things.

"There'd been an attempt to prosecute him. For that case, for what he did. The previous victim stopped cooperating. I keep asking myself, what if something had been done in that case. What if something could be done with ours? Who might it help? Some other child, some other family wouldn't have to have their world shattered."

The tears began then. I had to presume they were real and not calculated. She had every reason for them to be real.

I didn't move. These were haunted people connected by a single purpose with all else behind them lost, including any love that had once been there. They were clutching at something, hoping.

"What is it you want me to do?" I asked.

"We have a proposition," Grace said, dabbing at her eyes so that the little black square of a napkin caused minimal irritation. She put the napkin aside and stared across the table at me with more fervor.

"We want you to kill the devil, Mr. Reardon."

CHAPTER 3

Of course, I said no.
Hell No.
Fuck No.
Before there could be further discussion.
Before there could be debate.
Before they brought the demitasse cups.

The meeting had been set up well. Happenstance in a public place. If anyone could even be found to recall a guy in a suit passing through the dining room. If any security footage was found. If a crime were actually committed and an effort at establishing a criminal conspiracy came somewhere down the road.

I'd worked a case once where we believed a businessman had had his business partner killed for the payout on an insurance policy. The defense attorney had made his meeting with the trigger man an asset. "Jake Gremillion is a prominent businessman. Would he be stupid enough to go to a meeting in the middle of town at the murderer's place of employment?"

The triggerman had not been the most competent of professional killers, a sociopath who managed a retail establishment. He'd seemed innocuous enough until you looked at the record he lied about to get that job and knew he had no connection with the victim except through the partner.

This meeting would be even more easily dismissed. No explaining why I'd been at a private residence, no real connection. Just "the restaurant was crowded and we got thrown together." It wouldn't seem out of the question a guy not long out of lockup had wanted a good meal.

But I still beat it the hell out of there. I couldn't be connected with the fumes of anything illegal. I wasn't technically a convict at the moment, but a second offense wouldn't look good on my record. I didn't pass Go and didn't wait on the curb for Rose to turn up again.

I hoofed it up to Bourbon and insinuated myself into the stream of tourists and gawkers, a thick, interwoven mass of humanity that marched past barkers and promises.

"We've got the prettiest boys in the city...."

"Men for the women, women for the men. Come right in. Come right in."

"The show is just beginning...."

It'd still be just beginning at 1 a.m.

Bourbon's a surreal carnival any time, and that night I felt more lost in the middle of it than ever, jostled by tourists, caroming. I let the odor of beer and drinks in red plastic Solo cups fill my nostrils, dodged drunk guys dancing, gaggles of tourists four abreast giggling, let the noise and the insanity envelop me and let myself believe nothing was real.

Then I was in a bar around a corner from one of the strip clubs. I had a glass in front of me with something else amber on ice. I sipped and I watched a girl of about 22 in a white blouse and black slacks hurrying a new rack of glasses out for the bartender.

She wasn't Sandra, of course. The odds would've been incredible of just stumbling on her, but for a second, she became my ex-wife until I shook my head and sipped another swallow.

She was younger than Sandra, but Sandra's skills included bartending and, when she needed the work badly, the more laborious bar-backing, everything from washing glasses to lugging fresh cases of liquor from the stock room. It could be shitty work, but it meant she could be almost anywhere, under most of the radars that blipped when resumes and references were checked.

I'd heard mention of Florida from a friend who'd noticed something on social media. That seemed possible. It put a good bit of distance between her and Louisiana while offering a world not too alien the way a northern city might. A search, with the restrictions of a prisoner had made confirmation seem like a search for a raindrop in river rapids. Even these days.

Whether it was true or not, I often pictured Juliana walking in the surf, sea wind tousling her hair, her tiny feet leaving faint impressions in damp sand. I wanted to be with her there, running with her, splashing in incoming waves. Instead I stared at cinder block walls or at a sky framed by the correctional center's surrounding fences.

"There are ways to find your ex," my friend Jasso had said during a session of catch, his greying mane tousled by wind at his back. "Some calls, friends of friends. She's on planet Earth, she can't hide."

"I'm not interested in having her intimidated."

"Nobody said anything about intimidated. Found." It still sounded menacing.

"Not right now. It starts looking like I really might get out, that search could do some good. I'll get back to you."

"Suit yourself." Words dragged across his tongue in a laconic drawl that seemed to add vowels.

I stared now into glistening glasses dangling from overhead racks and rows of whiskey, rum, and vodka bottles. Sandra's job would have been washing and polishing those glasses, placing them carefully, among other tasks. She'd hated the hours and the dish washing, called it soul destroying when I'd met her while canvassing for possible witnesses, trying to find a guy who'd mugged an old man.

She had despised the hours, the toll on her back and her hands. She'd been happier when she got an office gig once we were married and had toyed with courses as a radiology technician, but bar work would do to take her far away from me.

I'd lost a lot for a stupid, off-the-books effort with my partner. I didn't need to make more mistakes. I ordered another drink. Speaking of mistakes, I'd left my bottle stashed in Rose Cantor's car.

CHAPTER 4

The thought that I should check into Rose Cantor further crossed my mind, but I had other priorities the next morning. I woke looking up at the canopy of the antique bed in my little guest house room. It was better than waking on my prison bunk, and I just didn't feel that inspired to call people who might have given her my name. They'd just rejected me anyway.

Someone must have meant well.

I had one more old friend to try for work in my field before I went to job listings on Craig's List where I'd been told the opportunities in New Orleans might be interesting.

I checked my reflection in an antique mirror with a dark wooden frame. I looked slightly younger than the oak, but my sandy hair was only a little neater than Trotsky's. Dark circles formed chasms under my eyes, and my upper lids were puffy. I didn't need to apply for any male modeling gigs.

As I stepped back, I wondered what Julianna's face would look like today since children's faces change so quickly, and I hadn't seen her in a year and a half.

Sounds of her as an infant, the soft little gurgle from the crib came back to me. She'd gone from there to walking while I'd been kept busy by the job. Her little coos and babbles had turned into talking for her mother first as well.

A lot of other milestones had passed now. I had no idea what markers, but as I imagined a taller and clear-eyed version, I found myself willing to beg for a security guard's checkpoint tracker, or whatever they used in these high-tech days, and willing to put on any cap and uniform polyester shirt.

A blonde receptionist who looked about 19 put me in a small square waiting room off the lobby of Clement Security even though Jerry Clement had told me to drop in around 1 p.m.

I'd donned a fresh blue shirt with the courtroom suit and a crisp new tie, red with little blue diamonds. Someone in the shop where I'd bought it had told me it should be good for job interviews. I'd been clean-shaven when I arrived. I wondered how much of a shadow I'd have before anyone saw me.

I'd never really liked Jerry. He talked faster than an auctioneer and louder than Al Hirt's trumpet. He was showy and superficial, and somehow a lot of people failed to see through it. My curse was that I could, and he was still my last life preserver.

I read through a stack of issues of *Security* magazine and felt versed in the best software choice for physical security information management when I finished. All of it was exponentially more interesting than it would have been under other circumstances, even in my old bunk.

I was fighting the urge to yank the tie away from my throat and unbutton my collar when the receptionist stepped into the doorway, as cool, efficient and demeaning as any prison guard.

"Mr. Clement can see you now."

I followed her back through the lobby and along a narrow hallway. The building had been a residence once upon a time, but renovations had given it an innovative feel, and a decorator had placed edgy still lifes in steel frames and other strategic items to make it feel cutting edge.

Behind his cherry wood desk, more shiny silver frames featured pictures of Jerry with New Orleans leaders and Louisiana governors, the ones without indictments or convictions. I suspected the wall would face more editing after the next round of grand jury sessions. We were in New Orleans, and in the bigger picture Louisiana. Huey Long once said the officials serving under him would wind up in the penitentiary if they were ever left unchecked with the power he'd given them. After he was assassinated, that proved true, and it always seemed to repeat. Katrina washed away a lot, but not the corruption.

The current iteration of Jerry sat at the desk in a lavender shirt he'd never have worn as a detective. He poured over an electronic tablet. His hair had been clipped into spikes on top to de-emphasize the thinning. A comb-over would've done the job in his cop days.

"Have a seat," he said without looking up.

The guest chairs were covered in forest green vinyl. I managed to choose one that exhaled as I settled in.

"You've been on an interesting ride, Si."

"That I have."

"Technicalities are what it all turns on."

"They wanted to make an example of me." Speaking of trying to stop corruption post Katrina.

"I'm glad things turned around. My gut clenched when I read that first verdict in the *Picayune*. Then the sentencing. Jeeze."

He lifted his head from the tablet. His long face bore a few more wrinkles than I remembered, mostly around the eyes, but he had a nice tan. He'd either found some time for Aruba or a tanning bed.

"All a big show." He shook his head. "What are you looking for?"

"Something to keep me busy until I run for sheriff."

That brought a chuckle, but after a while he shook his head again. It seemed to make him sad and tired. He wished I wasn't there, but he didn't want to throw me out.

"Half of what I do here is image."

No shit, I thought, but kept it to myself.

"I didn't think you'd put me on the marquee, but I can handle the stuff that's not glamorous. I'm even ready to put on a uniform and stroll around warehouses."

"Word would get around. Wouldn't take long, I'd be the firm with the gunslinger on the payroll. Make some people nervous. Big clients."

It was the same song with more specific verses. Had everybody I knew gone to the same choir rehearsal?

"Maybe it could be a selling point."

That produced a little exhale that was part of a nervous laugh.

"Anything on the software side? I could get up to speed on

the cyber. I did a lot of reading while I sat around my cell."

"Then I got an ex-con behind their firewalls. I can't do it. You know the drill. I would if I could."

"Come on, Jerry. You've got people on your client list that have to keep their sleeves rolled up because they're elbow deep in so many cookie jars."

"Different kind of dirt, my friend. Best I can do is be a reference, say I'm confident you're on the straight and narrow."

"Where the hell else am I going to go with that rec?" If he referred me to Gilbert Lombardi, I was ready to throw a punch. "No offense, Jere, but you weren't my first stop."

"No offense, but that means I'm not the only one with regrets." He stood and offered a hand. "Good luck."

I let his hand stay open, waiting for a while, but finally I accepted and gave him a shake.

Then I thought about dialing Rose. To find my bottle of bourbon.

CHAPTER 5

I walked the Quarter a while instead, turning down shoe shine offers and looking for something to take my mind off my problems. I'm not proud of that fact, but that's what I was doing when I noticed the guy on my tail.

Maybe the wraparound sunshades provided my first tip or maybe it was just instinct. I'd been a cop trying not to look like a cop a time or two in my other life. This guy had a bit of that tinge. To go with the shades, he wore a light black jacket in the Members Only style over a black tee with a tight little rope of stones around his neck just above the collar. The stonewashed jeans had a lot of white stitching. Maybe that had become the style while I'd been inside. I hadn't had a chance to visit a GAP or whatever shop the kids were frequenting to figure out what the cool crowd was wearing.

Showy watch, rings. Silver band on the right wrist. Could have been bad taste or the kind of thing a cop might choose to accessorize. Same thing with the hair. Dark with iron grey encroaching, combed straight down in front, probably with too much attention and a bit of styling spray. Every time I looked back along Decatur, he was 300 feet behind me, taking an interest in something in a shop window or on the other side of the street. He had to be either working for Rose or one agency or another who wanted to catch me stepping out of line. Prosecutors tend not to like hangnails, and they've been known to keep picking at them.

I worked my way through the crowds over to the French Market. If he followed me there, I'd have a pretty good indication we weren't just seeing the same sights. He didn't look like

someone in the market for garden vegetables. Maybe costume
jewelry.

Once I'd moved through the market's entry arch, I strolled
a while under the canopy past purses on posts and alligator on
a stick. I had to weave around guys in polo shirts and soccer
moms in sun visors, but I'd soon found my way deep enough
in to pause in front of a hot sauce display and take a look back.

He'd managed to keep about the same distance. He was
testing the texture on a tote bag with New Orleans printed on
the side and featuring a rendering of the Quarter by an artist
imitating LeRoy Neiman. The guy acted as if a purchase might
be imminent.

If he wanted a souvenir tote, it'd be to conceal a handgun.

I made my way along the path between the displays until I
could get into the open again. Then I moved at a brisk pace onto
the Decatur sidewalk, heading on around a corner of a narrow
street called St. Philips. Casual pursuit on his part had ceased
to be an option.

I had to hoof it further than I wanted to find a spot to slip
into, moving up the street past little cafes, small businesses and
residences with black ironwork along second floor balconies.
Iron gates also covered a lot of doorways. That meant locked
gates.

After a block and a half, I found an open alley between pale
buildings and ducked in there, then peeked back around the
corner. I'd managed to disappear in an instant the tough guy
wasn't looking my way. He strolled the sidewalk, turning his
head fractions to each side, the shades looking like a scanner
gradually panning the perimeter.

A cell came out of a hip pocket, and he spoke to someone. I
welcomed the distraction. I waited, leaning against the wall, my
heart picking up speed beyond the exertion I'd expended to get
here. I countered that with deep breaths and still had to wait a
few more seconds before he neared my spot.

I didn't catch what he was saying just before I grabbed
handfuls of his jacket. That interrupted his thought, and he
babbled a complaint just before I yanked him from the sidewalk
into the space between the buildings.

As I slammed his back against the wall where I'd been pressed and leaned in on him, jamming a forearm against his throat, I noted the newness of his clothes. They were crisp and fresh and had been on the rack recently.

He tried to struggle against me, so I grabbed the cell and listened as I stepped back. I caught just a snippet of a woman's voice before a sentence finished.

"Hello," I said.

Whoever was on the other end didn't respond to a new voice and the screen's face logged the caller as unknown. A disposable cell like mine? I listened until the connection broke. Redial just got me a series of unanswered rings then a generic electronic voice mail message.

I tossed it back to him and stayed out of swinging range. If I'd wanted to fight him, I would have taken my coat off. I didn't want to be slinging punches when and if his sidekick showed up. Effective surveillance usually requires two.

"Why are you watching every step I take?"

Maybe I'd plant a musical earworm that would annoy him all day if nothing else.

He grumbled something that trailed into: "...the fuck you're talking about."

"Buy any produce or hot sauce in the market?"

He just aimed the sunshades my way.

"Cop?" I asked.

That produced kind of an angry sigh, like I'd asked the inevitable question he didn't want to answer. He slowly pulled out a badge case. Joseph Culler.

"I'm not on the job."

"Take it from me, that can get you in trouble. Who asked you to follow me?"

"I work over in Destrehan."

"Who?"

"Ronnie Lehto's widow."

"How long you been following me?"

"Part of yesterday, 'til you walked out of Gilbert Lombardi's office and bought a bottle. Figured you weren't going on another job interview with that."

Wrong about that, but at least he hadn't seen me being party to an illegal offer.

"What does Joy care what I'm doing?"

He shrugged. "She called Gilbert after you left. Wanted to make sure he didn't hire you."

"Same with Jerry Clement?"

"Don't know if she called yet, but she knows where you went today."

"What does she fucking care?"

"Her husband's in the ground. You're walking around."

That wasn't exactly my fault.

"What are you to her?"

He was a little chagrinned, probably for what he was doing and a little for getting caught. Fortunately, that was keeping his natural cop belligerence in check.

"Friend of her brother-in-law. Sister's husband."

The news gave me a sad, sick feeling. I was on the bad side of a cop's widow. Ronnie had been on the wrong side of the line with me, but in the ground made a difference. That had a way of absolving sins.

Didn't matter he was the one who came to me, pissed off that some muscle for a drug dealer named Rahel Nebay had fucked up his old partner in narcotics in an altercation. They'd slithered out of charges, so he'd come to me to ride shotgun as he kept an eye on them. He hadn't bought any bubble gum. He imagined we'd be kicking some ass.

We'd been sitting in a personal car, watching the sidekicks and Nebay himself, who'd had a big transaction going down.

Turned out it was an intended show of force for Nebay. The other guys had anticipated that. Some black limos had pulled up at the secluded meeting place that was nowhere near our jurisdiction. All the cypress and hanging moss you'd expect.

Ronnie and I'd been dressed about like Culler, though the jeans showed a little more wear and the shoes had a few more scuffs. We hadn't bought the outfits just for the occasion the way Culler had.

One of Nebay's men made us, and suddenly all of the guys focused on us, and we were in a firefight.

Bullets sprayed. I'd pulled a service Glock. Ronnie had yanked his weapon from the spot on his belt he'd wedged it, trusting the safety a little more than I would have. At least it had been handy and let him go down looking heroic.

He got the guy holding the weapon that ended his life. I shot a greasy blond kid about 25 named Leo Maier from Nebay's opposition. He'd been pulling out something that looked like a Howitzer. He'd had aspirations. My bullet went into his throat before I got a demo of how his weapon's sound suppression worked.

When the smoke cleared, Ronnie'd been on the ground. I'd debated how to call it in while I got a wadded windbreaker pressed into his chest wound. There hadn't been a way to spin it. It was what it was, and I still had hopes of keeping Ronnie breathing in the moment. I'd been conscious of his house note, his boat and his wife.

He died in the air ambulance they dispatched since we were in the middle of nowhere, and they found all kinds of interesting charges to throw at me shortly after the bagpipes played and uniformed officers folded the flag on his casket into a neat little triangle.

Photographers had snapped pictures as blue uniforms presented it to Joy, and I'd wound up dodging photographers, the vigilante cop who got his partner killed. It was in a moment the department was polishing its image, so the manslaughter charge stuck.

I tossed Culler back his credentials.

"I could hit you with an assaulting a police officer charge," he said.

"You want to? When my name goes out, they're going to come and take pictures of you in that getup. How's that gonna play?"

He threw up a dismissive gesture.

"Good luck to you," he said.

That made me feel like crap, this costumed wanna-be tough guy feeling sorry for me. Meanwhile, Joy, who I'd been thinking of, had done the damage she could. I guess she needed someone to blame. She was in pain. I was guilty of not being the one who'd died.

She didn't need to know every move from here. She'd poisoned the sea. The tide would take her message where it needed to go.

Maybe it was time to think about a new town.

CHAPTER 6

If I had to rank the levels of hatred toward me by temperature—and why not, we're talking New Orleans—Joy would have been in the range of 102. My ex-wife Sandra, I'd have to put at 120. Her mom, Charlotte, was a few degrees below that, maybe even the comfortably balmy 90s.

I made a few calls among other family members and listened to assessments of me that peaked in the mid-80s with currents of profanity cresting between minced oath and coarse trends about my parentage. For my trouble, I wound up with Charlotte's phone number.

Her post-salutation greeting spiked into foul territory before she calmed and listened to my pleadings. Charlotte had trouble with her knees. Sitting still for a while probably didn't require too much persuasion.

"She doesn't want to see you," she said after I'd babbled a couple of minutes. "But she probably needs to."

I hadn't quite expected that.

"What do you mean?"

"She's seeing a character named Finn Alders. I don't like him."

After a while, I gleaned that the couple enjoyed recreational substances. I had to hold back my stomach's contents when layered-on suppositions were articulated—Julianna neglected while they were high was the least of them.

It could have been Charlotte wanting to fuck with my head, but the real intentions of men drawn to single mothers with young daughters rang true enough to concern me.

"Has anything happened yet?" I asked.

"I don't think so. I just have a sense there are aspirations. Could be he's just being good to her."

Second dad was enough to make me psychotic. Someone named Finn laying hands on Julianna pushed me to the outer darkness.

"Does Sandy have any inkling?"

"Have you ever known her to listen to me? She wouldn't listen about you. She never listens to anyone."

"Even about concerns for Juli?"

"He can do no wrong. Isn't a threat. It's all my imagination."

"Where are they, Charlotte?"

"She'd kill me if I told you. You know that."

"I need to go check on things, at least get a look at the guy."

"I promised."

"If Julianna is in danger, that should override a promise. You're her grandmother."

"I'm sorry. I'm gonna have to think about it. How do I know you aren't going to go there and hurt someone else?"

"I shot a drug trafficker in self-defense. Just happened not to be my job. Don't be absurd on anything else. On the worst day I never did anything to Sandy. You know I'd never hurt the child."

"Yeah, but I don't know how much good it would do if you find them and go all Amber Alert on things."

"Dammit, Charlotte…."

"I think I'm going to hang up for now, Si. I'll give it some thought."

"At least take my number."

She acquiesced at that.

"Try to calm down," she said after she'd written it down. "I'll sniff around a little more. Maybe I'm overly suspicious. If I think Finn's seriously a problem, I'll get back to you."

I shouted her name into my phone several times after she broke the connection. Didn't do much good, and I was left with visions of negligent parents worse than every case I'd ever seen and every cautionary drug propaganda film or *Dragnet* episode on record.

I couldn't just stare at the ceiling after that. I looked around the small room and found the folder with my rent agreement. There'd been a printout with a few of the extras I hadn't really cared about when I'd been looking for a roof.

It seemed a little out of place in this house of antiques, but the printout stated a small business center was available with a computer, printer and Internet. I hadn't intended to do a lot with social media, so my phone didn't have bells and whistles like apps yet.

I went down to the nook under the stairs and stood with my arms folded, sighing a lot. That got me nasty looks from the snotty twenty-something who was using the aging Dell. There's always someone using the computer when you need it. After a while he got the hint that I didn't think it was for the casual use he was putting it to, saving himself a headlock he must've sensed was coming based on presence and body language. I did everything but crack my knuckles and drive a fist into my palm.

When I was finally seated, I googled Sandra and Finn Alders.

I found mug shots and public record booking reports for minor infractions. I had to interpret the local codes on the fragments of the arrest records, but it looked like burglary on a small scale. The kind perpetrated to support the purchase of recreational substances. These had been six months back in a town called Casselberry, Florida, somewhere outside Orlando. Maybe they'd moved on or maybe they still hovered in that vicinity. I wished for the databases I'd had on the job. That would have made things easier.

I stared at one of Alders' mug shots, one of a collector's set of several. He gazed into the camera, eyelids drooping, tired but defiant, stubble on his upper lip, scruff on his chin, a scrape on his neck and a cut above one eye. I'd collard hundreds like him and knew how cuts and scrapes happened. I couldn't read in his eyes whether it was true he had an unhealthy interest in little girls. I'd have to use a favor to get someone to pull his jacket for that, but Julianna didn't need to be around him, regardless.

I started turning costs over in my head. A custody battle would mean more dollars, on top of any fees if my case was re-filed.

I don't know why I tried to sleep after that. I lay under the bed's canopy in that gray dark world that emerges after your vision has adjusted to the lights being out. As I stared past the thin folds of gathered fabric at the ceiling, demons whispered of horrors that might already be occurring. If I dozed at all, I saw Juli crouching in a dark, dank and grungy space in tattered clothes, weeping and filled with terror, and the worst version of Finn possible loomed in the shadows, a lean and sinister devil-man still possessing those droopy eyelids from the mugshot.

CHAPTER 7

Just after dawn, street sounds woke me, and I fixed coffee in a little one-cup maker that came with the room and watched the antique clock like you're not supposed to. The hands refused to move. I waited for business hours.

After the coffee worked on the numbness a while, I showered and shaved and waited more, the gnawing feeling relentless.

I talked to Clinton Laroque's answering service not because I expected anything, but it gave me something to do, though it came with rejection. When the law office opened, I got a secretary who told me it'd be another hour at least before I heard back from anyone.

It was two, and I was feeling like I couldn't breathe when Clinton came on the line.

"I need to be in court soon," he said. He was in a public place. A crowd buzzed around him. So, he'd be in a suit, seersucker if he stayed to form, holding his briefcase, me pressed to his ear, trying to take in as much of what I said as he could with the noise.

I gave him the gist of it.

"It's gonna come down to what you can prove, and if they're not in state that's an issue. Let me lay it out for you beyond that. The judge is going to take child safety into consideration, but for custody they're looking at employment, food and shelter, emotional support for the child. You have no stability and a possible re-trial hanging over you. You're likely going to get her taken in and put in foster care. There's a chance that's better than where she is if what you're hearing is right, but not ideal."

"I need to do something."

"Try to confirm the danger. That's got the potential to sound like you stirring up cause for concern, and try to get your feet on the ground and get some money coming in. It's step-by-step. Gotta go. Judge. Waiting. Not good."

And I was in the empty room with silence again. Except for the clock. I could hear it ticking, but the hands still didn't seem to want to move much.

The afternoon crept like the morning had, but the temperature climbed quicker. I took my jacket off and sat at the bar in a seafood restaurant in the Bywater area not far from the Gulf Outlet Canal, part of the area where Katrina was most unkind. I thought about keeping my shades on. My eyes were tired from the lack of sleep and probably looked like I'd been using something the law didn't allow.

Lt. Patrick Abshire worked the 5th District out of the newish white and orange station on North Claiborne. I'd passed by it, but he hadn't wanted me to drop in for a visit. It wasn't about the bleary eyes. It was my general stench.

We'd compromised on the restaurant. It was a small, dimly lit place with the smell of rich fried oysters. I ordered an appetizer and a local beer with an alligator on the label because I hadn't eaten all day. I got a fried eggplant. I didn't want to risk oysters on the half shell in a month with no r. Not with so much to live for.

Pat came in a half hour after he'd promised and raised a hand to decline my drink offer. On the job. He was in the kind of suit he'd always gone for. Crisp, perfect cut, light fabric. His skin was just a shade darker than the pale tan, his eyes gold-tinted and one shade darker than his skin. He carried an envelope he probably shouldn't have had under one arm, but I was a friend and I'd asked.

"You remember these days they watch the jackets you pull and the records checks you run," he said, sitting beside me and sliding the envelope along the bar to me, stopping just short of one of the rings a beer had left behind.

"Do they charge for the copies?"

He gave me a glance and an annoyed smirk.

"Just reminding you. I can square this, anyone asks. Just

doesn't need to become frequent behavior, your ex starts to date around or anything. I can't be looking up all her boyfriends."

"Let's hope it doesn't come to that."

I opened the envelope and looked at the pages he'd compiled. A different mug shot of Finn graced a sheet on top. Same sleepy eyes. Different haircut. Lots of asterisks served as dividing lines and brief narratives summed up his offenses. He'd been picked up for a Metairie burglary, just like Florida. He had some drunk and disorderly charges as well and he went through a phase of breaking into cars.

"He's been popular with our kind for a while, flip a little deeper," Patrick said.

I found a younger shot of him. His hair was longer, head tilted back, chin jutting out a little more. The arrogance didn't show quite as much in the next. He looked resigned and a little tired, still feeling the effects of the controlled substance he was charged with possessing.

The stack went on with a few more infractions over a few more years.

"He had some juvie stuff. I couldn't get at all of that. It's not guaranteed to be a lewd and lascivious. He's not registered as an offender or predator."

I almost felt better for a second, but then he pulled out a sheet he'd dog-eared.

"No prosecution. Went nowhere," Patrick said. "But there was a call related to a younger female cousin staying in his family's house."

The appetizer and beer I'd consumed threatened to come back up in an instant, because I knew how many incidents went unreported. I knew what got covered up in families, and I knew what patterns of behavior indicated.

"Maybe he's just got designs on Sandra," Patrick said.

"She's a catch," I said.

He was a cop. He didn't have a bedside manner. He wasn't very good at making me feel better.

"You still good with mental snapshots?" he asked. "You know you can't keep this."

"There's no name? On the cousin?"

"No. That's sealed. She's in her twenties now." He put a sticky note in front of me with a phone number. "We've moved into you-owe-me-now territory."

"If I'm gonna owe you, can you get a line on this guy? At Disneyworld or wherever he is?"

"We'll see. Don't look for too much help on anything within the department."

"I was helping my partner." That case had been made before. I just felt the need to repeat the point.

Pat lifted his hands.

"Every police agency has public perception to deal with these days. We've got a commitment to commitment to 'transparency, accountability, collaboration and integrity.' The world hasn't forgotten Danziger Bridge, and it's a rough city, tough one to police. A guy like you….."

I tilted my head and raised my eyebrows.

"It's not a good time to have cops making it look like the wild west, going after people with guns blazing."

I started to speak but he raised his hand. He knew the story and he didn't care. "We got guys out there and they're gonna have to defend themselves from time to time. Rep needs to be pristine. Let me reiterate. Don't expect any more off the books help from the department. And good luck to you."

He collected the folder, gave me a pat on the shoulder and left me sitting there over my beer and eggplant.

I called the number on the sticky note a while later, when I felt strong enough.

Finn's cousin lived in Monroe. I could have visited her easier from N-5. If they'd let me out.

"How'd you…?"

"I was a cop."

"Sealed records only mean so much."

"Something like that."

Her voice was measured and a bit deep, not letting out much emotion.

"I try not to look back on the past," she said. "It's all behind me."

It wasn't the kind of case I'd worked, but I could read that that wasn't really true. Nothing's ever fully in the rearview mirror.

She wouldn't talk long on the phone, even when I managed to wedge in my concerns between her protests, though she finally heard "daughter."

That made her go silent for a while.

"How old?"

I told her.

There was more silence, maybe indicating a personal debate, but it seemed to have been enough to give her a nudge.

"Maybe you have reason to worry," she said.

There was no more she was willing to say.

She hung up.

I needed that damned bottle I'd left with Rose.

CHAPTER 8

I had the fresh bottle in a brown paper bag and my tie in my pocket when I spotted the brunette who looked like a college girl. She was hanging out in a shady spot near some street vendors on Decatur across from Jackson Square and not far from the old Jax brewery that was now a mall.

Short navy skirt, dark blouse, handbag over a shoulder. The eyelashes were exaggerated, the hair a butt-cut, but she was subdued for the Quarter. That let her linger in spots a lot of hookers might have been spotted and shooed.

I sat on the metal railing near a historic marker and said hello.

"I'm meeting someone," she said. "A date." Emphatic.

"I'm not a cop."

"I didn't think you were on the job." Her dark eyes were stone when she looked my way. "But I'm busy."

I opened my jacket where the tops of bills showed in the wallet pocket. I had fanned them before slipping them in after the bourbon purchase.

With a glance, she turned her gaze across the street, away from me but not really focusing on anything.

"I work by appointment."

That explained it. Casual encounters enhanced the pre-arranged experience. No wonder she didn't look like a real streetwalker. To the untrained eye.

"In college?"

"Didn't like the course load."

"Double to break your date and have a drink with me."

I crinkled the paper bag.

"My boss wouldn't like that."

"A regular today?"

"Tourist."

"They can send someone else, and you can pick up a nice tip."

"He liked my picture."

"She can say she got a new hair style."

"I don't know you."

"You know me better than a tourist you haven't even met yet, and if you have an appointment, I bet you have a spot ready."

I took out a couple of bills and worked them between my fingers so the denominations showed. She eyed them a while then nodded slowly. She had rent to pay even if the textbooks had gone back to the store.

"Give me a second."

She told someone on the other end of a call she was Crystal and needed a sub, that she was taking a walk-in or something like that, jargon. She assured her contact she'd be safe and gave my name after I mouthed it. That didn't make me feel proud either, but when she was off the call, she took my arm, and we walked along Decatur like a couple.

The motel was tucked into a little pocket on a side street just a few blocks away, the room she unlocked functional but clean enough. When I returned from the ice machine, she'd slipped off the blouse. Stood in the nook outside the bathroom running water in the washbasin. A lacy black bra lifted her small, firm breasts, and the skirt shimmered around her as she turned toward me. Seventies porn music should have been cued.

The onyx eyes rolled toward the water.

"You're serious? That's what you're worried about?"

"It's one thing we can take care of. I'm sure you know the drill from that house trailer bordello where you lost your virginity."

"You study the history of the trade or something?"

"I just know Louisiana."

I kicked off my shoes and walked into the hard, white light of the fluorescent bulbs. While I peeled paper off a couple of the plastic tumblers in front of the mirror, her fingers moved to my belt buckle. I dropped ice cubes into the glasses and tossed back a shot. Then I rattled melting cubes and refreshed and poured a drink for her.

She gave it a light sip and sat it down. Then she unzipped the skirt, letting it drop around her ankles. Stepping out of the fabric circle, she picked up her drink again and walked in her black thong, bra and heels to the bed, her alabaster skin and slender form making her look like the most ethereal of demons.

I followed and sat beside her in my now open shirt and boxers and touched plastic to plastic then sipped again, letting enough bourbon down my throat to produce a burn. It wasn't hot enough to sear the bitterness and remorse.

She sipped a little more, working for seductive, then she reached over and touched my cheek. When I didn't move, she leaned in for a soft kiss. That might have been off the table for some. She was used to playing a girlfriend, and she sought to make it a familiar greeting that would move things along.

I took another swallow. She looked far different from Sandra, who had sandy hair, but I couldn't stop thinking about my wife. Thoughts of her brought thoughts of Juli. That didn't make want me want to snap a selfie in this setting, even if I could figure out the fucking phone.

"I'm glad we could be alone," Crystal said.

She slipped her arms around me, holding her glass at the nape of my neck as she gave me a deeper kiss and pressed into me.

She wore a delicate perfume, and her flesh was warm, soft, not flawed by track mark nor decorated with tattoos. Her employers probably mentioned that in her promos. I slipped an arm around her waist and pulled her close, trying to think more of where her tongue was going than where it had been.

I had enough cash to keep her around a while and to keep the numbing drinks coming from what passed for room service, a skinny African American kid whose retro 'fro almost touched the top of the door frame.

Crystal offered to get meth. Heroine, when I said no to the

chemical composition of the meth. Some lingering fragment of self-preservation wanted me to keep my teeth white.

I said no to the smack too and just kept to the whiskey. I wondered if it somehow signified a change in my luck, that I'd found the best call girl in the *View Carre*.

Flashes of her hair and body drifted through my consciousness, the comfort of her touch inevitably giving way to more thoughts of my family.

They sailed somewhere in the Atlantic while I watched from shore, wishing I could get to them. Juli waved, her arm pivoting from the shoulder in her fervor. Sandra refused to look my way, focused on steering the boat away from me.

They disappeared into a fog so gray and thick it enveloped all and gave me a feeling of disorientation as well as despair, and I knew Finn, the demon with drooping eyes, was somewhere near. Snippets of high school excerpts from Dante hit me. Did I mention I went to a really good high school? I thought of the opening part where he talks of being lost in a dark wood in a place "scarcely less bitter than death."

In one of my forays into Facebook, someone posted one of those little quote images that stuck with me, a bromide, I suppose, from Norman Cousins, that *Anatomy of an Illness* guy. "Death is not the greatest loss in life. The greatest loss is what dies inside us while we live."

I suddenly understood it better in the midst of my stupor than at a desk scrolling past recipes and cat pictures. Death would have had no feeling, but in my gut, the damaged spots were raw and toxic.

I'm not sure how long it lasted. At some point the girl went away, probably when the cash I had with me ran out. So much for the hooker with the heart of gold.

I lay staring at the grimy ceiling, tangled in sweaty sheets, drifting until a new face floated into the void.

"How are things here at the bottom of the ocean?" Rose Cantor asked.

CHAPTER 9

Rose gave me water then a sports drink so green it glowed. I felt hot as hell, and I must have kept babbling because then some guy came in with an IV and a plastic bag.

"How far the fuck gone am I?"

My voice cracked as I formed the words.

"You're dehydrated, but you just formed a cogent question. That seems to be an improvement."

"So, to what do I owe this intervention?"

"While she was cleaning out your wallet, your girlfriend got a little worried about you, found my number in your things and dialed my disposable cell from your disposable cell. Did you have any credit cards? You might want to think about cancelling them."

"I was told not everybody's right for an American Express card."

"Well that's one thing."

"Do you do this for all your clients?"

"You're not my client."

"I meant your other clients."

She sat in the room's desk chair, legs crossed, tall paper coffee cup on a chair arm, watching the guy check my pulse and blood pressure.

"He's a nurse. Had some licensure issues. Sometimes sings the national anthem at high school sporting events, though."

The guy looked down at me and smiled.

"How's your Pagliacci?" I asked. Yeah, I went to a really good high school.

He just focused on the drip.

"So, all this trying to get me to work for your clients?"

"They weren't willing to take `fuck no' for an answer and asked for one more conversation. If this is what it takes." She lifted her shoulders.

I massaged my forehead a bit. "I did say that. Sometimes cops dispense with the pleasantries."

"I've worked with cops. I'm aware. Should I enumerate the reasons you need the gig about now?"

"My attorney already did that. Actually, it was more of a list of reasons I need to win the lottery, but same difference."

I sat up carefully, adjusting the sheet to protect my modesty while the Singing Nurse gave me a little play in the IV tube.

"A prosecutor may decide to take another run at me, my legal fees are already in orbit, and you can't win child custody when your life's in the toilet. Is there any more of that coffee? Meanwhile, the wife of my dead partner's taken it upon herself to make sure I never catch crooks in this town again."

Rose passed me another bottle with liquid that glowed green.

"Caffeine's not good when you're dehydrated."

"I'm in a cheap hotel drinking alien's blood, and I have no idea where my ex-wife took my daughter. With a guy named Finn. Who might like little girls. Caffeine's the least of my worries."

"I should mention my clients are willing to pay for this next conversation. Regardless of your decision after. So, any thoughts about what you'll do once we give your pants back?"

"I suppose the cash the hooker took is long gone."

She took a latte sip and sat quietly.

"I could probably take a meeting," I said. "Let me powder my face."

A day later, Mrs. Holst had had a new haircut.

I think they call it a bob, mostly chin length all around with a longer parenthesis of blond on the right, curling under the slight cleft in her chin. When there are things you can't control, you fiddle with the things you can.

I kept my shades on as I neared the bench where she sat near the Riverwalk. Her dress was mint green, almost the color of the sports drink and a little blinding in the midmorning sunlight.

"Your husband couldn't make it?"

"We thought a crowd might draw attention."

She picked up her purse, got to her feet and started along the sidewalk so I fell in beside her, matching the pace she set with long legs.

I'd dropped my courtroom slash interview suit at a dry cleaner, so with jeans and a striped sports shirt under a light tweed jacket, I looked enough like a slightly upscale tourist.

"So, you wanted a little more conversation?"

"You left so abruptly, we never got to an offer the other night. Let me cut through the small talk. We thought the dollar figure might help convince you."

We made our way down to an outdoor café where bistro tables with bright flowers as centerpieces were shielded from the street by vibrant green plants in planters. We settled a few tables down from other patrons.

"What do you think?"

"Seems nice."

"I meant about what we were discussing."

"He's clearly a man capable of terrible things."

"Finding someone capable of dealing with a man capable of terrible things isn't as easy as you'd think."

A waiter arrived and selected a couple of glasses from the assortment in front of us, filling those with ice water. A Bloody Mary would have been nice, but we ordered a fruit plate and sent him away.

"Nice you think I'm capable."

She let that ride. "We're prepared to make the offer of $250,000 delivered in two increments," she said. "One fourth now. The rest when your job's complete."

"That would take care of the gap my money manager has spotted in my retirement fund."

"We don't have to worry about college funds now. Before you ask, if things should go wrong, we realize it might be hard to get a refund on the early portion. That's why it's small, but it's also a show of good faith."

I nodded.

"You need the money, Mr. Reardon. Ms. Cantor is good at what she does. She's filled us in on your situation."

I wondered how much she knew.

"I have to ask one obvious question," I said.

A tick of her head suggested I proceed.

"What if I could find some kind of proof that would lead to an arrest?"

"We've had private investigators from a couple of big firms and paid a lot of money, hoping."

I suspected I'd visited some of those firms recently.

"I don't think some one-man Sam Spade move on your part's going to get anywhere," she said.

"I'm going to have to sniff around anyway to prep for anything. If that avenue were to become feasible?"

"It's unlikely, and you couldn't guarantee a conviction, could you?"

I lifted my hands. "People get out of jail all the time."

"Forgive me then if I've hardened to the promise of a victim impact statement in court providing any kind of closure. Mr. Alexeeva is better connected now than he was a few years ago. He has friends and he has good lawyers too. He's aspirational."

That inner cold I'd noticed at dinner became evident again. A sunny day and a bright colored dress couldn't hide it.

And slowly it sank in. Regardless of him being a bad man, even the devil, we were sitting here putting a dollar figure on a man's life. As a cop, I'd always been cognizant of the fact I was sending someone to a grim fate as I put a case together. Usually it wasn't a death sentence, but Angola, where the state prison sat, always loomed as a possibility. You may have seen documentaries about the place. The farm. The inmates wear white. Some of them are even sorry, but they're not leaving. I always had to keep in the back of my mind I was working for the victims, looking for someone who'd harmed someone else.

One kid, we'd tracked down for raping and murdering his date. He was a true product of the system. He'd been in and out of lockups since about age 13. He'd been abused in multiple ways even with the protections that were supposed to be in place.

He'd been out of lockup about two weeks when a friend introduced him to a girl. They'd gone for pizza, a movie and then they'd looked for a secluded spot off a roadside for privacy. Everything that had been done to him had emerged again in the front seat of the car he'd borrowed from an aunt.

We ran him down easily enough when the body was found, dumped by a canal. DNA confirmed everything that had happened. He hadn't quite looked like a monster when we'd cornered him at his aunt's in a back bedroom. Sweaty, disheveled, wild-eyed, he was like any other scared teenager we collared.

The whole time the trial was going on, I kept the autopsy of the victim in mind and all that had been done to her. The kid dodged the death penalty with the diligent effort of his lawyer, and they sent him to the farm. Life sentence.

Justice was done as well as justice can be these days, but when the news came that inmates had held him down, helpless and screaming, and cut his testicles off, it had hit me hard, a cold, clenched horror in my gut.

Being asked to carry out this sentence still seemed a little different, even with word of the Holsts' dead girls, but I willed my insides to calm. I had a living kid to think of. I had a possible retrial if I was seen stepping out of line, especially to do vigilante work.

"What about expenses?" I asked. "In theory, I'd need a weapon, some details would need to be worked out. I may need to enlist someone to help me."

"How much attention to logistics is needed?"

I could see why her husband had sent her to negotiate.

"You're well aware he's never going to be readily unguarded. He's got to be isolated at the right time. The deed has to be done...."

"Corner him, tell him why you're there and put a bullet in his brain."

The cold core was very real.

"You'd like to see the deed done. I'd like to ride away from it. This hefty amount is going to go fast if I have to spend it on defense against a murder charge with strikes already against me."

I felt cold sweat just thinking about that. I had a flash of myself playing catch with Jasso for eternity. It wasn't a good flash. I didn't want to go back.

"How much do you foresee?"

"Could go another $100,000 just in preparation."

I had no idea how much I needed to kill a man, but I knew the take home pay needed to be high, not incrementally eaten away. Worst case, she'd say no and I wouldn't have to kill a man.

Another man.

I'd still be broke. Everything has a down side.

"I'm going to need to talk to my husband."

She slipped a hand into her bag.

"I'm going to recommend not doing that over the phone."

"I can be discreet, Mr. Reardon."

She slipped up from her seat and over to the edge of the sidewalk, pacing parallel to the little black fence that bordered the sitting area, cell to her ear. I sipped my coffee.

"Okay," she said when she returned.

I should have asked for a full half a million.

CHAPTER 10

Speaking of discretion, I needed help from Richard Jasso, and a phone call obviously wasn't an option. That meant some of the expense money would go for the four-hour drive back to North Louisiana for a face-to-face on a visitation day.

My name on the visitor log would be recorded. That might not look good, but the conversation wouldn't be recorded, and Jasso was serving enough life sentences that he wouldn't cave and testify for any new accommodation short of being set free at this point. The state didn't have that quality of mercy.

I'd had plenty of talks with him over the time we'd been in N-5 together. Jasso had offered long tales on longer, hot afternoons. I think he'd decided to become an informant because he'd grown weary of general population and having to look over his shoulder anyway, but he had it as good as it was going to get for him.

He liked being away from the world of Angola, though David Wade was still prison. Don't make any mistake about that.

I think he missed Angola sometimes too. He'd regaled me with accounts of stupid cons he'd known through the years either on the street or in the bunk houses, guys who'd burglarized houses while wearing ankle monitors or fallen asleep in cars they were trying to steal.

He also told me tales of successful criminals. Some were involved in activities in which he was a participant. Others he'd learned about since being locked up. It wasn't hard to ascertain some of the pseudonymous tales from people carrying on his work on the outside.

Those were the guys I needed. They were the ones I anticipated paying some of the Holsts' expense money while maintaining plausible deniability. I hoped to avoid being one of the stupid criminals too and to always give an attorney wiggle room to argue reasonable doubt.

Why did I visit Jasso? Well, life's tough on the inside, and I wanted to offer moral support to a guy who'd protected me.

My gut tightened as I tooled past a nondescript white fence and approached the manicured entrance where a neat rectangle of shrubs bordered the white-on-black sign that proclaimed I'd reached a correctional center.

The grounds, with numbered brown towers and coils of concertina wire were further off the main road, and I felt my mood take a downturn as I headed toward the parking lot with all of that in sight. It's considered medium security, and I've written of the protective unit, but it's not the country club you might be thinking of. There are lots and lots of bars inside. Lots of men locked up, and a lot of punitive turning to vindictive. A guy escaped sometime back, touching off a lot of scrutiny about procedures, and that led to tightened screws, no play on prison language intended.

I suppose I owed the place a debt. It had kept me alive and all my body parts attached, and I'd read a lot of books in there, more than at that great high school. More than in the time I'd spent in college.

I'd dabbled with correspondence courses as well. Still, I didn't harbor warm feelings. I didn't really want to go back in and revisit the library or see my old cell.

I knew the fear that they would not let me out again was irrational, but it made me question my contemplated course of action one more time, especially once I'd stepped through the metal gates and a black door that had windows but still slammed and locked behind me. I endured ribbing from guards who recognized me. They had nothing really original to say, but the suggestions about the outside and refuge I must have felt here darkened my mood even more.

I waited a while, though it wasn't as bad as some Saturdays from what I'd heard, and eventually Jasso and I were facing each other in the visiting area where families posed for photos in front of colorful backdrops that included a seascape and one with cartoon characters for families with kids. I'd tutored a few guys who had to live with only those snippets of real life. It always reminded me Sandra had never brought Juli up here to see me.

For the best, I told myself, though it reminded me that she would never bring her here if I returned. I'd have to hope for the kid wanting to know her father when she reached her teen years. Or older.

Jasso wore familiar blue chambray like the other inmates, his lion's mane looking a tad more grey, his face a little more wrinkled even though it hadn't been that long since I'd seen him, and he had a thinness that came with age and showed in his forearms and the way the skin fit at his neck.

"Couldn't find anyone to talk to you on the outside?" he asked as he settled, drawing a squeak from the plastic chair.

"I realized we didn't have pictures together and I thought I'd rectify that before you got older and died."

"Well, cheers," he drawled from deep in his throat. "Surprised they let you in. As a guest."

"I filled out all the paperwork."

Praying it wouldn't become an evidentiary exhibit somewhere down the road. The optics weren't good on any front, but I was just a guy who'd made it out paying an obligatory visit.

"Besides," I said, "when they heard it was a pilgrimage for a fresh dose of your wisdom, they opened the gates on religious grounds."

"You'd think more people would seek me out," he said. "I need better PR. I could be quite a consultant on Zen and the art of tractor repair."

Jasso read a lot too.

He coughed now, rattling phlegm somewhere in his chest.

"You doing all right?" I asked.

"It's not bad." He cleared his throat again. "Nobody's slipping me extra cigarettes, so that'll actually improve. They've got some new investigators in sniffing around, so everyone on staff's got their backs up, but you know how it goes."

"What are they investigating?"

"Something new on that escape. Who knew what, when. That sort of thing. How's life for you?"

"Rocky but better than in here."

"Shittiest day free better than the best inside," he said. "Exit through the gift shop, you'll find that on a tee shirt."

I chuckled with him for a while: The Saints, state of the world, what the girls were wearing on the streets of the French Quarter on hot days. It was easy to forget his past, and easy to forget what I was up to. Just two guys shooting the shit.

"What do you really need, son?" he asked following still more small talk. He could have read it in my manner and body language, though he knew I hadn't come just to see his face.

I provided a vague outline, just enough to give him a sense of what I needed without offering anything he could testify about. Maybe he could be swayed by a promise of more cigs.

He slouched in his chair and leaned an elbow on the chair back. He was more than six feet, and he looked like an aging basketball star for a moment.

"Is that really what you want do with your life?" he asked, reading between the lines.

"I had a father, Richard."

He lifted his hands in surrender.

"I've turned it over a few times," I said. "Stupidity looks the same from all angles."

He laced his fingers behind his head. "It's a pleasure to see the student aspire to be like his sensei. Keep it up, you'll find yourself in the desirable position I've attained."

"I don't have a history of great decisions," I said. "Or weighing risks well."

"There's not any other way?"

"I'm in a hurry. I don't have a lot of options and a kid to think about. More problems than we need to go into."

"That's how a lot of people you can look around at right now got where they are. A lot of these guys never had any options. Society doesn't quite know what to do about that, so they just get dumped in these luxury accommodations. `We whisper together. Are quiet and meaningless. As wind in dry grass or rats' feet over broken glass in our dry cellar.'"

Eliot's *The Hollow Men*, interesting spoken in his draw. As I said, Jasso did a lot of reading in here too.

He unlaced his fingers, sighed and leaned forward to look me directly in the eye and repeated his other aphorism. "Life's a fool's run on a crooked road. You have to find the best route you can."

"Maybe you are worthy of a pilgrimage," I said.

"I try to be."

He had a general sense of what I needed. I locked on his gaze now and didn't waver.

"You got any names for me?"

"There are people I can send a cop to see. But maybe a quasi-legitimate businessman."

I left with a name, and I was happy to get the hell out of the place.

CHAPTER 11

Archie McCluskey was actually Jasso's nephew, his sister's boy. That was actually one of two names he gave me. Arch's younger brother, Kenneth, Jasso warned, could be handy too but was a few bricks shy of a cube.

"Don't get 'em in trouble," he said. "I know other people."

"Got you."

He also warned me not to get in a political discussion with Arch. "Boy's never been inside, served overseas and he's subject to the influences that swirl around everybody in the South if they watch too much of a certain cable network."

Arch had served tours of duty in unpleasant places including Afghanistan and Iraq where he might or might not have perfected black-market practices that he possibly carried on stateside. He also led hunting and fishing tours and offered "hunter safety" training, enlisting his brother's assistance since his work in an autobody and wheel realignment shop had ceased to challenge him.

Jasso had spoken of them with pride, eschewing the easy and lucrative path of meth cooking and distribution and other activities of the rural South. He'd known I wouldn't share with anyone.

I drove out to their fishing camp, following directions Jasso had provided. Once I'd found the right winding dirt road, I tooled through stands of cypress and oak trees with grey-green tangles of Spanish moss looking like *Duck Dynasty* beards.

A metal gate blocked the roadway a short distance from the lakeshore, so I pulled to a stop and climbed from the front seat, trying to look non-threatening. I kind of expected that I'd be met here.

The McCluskeys didn't disappoint.

As I leaned on the top of the gate and looked across, for signs of more than reptile or bird life, a voice drifted over from somewhere to my right.

"You come down that road, you either have business with us or you mean us harm. Who the fuck are you and what the fuck do you want?" It was a version of Jasso's voice without as much vocal fry. But with a lot more malevolence.

I kept my hands extended, showing they were empty. I'd dressed in jeans again and a new crew neck shirt with a windbreaker, striving to look less threatening and less official than the courtroom suit. Still it's hard for a cop to look like anything but a cop.

"My name is Silas Reardon. I'm a friend of your Uncle Richard's."

"Funny, that's just what an undercover ATF agent would say."

"Your uncle led me to believe you were smarter than to call out the name of the agency you suspected might be looking into you."

I heard a chuckle. "First one that came to mind, and if I said revenuer I'd sound like a hick."

"Or slightly anachronistic."

"Feds aren't above bustin' a few stills when they're between looking for guys named Muhammad."

"I'd think white lighting would be the least of their worries in these parts. But you can generally bust a still without touching off an explosion."

"We don't cook."

"That's what I heard."

Some foliage shuddered to my right. Then a patch of the swamp flora detached itself and moved toward me. I caught flashes of camouflage fabric among the wiry coils of jute twine, moss, and tree roots. The custom ghillie suit impressed, but the compound bow really held my attention, threaded as it was with an arrow featuring a nasty triangular tip with primary and secondary blades looking razor sharp. I studied them carefully. I couldn't help but calculate how much weight the system of pulleys would put behind them in propelling them into my chest.

"Can we have a conversation without that?"

"Who are you again?"

The guy in the suit who was tall enough to trigger reports of Bigfoot wasn't the one talking.

"Silas Reardon. You may have heard about me."

To my left this time, I heard more fabric rustle, and a guy slightly shorter and a little more dressed down emerged. He had on a camouflage jumpsuit and a matching camouflage cap that looked like it was cut for the German military. A neatly trimmed red beard masked his lower face. Had to be Archie.

"Where?"

"From your uncle who probably spoke of me fondly. Or in the news."

"You're that cop?"

"I'm pretty far from cop now."

"What brings you out here?"

"I needed to talk to you about some hardware."

A few minutes later I was in their kitchen, which was neater and cleaner than I had expected, though their house skewed a little dark both in the lighting and the paneling. Dark brown leather furnishings in the living room didn't add any cheer.

A television they could have put at the Superdome did offer a little glow, though. At the moment, a couple of soccer teams from Spanish-speaking countries were squaring off in the latest iteration of HD. You could see nostril hairs.

We sat at a little table near a back window overlooking a lake and a pier. The coffee wasn't bad. They had a Keurig. I drank French Roast.

"Your dad was a sports fan?" I asked as I sipped from a black mug with a gold Saints helmet stamped on it.

"Through all the rough years," Arch said.

Those would have included eras when Archie Manning and Ken Stabler had served as quarterbacks and hope had sprung eternal in the hearts of fans. My old man had spent a lot of

Sunday afternoons alternating prayers and swearing.

Stabler had led the Oakland Raiders to a Super Bowl victory, but he'd been a little older when he'd come to New Orleans when I was a kid. Hadn't deterred optimism that "the Snake," as he was known, would be a savior.

"I'm technically Elisha Archibald," Arch said, straddling a chair that was turned backwards toward the table. "He's Kenneth Michael. The old man didn't make it to see the team win the Super Bowl. He woulda legally changed one of our names to Drew Christopher."

Drew Brees had led the team to a Super Bowl win in 2010.

"So, what do you need?" Arch asked.

"I've got to do some hazardous surveillance work. I need something small, easily concealed but accurate. Doesn't have to be the latest and greatest. No questions asked."

"Might go to the Russians," Arch said, looking like he didn't buy any of my story.

"Russians, really?"

He shrugged. "They invented a little flat job for their diplomats that I was shown recently. Goes nicely in a waistband."

"For when diplomacy fails?"

"Somethin' like that."

"Boom, boom," Kenneth said in a voice that was higher and squeakier than his size would've suggested. I thought he was screwing around until later when he talked again. For now, he zipped it, following a sharp gaze from his brother.

Out of the ghillie suit in his own camouflage jumpsuit, he was inches taller and much heavier than Arch, who was angular like their uncle, his beard thicker, but rounded, nothing to rival the Spanish moss or ZZ Top or Phil Robertson. He could have put on a green robe and a holly wreath and been the Ghost of Christmas Present, though.

"Might work. Got it in house?"

"Nah, it's called a PSM. That stands for something in Russian, what is it Kenny?"

"*Pistolet Samozaryadny Malogabaritny.*" Kenny's skills exceeded what I'd expected.

"I thought in Louisiana a *pistolet* was a bread roll."

"It just means it's a self-loading pistol," Arch said. "I can get it. One I'm thinking of is the ultra-thin version the diplomats would have brought in and not the version that's allowed for import. But no show models, sorry. This is an innocent fishing cabin for two brothers when they take a break from auto-body repair, logging, and serving as hunting and fishing guides."

"Is that what they call your work these days?"

It was a good label for providing off-the-books collectibles to businessmen.

"You'll need to be close with it if your surveillance goes wrong. It's not known for stopping power, but it's got some features."

"Wi-Fi?"

"It uses a specialized ammo, and we can get some boxes of cartridges. It's not a Glock, but close enough in, it'll pierce soft body armor. When do you need it?"

"Few days?"

"Doable. You'll probably want to get familiar with it. We've got an outside range. We can put up some body-shaped targets."

"The fishermen use those?"

"The business executives on weekend getaways do. Makes the white-collar types feel like they've got a pair."

"Ah huh."

He calculated how much I was going to take out of the Holst's expense purse and wrote it down.

I said: "Okay."

CHAPTER 12

The club had been named The Runnel. It was an odd choice. The word essentially means a small stream. Clubs have to be called something, and someone must have convinced Alexeeva it had marketing value for the element he wanted to attract: *It's a hip word, and people will realize they're going with the flow, baby!*

If you were able to flow past the doorman, you were part of an in-crowd.

From what I'd picked up in word of mouth, it represented one of Alexeeva's steps up over the last few years, though the opening had come after even the last reports from detective agencies that the Holsts had turned over to me.

It was close enough to the Quarter to be chic, but outside, in daylight, it kind of blended with the rest of the district, which trended brown brick. Word had it renovations had made it much more exciting inside. Colorful lighting, loud music, dancers, enough to compete with a neighboring club backed by Harrah's.

It would be a signature location for Alexeeva, more glamorous than his other businesses. His hope was to preside and host an ongoing, raging party for a few hundred of his best friends. He longed for some extra air of legitimacy an in-spot could afford.

I walked by, studying the entrance and the awning while remaining casual. I'd found a white, double breasted chef's coat. I looked like I was due on the line in the kitchen of a nearby restaurant. Maybe I was out for a walk and a smoke. I even put a meat thermometer in the sleeve. Si Reardon, master of disguise.

If this was going to be a place Alexeeva hung out, I'd wanted to at least be aware of the location as I tracked his movements. I wanted a good feel for all the spots he frequented so that I could formulate some sort of plan. I had to keep reminding myself my purpose wasn't the same as it had been in law enforcement. I had no case to build unless I got lucky.

I was reverse engineering everything I knew.

I didn't need to document times and dates as evidence, just to know his movements, locations, habits and how many goons were usually around him.

Since the Holsts had the "let him know who's behind it" request, and since I wasn't a sniper anyway, I was contemplating how close might work. He maintained an entourage, I'd learned, with Taras Seleznyov and Nestor Zhirov, who Adam Holst had named when I described them. They were always on hand along with assorted disposable goons armed with concealed weaponry that would make the McCluskeys envious. The goons with Taras and Nestor formed a phalanx. Doing some Jack Ruby-style approach in a public place while he shuffled from a car to a building didn't seem viable.

Or advisable.

Apparently the lean and smaller Taras served as a sort of CFO and could keep details of Alexeeva's business written on the hard drive of his brain. He carried a weapon concealed somewhere in his dark suit, but he wasn't my biggest concern.

That would be Nestor based on what the Holts had told me. Nestor was a Russian tank.

He stood a couple of inches over six feet, but he was also wide and solid. He didn't try to button his black shirts at the throat. He wore a thin rope chain, the kind that retailed for a grand unless you had a 20 percent off coupon at Macy's. He could probably catch a bullet in his teeth. If he missed, he could just swallow it. Couple of slugs in the abdomen would go unnoticed like mosquito bites. I suspected he already had a few scars from getting in the way of things aimed at Alexeeva.

He'd be one of the biggest impediments to my getting away. And, ideally, getting away would still be part of the plan, unless I ramped up my life insurance and made my daughter a beneficiary. That still didn't address the Finn problem.

So, if I could get through assorted accompanying goons plus

Nestor and the wiry Taras, who'd yank some kind of weapon from his suit, how would I flee if I popped Alexeeva? Anywhere.

At the club—a crowded, loud, active venue—he'd be vulnerable in ways he wasn't in a private office, the street or his garage. In a VIP room or even at the bar, the phalanx would be a little more relaxed and reluctant to bring out automatic weapons. But you can't move well in a club under the best of circumstances. I'd be fighting a crowd to any exit, and with the boss dead the goons might just shrug, or they might not worry about collateral damage and spraying lead.

I contemplated the life insurance again. I'd have to pass a physical for coverage, but an actuary wouldn't have my morally corrupt intentions to factor into the premiums. Short term it might be a good move. It just wasn't what I liked to think of as optimal.

So, back to: Succeed and Escape.

Getting close even in the crowd would be an issue.

What if I threw on a breakaway coat over my chef's jacket and went out through the kitchen? A firm Plan C or D. It came right behind getting a job as a limo driver and popping him in the garage where he'd offed the Holst kids.

The poetic irony of that had to be weighed against the complications.

Getting a chauffeur gig, given my recent employment problems, might be difficult, and it would mean leaving a trail worse than the shiny stream of slime I'd already generated. When the investigation of his death started, I didn't want obvious, visible connections to Alexeeva if I could avoid them, activities I'd already engaged in aside. At the very least I wanted to avoid giving people good long looks in well lighted places.

Short of going the other direction and getting a sniper rifle, I needed a shadowy way to get close. Developing intelligence would be the best way of getting an idea what might be possible. Once the Russian weapon arrived, and I slipped it into the small of my back and started to get used to the feel under an un-tucked shirt, I could move on from visiting locations and track the entourage a little more closely.

I'd found a good used car, a tan Chevy Malibu from the early aughts with a few dents that wouldn't capture much attention. I'd also purchased a little silver camera with an automatic zoom. Again, I just needed images I could work with, not anything sharp enough to stand up in court.

I picked up the crew early one day at the garage. Alexeeva and Taras were busy inspecting the dent in the front fender of a white stretch Escalade parked just inside an open doorway. Looked like it had absorbed a pretty good blow. From the graveness of the expressions, they were either contemplating insurance issues, a potential lawsuit, or having someone shot.

The last possibility started to appear more likely when Nestor brought out a guy who looked like he'd slept in his black suit. The body language said he was pleading his innocence while Alexeeva's suggested a rising temperature. Arms flailed. Gazes turned toward the dent. I got the impression it might be Alexeeva's car and not just another brought in for body work.

The guy gestured with open palms, saying something. Alexeeva flailed more and turned his back. Looked like he said something dismissive. The guy tried to speak again, but Taras stepped in, took his shoulders and turned him away.

He must not be just any driver on a vehicle that had been brought in but Alexeeva's driver. It didn't look good for him. I looked at Nestor to see if he was drawing a weapon, but he just listened to Alexeeva and nodded. The guy walked away, looking like a sad kid with a bad homework grade.

You seek intelligence where you can find it. I located the guy in a little bar on a side street, a nook with exposed wooden beams and a small army of gleaming bottles on display behind the bar. He sat on a stool with a beer. He'd slipped off his suit coat, rolled up the sleeves and loosened the tie. I ordered Bourbon with some ice and rattled the cubes a bit before taking a sip. After he'd finished a couple of drinks and his judgment seemed suitably compromised, I pretended to notice him with an absent glance in his direction.

"Everything okay, buddy?"

"Lost a job. Wasn't my fucking fault."

I studied him, gave him a minute. Sipped. I didn't really want too much in my system this early, but I wanted to look realistic: The Guy with Worse Problems Than Him.

"Been there," I said.

"Car slammed me last night at a corner. Didn't see it. Car full of college kids and a hooker. I hadn't been drinking or anything."

"Lot of noise?"

"One fuckin' loud kid. Kind you wanna punch. The car was still at fault but I got canned. Boss was...insane."

"That empty? I get you another?"

He tilted his bottle, nodding, and I made a replacement magically appear.

When we moved it to a little table across the floor of red-and-black tile, he was telling stories because I'd asked: "Who the fuck is this asshole?"

"Maniac Russian or Ukrainian really. Tries to rule everything." He ran a finger into the waistband of his pants. "Had to keep trim and be perfect to be one of his drivers."

"Sounds like quite a guy."

"Dangerous as fuck. I've said too much already."

"I'm not working for him."

He upended the long neck and emptied it. I gestured to the bartender for another.

"You're having a bad day," I said.

"Could have been worse. I need to remember that." His head bobbed downward, and he shook it in a slow side-to-side. "I looked the other way on a lot of stuff."

They rustled up a barmaid who brought over a little round tray with a fresh bottle. He took it and thanked her, sipped. Then he reiterated that he shouldn't say too much.

We talked about the weather and the Saints for a while. While he was focused on his bottle, I befriended the barmaid, and she brought whiskey after a while. He downed that without really noticing the transition, leaving the regret to me as the conduit for his deepening misery.

"He got mad at this call girl last week," he said as his tongue loosened. "She was supposed to be helping schmooze somebody he wanted to get close to, businessman. Didn't turn out like he wanted. He had me drive to this deserted parking lot. I thought he was just gonna slap her around in the back. That's where it started."

It sounded right in character.

"What'd he do?"

"Slapped her and punched her in the back, then dragged her out the door by her hair. This was a beautiful girl, too, escort type, not a meth whore. He shoved her onto the ground. Had his big boy at his side, you know. She crawled, trying to get away. He stomped her in the ass, flattened her. Then he took a gun from his sidekick, put it to her head, and starts yelling `yzha' `yzha.' Took a while to figure out what he wanted, his face getting' all red. Finally, his goon, Nestor, explained he was saying eat. He'd had me drive to this gravel lot. Girl's face was already scratched up and bruised. Makeup's runnin'. She has to sit there and eat rocks. God knows what that did to her."

Another business deal gone wrong. He clearly hated when that happened, even as he worked toward a higher degree of respectability.

If I'd needed it, I had more confirmation he was a very bad man, but I didn't find it soothing.

If I'd been a cop, and I could turn up the girl wherever she was recovering, I'd have the beginnings of a case, but the Holsts wouldn't really be interested in an assault charge, not even a heinous one. I needed info on Alexeeva's patterns and habits.

The guy killed another long swallow as he relived his memories.

"What was so important that he got this upset?"

"He was trying to wiggle into some financial deal a company was running, I think. The guy was supposed to know some details that would give Mr. Alexeeva a way in. Something about money being forwarded from one person to the next. The guy didn't give as much detail while he had his dick in the girl's mouth as he was supposed to."

I tucked that away for later and bought the guy another round, and the driver remembered the name of the businessman Alexeeva wanted info on was Ryan Moates because he'd thought it sounded like a castle.

I cataloged that too using the same mnemonic, and as he grew more sloshed, I pumped him for what he knew of Alexeeva's schedule, gleaning the details he knew about when he tended to visit his club and when he spent time at the carriage concern.

When he grew so sloshed he ceased to be useful, I paid for a couple more drinks so he wouldn't remember me well, felt around his coat until I found a phone, called him a cab because I didn't know how to use Uber and left enough for the fare tucked in his shirt pocket, hoping for the best for him.

CHAPTER 13

Rose slipped into a chair across from me, looking fresh and comfortable in a grey cotton dress that let her appear professional without wilting in the later afternoon humidity. I wasn't faring quite that well with my sleeves rolled up and shirt un-tucked even though I'd changed and showered before our meeting.

We ordered mojitos that came in tall glasses and looked impossibly refreshing with the mint leaves diving amid the ice cubes.

"You aware of any Ponzi schemes in town involving a guy named Ryan Moats?"

With a long, dark nail, she encouraged a lime wedge to swim a bit.

"If I knew of anything like that, I'd be required to report it as an officer of the court."

"Unless you represented him or his firm?"

"I don't really do financial cases."

"So, who do you hear rumors about?"

"Moates is at an investment firm called Ruffin and Whitehead."

"Top of your head? Really?"

"Everywhere's a small town, and I work with a big firm. We know where the big players are. No indication I've heard of that they're doing a Madoff."

"Could he have something going on the side?"

"Anything's possible, some investment scheme doing a money-in money-out game, but his reputation's above board. Why does this matter?"

"Thought it might be something I could work with. Details you don't need to know and I don't need to leave a paper trail about."

It would probably be better to look for another opportunity to isolate Alexeeva. The more complicated, the more likely I'd be to get nabbed, but I was in an exploratory phase.

"Let me ask around a little just in case it helps," Rose said.

I watched her hair brush her tanned shoulders for a while as she sipped her drink.

"So, you're not into family law, either?" I asked after tearing my attention away from her skin.

"Not my specialty."

"What do you think I'd have to do to win sole custody of a daughter?"

"Sole custody's hard."

"If you're technically an ex-con? My lawyer didn't include rosy in his pallet for the picture."

"It's hard under better circumstances than yours. Physical well-being of a child's an issue. So's psychological. If the mom's living with a dangerous boyfriend or if she's abusive herself you can get a toehold. If she's a single mom doing the best she can, gets more complicated. What about joint custody? Better than the none you have right now."

"Sounds like either's a tough game. I think we have the dangerous boyfriend angle covered. I guess knowing where my ex and my daughter are might be helpful."

"I don't suppose you have a lot of time to look just now."

"Yeah, I'm a little preoccupied."

"Maybe I could put some feelers out. Text me what you know."

"Billable-hour clock running?"

"A courtesy."

"I'll give you her mom's name," I said. "Last known address is Casselberry, Florida." I added Finn's name. Didn't say more. Less she knew the better if all else failed and I had to take a diplomatic approach with him too.

"Should be a start. Is she unfit?"

"Possibly."

"Does she hate you?"

"Now, yeah."

No one sets out to marry the wrong person, the person that combusts when combined with you or who makes you combust. Things always look good up front, when you're staging the fairy tale in your mind. I'd met Sandra on the job. She'd been bartending at a pretty nice place in the Quarter where an argument had escalated into a shooting. She'd been mixing the place's version of a Hurricane for a tourist when the gun had come out at the little table near the window.

She'd been wearing little makeup that night, and her hair, brown then, had been pinned in a tangle behind her head. Sitting at a barstool when I walked in, black tee shirt, black jeans, she looked nervous as she talked to a uniformed officer.

"She got a pretty good look," he said when I walked up.

I lowered myself a little so we could see eye-to-eye and tried to calm her. She didn't know names, but she'd seen the guys in the place regularly. Buddies. Until they weren't.

Nobody would have called her beautiful that night, but I saw something in her eyes as I talked to her, working to calm her down. She was scared of having to testify. A common thing. I told her she probably wouldn't need to. People usually like to hear that.

Sometimes it's true.

I got a story or two about cleaning up vomit out of her, learned she took classes at Delgado with an eye toward something related to early childhood development and finally coaxed a description out of her.

Connecting the dots didn't prove that hard.

We found the guy in the cheap hotel where he was hiding out, and he confessed when questioned. Sandra really didn't have to testify, but I'd managed to get her number as we talked. I called her a few days later, and we went for a beer.

She'd changed her hair color to blond by then, and she wore it unpinned and coiffed in soft waves with a sequined shirt and black jeans. She laughed a lot that night and talked a lot about the work she planned once she'd earned her degree. She'd be helping kids with pervasive developmental disorders. She was working on a paper on something called Rett Syndrome. With my days devoted to dealing with street crime and dead bodies, she'd seemed like a princess.

"She's not really up to date on who I am these days," I said. "She was happy enough with having a little money when we were together. Less happy being tied down, I guess."

"You paying child support?"

"A trickle. I had an account set up before I went in. There's not a lot left in it."

"You need to improve the flow, but don't get crazy with the infusion. Someone who shouldn't might notice that. I never said that."

I nodded, and she let another sip of her drink pass her lips. "I should be going."

I stood and watched her weave away through the rows of tables, then slipped the disposable cell from my pocket.

It would make me more vulnerable, but I was going to need some help. I tapped out the number to check in with Arch.

CHAPTER 14

The PSM was ready on my next visit to the McClusky compound. Kenneth presented it proudly in a little case on a bed of grey foam. It was black and shiny, as small and thin as advertised, looking like it came right out of a spy movie. I said as much.

"You might say it's a cousin of the James Bond guns," Arch said. "Or maybe the cousin of the bad guys' guns."

That kind of fit. I was one of the bad guys now.

I tested the weight of it in my hand, tested the fit and looked at the cartridges that came with it, recalling the promises.

"There enough of these to try it on your range?"

"More where those came from," Arch said. "It's out here."

He flapped open a back screen door, and we trudged out to an area that had been cleared for a target array, a row of head-and-torso silhouettes on thin posts. Numbered white circles within circles decorated the figures with a couple of orange priority areas indicated at the head and center of the abdomen.

"Kenny put out a fresh set for you."

"Just for me?"

"Nah, these are the ones the business executives like to use when they're here. Makes 'em feel like real men, I guess."

I'd qualified on ranges throughout my law enforcement career. I'd been competent, never aspiring to be a marksman or join competitive shooting teams. I knew a guy who'd shot himself in the leg while training on one of those. The other cops had called him Shitty Shitting Bang Bang after that, Bang Bang for short, not the respect he'd hoped for in joining the team.

I wasn't sure I wanted to test my skill level with an audience, but I loaded the PSM as Arch looked on. When I tested it in my hand again, the weight and fit were still comfortable. I'd been expecting it to feel a little awkward like one of those miniature plastic forks they give you at picnics or the Colonel's. With the grip in my palm, I still had about an inch of lower hand showing. I leveled the weapon between both hands, sighted down the barrel and worked to get a feel for it, then planted my feet.

"Go ahead," Arch said.

"Kenny's not out there somewhere behind it is he?"

He called to his brother and got no answer, so I tried squeezing the trigger.

A tuft of ground kicked up somewhere off to the side of the targets.

"Been a while, eh?" Arch said.

"Small arms training wasn't something they offered or encouraged at David Wade."

I adjusted my stance, sighted again, drew a breath, held it, squeezed, and winged one of the silhouettes as the grip snapped back against my palm with a mild recoil.

"You're likely to be in close when you need that, right?"

"I'd rather not have to be."

I leveled again, took a few seconds to calm myself, pretended Arch wasn't looking and managed to get inside one of the numbered circles. One of the larger ones.

"I think it's pulling," I said.

"Really?"

Arch took the weapon, stepped into a spot facing the targets, raised the barrel and squeezed off the rest of the clip, sending the rounds into the priority region of the chest.

"It's windy where I was standing," I said.

He grinned. "A few pointers?"

"If that was my old service weapon, those figures would be on gurneys now," I said.

After we'd reloaded, I let him suggest the position for my feet then let him move my arms a bit, and in a while, I was showing signs of improvement.

"You're not stopping a subject on every shot, but you're getting better," Arch said. "After lunch, you may be ready for the maze."

"What's the maze?"

"After lunch."

He made Italian poor boys, which we call po' boys in Louisiana. It took him a while. I watched European sports via the satellite until he finished.

The sandwiches were as good as the best shops in the French Quarter. I felt a little sluggish after the thick bread and slices of ham and soppressata hit my stomach.

I didn't really care about televised Snooker, but it passed the time until early afternoon when we ventured outside again, departing the cleared area and following a trail back through underbrush until we came upon a mass of camouflage netting featuring a pattern of mostly green and reddish brown.

"Why don't you wind your way through and see how it goes?" Arch said, peeling back a flap that offered an entrance.

I shrugged and stepped inside, into a narrow and shadowy passage. Only a few pinpricks of light slipped in here or there.

"The businessmen really get a kick out this," Arch called from outside. "I think they usually pretend they're stalking their CEOS."

Not too far removed from what I was up to. Maybe it would be helpful.

I crouched a bit, got the PSM between my hands and let my eyes adjust from the sunlight, taking note of plywood and two-by-fours that provided the structure's framework.

The ceiling dipped lower after a short stretch. I crouched and checked around the first turn where the shadows deepened and then moved forward.

I felt a bit of tension at my shin, and my heart jumped into my throat when a light came on about four feet ahead of me, illuminating a grey-green figure with bright red streaks from its chin down its chest.

I pumped a shot into almost instinctively. Given the range, I scored a hit just to the right of the sternum and blood began to bubble out of the puncture, or red liquid.

"The fuck is this thing?" I asked.

"It's a zombie," Alex called from outside. "Don't let him bite you."

I fired a round into the forehead and produced more syrupy crimson. It was supposed to be a game, but the faux realism was sobering. This was what I sought to accomplish.

"It's done for," Arch said.

I snapped out of it and snaked on, stooping, crouching into two duck walks in even lower spots, and I scored reasonable hits on printed targets that looked like terrorists, criminals and a couple more grey torso figures with ill-defined features, though they were man-like enough to make me think again about what I was really up to. No illusions allowed.

That took away any of the zippy joys the vice presidents might have felt in the maze. Even though he was a man who'd make a beautiful girl eat rocks, Alexeeva was a man, and I'd been task with deciding on the end-of-the-line.

I knew what it felt like to do that in a self-defense situation with Leo Maier.

I'd spent some time in talk therapy about it, tried then to find words to express the depth of the emotion, but it had been hard to put into words.

I knew, even with the consequences, I'd had to pull the trigger then. He would have pumped bullets into me. My partner was already shot.

So, guilt was not the term for what I'd felt. It was more a broad and complex sense of responsibility, almost something cosmic, an irreversible act and a conversion of a man from something to nothingness. It had left me feeling very alone, not the only one who'd taken a life, but suddenly not quite like everyone else and not really capable of expressing that. There was a dose of sadness in that mix too, if not mourning. I'd never known him. I could not mourn, but I could feel the distress of loss and the anguish of something I couldn't take back.

I had to ask myself if I could do it again not under threat but with strategy and dispassion. Pulling the trigger on a toy zombie or a two-dimensional paper figure could only help achieve accuracy. It couldn't predict.

I wasn't sure how I'd find the stomach for it when the time

really arrived. The provolone and pork in my stomach grew heavy as I thought about it, and the little black weapon ceased to seem cool and elegant if it ever really had. It was metal designed to hurl metal into human tissue.

I stared at it in a sliver of sunlight near a support beam.

It quite possibly had already done that in some cold back alley of New York or Washington. Maybe that thought was glamorizing its provenance, but it didn't seem out of the question that someone with immunity might have destroyed an enemy or a colleague who'd failed in some way. So, there I was, a lonely figure with a weapon perhaps equally damned.

Then arms came out from the wall and closed around me.

I found myself in an iron grip, unable to move my arms, unable to pull free, capable of moving my weapon hand upward but not of controlling it effectively. My lungs weren't expanding that well in the already-stale air either.

Then a shrill whistle sounded in my ear. A gotcha announcement.

A second after I was trapped, I knew it had to be Kenny, but the rush of fear didn't depart with the realization. I struggled at first then relaxed as a snicker and laugh hissed my way.

"You knew there had to be a Minotaur in a maze, didn't you?" Arch was outside but nearby.

I writhed a bit more, twisted, and then Kenny began to laugh and released me. I staggered away, beginning to laugh myself now as well, and suddenly sunlight flooded around me.

Arch had pulled back a flap of tenting and camouflage, and he stood in the opening with hands on hips.

I slipped past and breathed in fresh air.

"Kenny ever get shot in these games?"

"No one's come close. He's pretty quiet and agile when he wants to be."

Kenny's head emerged from the tenting and he smiled. "Boom, boom."

I flexed my arms a bit, celebrating freedom of movement again with the rush of fresh air.

"Why don't we go back in and let me practice sneaking up on him?" I suggested. "That might be a better task for me."

Arch's brow wrinkled a moment as he contemplated that, wondering, no doubt, how that would be useful to me and drawing some reasonable conclusions. After a consultation with his brother via eyebrow gestures, he nodded.

"We can give that a try," he said. "Good luck."

He pulled back the flap and made a gesture for me to step back inside, and we spent the rest of the afternoon with me stalking Kenny sans live rounds in the PSM. He periodically made me jump out of my skin with unexpected bursts from his whistle. I think the note affected the central nervous system.

Despite his size, when he wanted to, he exhibited, as I'd observed, considerable stealth.

He outsmarted me a couple of times the next day, noticing me before I could get close, but I maneuvered into situations a couple more times where I scored imaginary hits with a loud "bang bang."

The return of old reflexes was gradual, but it happened, though luck still played a big roll.

I reacted to each success with elation only to feel it slowly deflate as I remembered what I was really teaching myself to do.

Wandering through the businessman's maze had been survival training. I was modifying it into training for silent aggression. Despite the adrenalin and excitement, only the image of Finn of the Drooping Eyelid kept me going.

Eventually, Arch entered the maze with me and took me through a few techniques deployed in the Middle East for entering and clearing buildings. I needed to rely on more than luck, and that seemed a little closer to what I'd be taking on in pursuing Alexeeva.

I was sure Arch was beginning to suspect what my task might really entail when I asked if we could go through a few more maneuvers with Kenny heading through the maze and me working on quiet pursuit. We ditched live ammo, and we did pursuit, then a few scenarios where I hid and waited.

Kenny's senses were so acute, he drew down on me with an extended index finger several times. I got used to his squeaky "Boom booms."

"Let me show you a few things," Arch said after Kenny had tagged me another time.

We found a nook in the maze at the edge of a passage.

"If you stand really quietly here, and place your weight so that you can swing out a bit in a fluid move, you can draw down with a little bit of time and surprise on your side. Strike before he senses you."

He gave me a demo, back to a nook with the passage on his right. He shifted weight onto his right foot and stood with his feet apart.

"Come on up, Kenny, pretend you don't see us."

Kenny proceeded our way, moving almost silently, light on his feet in spite of his size.

Arch waited until he was a few paces from his position then swung his left leg out in a quick arc, following through with the rest of his body.

He was almost instantly in a shooting stance in his brother's path. He leveled his imaginary weapon and dropped his thumbs in hammer fashion.

"Bang, bang, bang."

Kenny clutched his chest, let out a theatrical grunt and staggered backwards.

"With the right rounds in the PSM, he's taken a pretty good hit," Arch said. "You got a grudge against him, you just evened the score."

It would be a little different in a corridor or on a street, but after I'd practiced it a few times I felt a little more confident.

I still didn't feel like a soldier. Not in spirit. I was something different than a defender, but on the technical side, I felt like I'd reawakened a few rusty bits of reflex and layered on a little more technique.

"What say, I take you out for a drink," I said to Arch.

"Where are we going?"

"A place I need to have a look around anyway."

CHAPTER 15

A rch cleaned up pretty well once I told him where we were going. He already had things he could testify about. What were a few more?

I found Crystal again, forgave her the cleaning out of my wallet as she babbled to itemize and justify the expenses, and she brought along Amara, a Creole girl with blue eyes, streaks of blonde and a beige dress speckled with shiny shards that sent out flashes of light. With Crystal in a tight, short and also shiny blue-black dress, no one would be paying attention to two guys in suits at The Runnell. Especially not with Arch's clean-shaven face and return to a near military haircut. Once he had turned his car over to an attendant, we didn't face much of a holdup at the door either, though the club was hopping.

We were shown a path beside the throbbing dance floor where mad patterns of red, green, violet, and fuchsia alternated, and spotlights with similar gels shined down. A tall bistro table with bar stools awaited us near one of two bars positioned just opposite each other.

The ladies tugged hemlines into strategic positions once seated, and we ordered a bottle that would raise the Holst's eyebrows on the expense account but wouldn't come with sparklers. I wanted to fit in, but there was no need to be dazzling.

Alexeeva and his friends were nowhere in sight. Looked just like a typical Tuesday crowd.

"Are we going to dance?" Amara shouted as she ran a hand along Arch's forearm. She probably thought I was a businessman entertaining a client. She wanted to do her part to make him happy.

"Maybe in a while," he said.

We were more interested in scanning the landscape. The dance floor displayed a scene from a dystopian future where the hordes looked like green laser lights controlled their thrashing movement. While the room opened to the rafters over the dance floor, stairs on either side led to a second-floor balcony that bordered the back and side walls. Tables lined it, packed with business casual types. Getting anywhere would be a challenge.

"Looks like some meeting rooms on the second floor," Arch noted with a tilt of his head. "Probably not offices."

I hadn't given him a specific purpose for my reconnaissance. Less for him to testify about besides the weapon, worst case scenario. All I'd asked was for him to accompany me to a club, but he wasn't stupid.

Near the front of the dance floor above a stage where a dee jay worked tonight. More doors led somewhere, probably to offices and the green rooms.

Second floor was no good. Bang bang in one of those rooms then it would have to be out along the balcony, weaving around tables and drunk patrons just to get to the stairs and attempt a descent behind someone in no hurry.

First floor might be the best option.

More doors opened off the back wall. Restrooms were along one narrow corridor there.

There should be a back way out.

In a room there—bang, bang during off hours and then to the alley? If I involved Arch further, it might be good to have him waiting with the door open, ready to deliver silenced rounds at anyone like body guards who tried to exit. Seemed viable given the desire for me to kiss Alexeeva on the cheek and not place a bomb in his car or use a sniper approach.

I'd need a better look at the physical layout and later the blueprints if I could get them, check escape routes vs. the garage. He was here more often of late, which I had to consider. He'd given up his leather jackets and gold chains for Tom Ford and the club suited the self-image he been trending toward. A look at the office space now while things were busy offered an opportunity for at least the physical layout.

"You guys stay here if you want," I said to Arch. "Dance if you want to."

That prompted Amara to clap and burst into a chorus of the old song. I gave Arch a wink in response to his grim expression and took Crystal's wrist.

Her tongue made a quick circle of her lips, and she followed me. My Russian diplomat's weapon that I'd palmed and played a moving game with while they had swept me with a wand at the security gate, felt snug holstered at the small of my back, though I was conscious of making sure it didn't slip down a pant leg.

After weaving a little way into the thralldom of the laser light, Crystal raised her arms over her head and began a little gyration coupled with a slow hip rotation.

I moved my feet a little, lifted my arms, tried not to look like my dad, though I felt like I was him, doing a stiff and awkward samba in his full-dress blues. What would he think of this mission I was on?

He'd grown almost violently angry one night when I was a kid and jumped a curb, driving too fast in my Chevy. I'd popped a hubcap and bent the wheel a fraction of an inch, and he'd turned into Mr. Hyde, railing about the importance of following laws, including traffic laws passed to keep idiot kids alive. Sorry, Dad. Shit happens. Sometimes you have to waste a bad guy when the law fails. If you really need the money.

I thought I heard him roll over in his neatly tended grave out in Metairie, but I put my internal philosophical debate on hold when I spotted Alexeeva and his entourage moving along the dance floor's edge.

Shifting position slightly and maintaining movement, I traced the group. Taras and Nestor flanked Alexeeva. Some other thick neck walked at his back. No telling what artillery he was packing under his blazer.

"Everything all right?" Crystal asked, taking my wrist and leaning in for access to an ear.

"Fine."

"What are we up to?"

"Just looking around."

"You want to find a bathroom stall? I could relieve some of that tension."

"Dancing's fine."

She took that as a cue and ramped up her movements, adding gyrations and twists that would have made some pole dancers look geriatric. I tore my gaze from the rise of her hemline and clapped my hands a few times as I watched a skinny kid in a hoodie moving toward the entourage.

With the head bowed and hands in pockets, I wondered if someone already had plans for the big man, but when the figure reached him, the feet arched to tip toes, and the hooded head leaned toward his face. Something was said into Nestor's ear and that prompted nods and hand gestures as he took the small figure's arm.

I'd decided it must be a female from the movements, though in the baggy clothes, the moves lacked the seductive quality of Crystal's. The entourage kept moving past the bar and through that door that seemed to open into a hallway.

Maybe it would be a good time to get a feel for the offices and that portion of the club.

"OK, you talked me into it," I said, taking Crystal's wrist. "Let's find a corner."

I led her along the path Alexeeva and his friends had followed, weaving around dancers. If anyone from the entourage turned our way, I could make things look exactly like Crystal thought they were, a guy with a willing girl looking for some privacy.

We made it to the same door they'd passed through without opposition and pushed through. The corridor was a lot less glitzy than the dance floor, drab brown walls lit with cone-shaped gold fixtures that looked like they'd stayed around only after a bribe to the electrical inspector.

Crystal brushed against me once the door closed out the noise and the crowd. Kisses landed on my neck. I turned and leaned into her, grabbing a taste of her mouth as I pressed her back against the wall and feeling the grind of her pelvis.

"Mmm, you're hungry," she said, sliding a hand in front of me, feeling for my crotch.

I caught her wrist.

"Save it 'til...."

She parted her lips and came after more kisses, as if she were trying to devour my mouth, really playing out the GFE. I kissed back and adjusted our position a fraction. That let me look over her shoulder even as I fought the burn in my groin, stoked by the press of her breasts.

The corridor stretched only a few feet. At the end of it, an oak door stood open about eight inches. Inside, a wooden desk and a couple of chairs filled most of the space. Alexeeva sat on the edge of the desk. The wispy figure leaned against the wall just inside the door.

"So how much were you seeing?" Alexeeva asked.

Something was mumbled.

The wisp seemed to be some kind of go-between. It was hard to tell which enterprise had shorted or offended the big man, but he wasn't particularly happy.

"You want me to get pictures?" the wisp asked. It was definitely a girl.

"You've done fine. We'll get on with it. You just go on home, wait for next assignment."

He turned his attention to someone I couldn't see in the office, somewhere beside the girl.

"Taras."

As Alexeeva started speaking, apparently instructions in Russian, the girl turned, slipping quickly through the doorway and stepping our way in a hurry, anxious to be back at the task of fulfilling her boss's commands.

I let Crystal continue her kisses and the grinding of her hips. This kind of thing had to happen all the time at the club. In fact, the girl slipped her hands in her pockets and started to move past us, averting her face. She couldn't pretend not to notice, but she could pass on gawking.

That would have been the end of it. She'd have slipped back into the dance area and out the front door, and I'd have feigned the discovery that Crystal and I were in the wrong hallway for a bathroom break, allowing me to guide her back to our table. I would have returned to Arch with knowledge of the office location and its dangers as a meeting spot since the quarters and the corridor were cramped.

But just as the face turned away, I noticed something familiar about the features only partially shrouded by the hoodie. She passed under one of the cones, catching enough of the glow.

I'd worked with enough missing persons cases and runaways to lock in on traits that didn't change easily like eye color and the shape of a nose, the cast of a jawline.

I couldn't be sure about the eye color, and I was catching just hints of blond hair, but even with a few more years on her, I could align the face with the photo I'd seen before. The photo I'd studied.

The girl in the hoodie was Dahlia Holst.

CHAPTER 16

I needed confirmation. Quick confirmation. I eased Crystal back just a couple of inches.

"Dahlia," I said, trying to make it just loud enough to be heard over the dance floor's throb that drifted our way.

She froze. The hooded head turned then, and I saw the frightened expression. That was confirmation enough. I grabbed her wrist as she tried to bolt. Then I pushed the door to the dance floor open, disentangling from Crystal as Dahlia tried to drag me along.

I wished for more hands. I wanted to grab my cell and the Russian handgun and hold on to the girl at the same time.

"The fuck's going on?" Crystal demanded.

I found her shoulder and pulled her in close so she could hear me over the music. "Get your friend and get out of here. Send Arch to the exit."

"What about our money?"

Dahlia was like a boat on a line struggling to break free in a storm. I locked my grip on her wrist and fished a fold of bills I had for tips from my pants pocket.

"Take this. Down payment. More later. Use the confusion. Get somewhere safe. We have to move, and you're not going to want the guys getting a good look at you."

"Which guys?"

The door pushed open behind her, giving enough of an answer to send her scampering. I shot my hand down to my spine as if it rested on a handgun, giving them a view that suggested what I might pack without showing it.

Dahlia shouted: "Let me go, asshole."

"Settle down. You're coming with me."

"They'll gut us both."

"Not if they don't catch us. Move."

We started around the dance floor, through throngs of tipsy and inebriated clubbers who swayed with the music, groped and chatted. I had the problem I'd envisioned if I'd been fleeing after a hit, and it was as bad as I'd expected and more.

At least Alexeeva's goons faced the same challenges. This was the good business. They didn't want to show their gats or raise much of a stir either. As I glanced to my right, at least Crystal seemed to be faring better, cutting a beeline across the dance floor. When Dahlia and I hit a yuppie roadblock, I pulled her in to me and pressed my ear against the hoodie.

"I'm working for your father. Let me get you out of here."

She looked up at me with a face that contorted in terror.

"Please, he'll gut him too. You've got to let me go back."

I wished she'd stop giving me that mental image. It made eating rocks sound appealing by comparison.

"Sorry," I said.

My heart was in my throat, but I was seeing a paycheck without having to pull a trigger, at least not as an assassin. I'd never been sure I could do it anyway.

The new possibility felt good even if the muscle heading for me didn't. I pushed through a couple of guys in suits who were trying to chat up a pair of girls dressed like Crystal, mouthing an "excuse me." Fully conscious of how much I looked like a predator, I moved on, threading, dodging, refusing to let go of Dahlia.

Temporarily, I let go of the gun and found the burner cell, thumbing Arch's number as I took a glance behind me. The biggest guy was bulldozing a path through the bodies behind me, a juggernaut for Nestor and Taras, who stuck close to his shoulders.

I couldn't hear anything on the cell, couldn't even be sure it was ringing. I'd have to count on Crystal to carrier pigeon the message. Clicking off, I pocketed the phone and put my hand back on the PSM at the same time we steered around a waitress with a round tray of Longnecks.

Dahlia caught the arm of a woman in a red sequined dress as we danced around the employee without incident. She tried to say something or maybe she did. The woman gave me a questioning look.

"I'm her dad," I shouted. "She shouldn't be in here."

That melted the expression a tad. I might not have convinced her, but it allowed a detachment, and we moved on, inching through the bodies, jostling people who only wanted to clap and giggle.

"Trying to get my daughter out of here," I said, maintaining the lie as an apology as people reacted to the jostling.

I could have told them a Spetsnaz battle tank would be a few seconds behind me, but I didn't take the time. I tried to maintain focus. The door was getting closer, but I encountered a column of college girls, dancing and twisting their way toward a restroom. They followed each other by some kind of bat radar, inches apart, tipsy, arms raised and waving with the music throb. It might have been a pleasant and provocative display, if you didn't have pain and death vendors bringing up your rear.

I couldn't get their attention to break through easily. I paused, watching them snake along. Dahlia seized the moment to make a fresh tug on her arm. I felt her forearm sliding through my hand and almost lost her when her wrist reached my palm.

Clamping tighter just before she freed herself, I realized I needed to do something. The co-ed procession wasn't getting any faster.

Putting ethics aside and letting go of the idea that I wouldn't be remembered here, I took the obvious action. I yelled: "Fire."

CHAPTER 17

The reactions along the conga line were immediate. Panicked expressions flared, and for a second or so girls looked at each other, left, right, eyebrows raised, quizzical, eyes wide. Then they bolted, looking for the door.

"Fire's in the back," I shouted to one frozen girl who for some reason looked to me like she'd be named Amber. That jarred her to attention. "I'm trying to get my daughter out of here."

She spun and joined the fleeing sorority, and collected a few companions in the process, and the crowd began to funnel toward the exit, dismay becoming viral.

I hoped no one would be trampled. Behind us Alexeeva and even his bull dozer were jostled as news was picked up by those over their way.

I let go of my weapon again and dialed Arch once more, hoping he'd made it outside. I pressed the cell to my ear even while wrapping an arm around Dahlia from behind and pressing forward with her struggling form.

She bumped into a guy who reacted negatively. I gave him a forearm smash with the cell phone arm and sent him teetering then returned the cell to my ear.

If I'd made a connection and if Arch was talking, I couldn't hear him. I kept it handy but concentrated on following the crowd funneling toward the exit. Behind me, the guy I'd smashed went into someone else, causing more animosity. Punches were thrown. That placed more confusion between me and Alexeeva's men. I couldn't complain.

Turning sideways, I tugged Dahlia through a narrow space, keeping my grip locked around her wrist like a handcuff. She did everything short of starting to gnaw her own arm off to get free. I managed to hang on anyway and found a spot in the bottleneck at the doorway that eventually pushed us forward, even as bodies crushed in on us from all sides. I worried Dahlia might get crushed and remembered old news stories of concert tragedies.

Pulling her toward me, which was like tugging someone out of quicksand if Tarzan movies are to be believed, I lifted her, wrapped my arms around her and forced my way into open space on the sidewalk.

In frenzied situations, people don't get to freedom and move in an orderly fashion to the side to let others out. They cluster where they emerge, blocking the way. We slammed through a group of club goers who stood with folded arms, chatting. They shrieked and complained but happily scattered.

I moved on through them, planning to step from beneath the overhang onto the street so that I could look for Arch, who I prayed was finding the vehicle. I didn't get as far as I hoped.

More shrieks and complaints sounded behind me. The bulldozer had emerged. He clapped an arm on my shoulder and mumbled something I didn't understand, but I got the impression he wanted us to come with him.

Un-diplomatically, amid the confusion, I slipped the PSM from my spine. I thought about aiming above the knee but trying to avoid his femoral artery. I wanted him to leave us alone, but I didn't seek to cripple him or cause him to bleed out, though I suspected getting him medical attention wouldn't be an immediate priority for Alexeeva.

I chose instead to hammer his lower face with the handle. He groaned and went down as his nose crunched under the weapon's force. I left him fighting the blood flow which held his attention. That dispersed the crowd a bit as well. They drew away, repulsed, sending rippling confusion outward where calm had settled.

CHAPTER 18

I towed Dahlia toward the opposite side of the street, aiming for shadow as I stuffed the diplomatic weapon into a pocket and found the cell again. The noise level remained high, but I thumbed Arch's number one more time and pressed it to my ear.

"Can you hear me now?" I asked.

"Got you. Where are you?"

"Front of the club. I hope you're getting the car."

I tugged Dahlia toward me, and we leaned against a stone wall as sirens filled the air and the clamor before us escalated. More people spilled through The Runnell exit, some tripping over the downed Bulldozer and people who'd knelt to help him.

"Finding it. I see a garage."

"You're never going to get it up the street here. We'll get away from this crowd and meet you at the garage exit."

"I'll call when I'm headed out."

"You're never going to get away. You're just going to get us both fucking killed." Dahlia looked up at me, eyes blazing with anger.

"Your mother wouldn't want you talking like that."

"She wouldn't want me getting everyone killed either. You don't know what he'll do." She tried to make herself an anchor. "He'll do anything if he hates you. He'll find a way to get even. To make you sorry you ever fucked with him."

I contemplated the repercussions of shooting her in the leg and just carrying her. She'd keep talking regardless, probably even get noisier with the inevitable whines and screams.

Her family could deal with her Stockholm Syndrome later. I

needed to focus on immediate concerns. Alexeeva and his pals had just emerged from the club, and he shouted instructions.

I looked to my right. A hurricane fence covered the mouth of a gravel alley. I wouldn't be able to get Dahlia over that. The area around The Runnell hadn't enjoyed quite the gentrification Alexeeva had brought to his club. We hoofed the other direction. I kept myself to the street side, masking Dahlia as much as possible as we moved past a drab cinderblock building with a barred window and a grungy beer sign. Beyond it, a parking garage's sign flared. Looked to be six or seven floors. Had to be where the valets were stowing Runnell vehicles.

The building beside us proved to be open for business. Canned music and beer fumes wafted through the open doorway at the corner. A few neon signs provided most of the light inside, but patrons had come out to see what was going on. They were grim, working class guys who'd already downed a few.

I pushed past them and a circle of still panicked girls in chiffon and sequins. Then we crossed the street. The garage's ramp, marked with exit only signs, was midway up that street and lighted. I didn't want to tarry there until Arch was close, so I edged Dahlia into a nook behind a dumpster where the garage parked golf carts, little maintenance vehicles and a shuttle to take vehicle owners to nearby venues. Had to be a security guard around but I didn't see him.

"Keep quiet," I said.

I tried to think of a viable threat as I watched for Alexeeva's pals, but she kept her mouth shut for the moment without inducement. Maybe a part of her wanted to go home or maybe she worried about what they'd do.

I tried Arch.

"Where are you?"

"They must have the cars on the seventh level."

OK, it was seven floors. He panted.

"It's getting hairy down here."

"Since when do you say hairy?"

He had the wind for that?

"Don't soldiers use that term?"

"Maybe in *Full Metal Jacket*. Embrace the suck and wait for me."

So, that was surly Arch in his debut.

On the Runnell side of the street Nestor and Taras headed our way, scanning the chiffon and blue collars for Dahlia. If I'd known I would have brought a prom dress to stuff her into.

I put my hand on top of her head and forced her down further beside a security truck, checking the handle as I kept my eye on the boys.

Locked.

The boys: across the street, scanning.

I willed them to move on, past the garage, on up the street. The next street would be a boulevard that ran in front of the convention center. Would they think that was a likely destination for a getaway?

What would I have thought as a cop, when I'd been on the other side of hunts like this? Probably that the shadows were worth checking but that this operation was well organized and that transportation waited there.

I didn't like being the one hiding. The one sweating. When you're a cop you can almost pick up the scent of that sweat and the fear. You're usually on the trail of a stupid kid who's botched a job that seemed easy enough when all the factors weren't weighed.

Now I knew how it felt.

Icicles were melting in my arm pits and spilling down my torso. I'd acted on impulse, thinking I could pull it off with bravado and will power. I was starting to feel like I'd knocked over a liquor store and found my car blocked in, forced to flee on foot.

Nestor and Taras must have noses like a pair of cops. They started our way.

CHAPTER 19

I couldn't risk a call to Arch now. Short of a coat hanger, lock jock, or tennis ball I didn't have an easy way into one of the security vehicles. I know. I know. The tennis ball trick's an urban myth anyway.

I raised my head an inch, looking across the hood of the vehicle we crouched behind. The boys were checking both directions but coming our way, catching just a little strobe from the police car that must've made it to the front of the club by now.

I dipped again, looking at Dahlia, who'd stopped making me grip her quite so hard.

"Don't you want to shout and get your friends over so you can go back with them?"

"I'm gonna get caned for letting you drag me this far."

"Get ready to run then. We're going up that exit ramp."

"They'll catch us in no time."

"I'm going make it seem wise to keep their heads down. Get ready to run."

I raised the weapon barrel up to press it against the vehicle window.

"Head down, sweetheart. Fingers in ears."

I pulled the trigger.

Sounded like a cannon blast and started a stitching pattern of cracks through the glass an instant before the slug shattered the window on the other side then exploded a window on the security truck parked beside.

If I'd been in their place, approaching, I would have dropped and expected Uzi spray. Or a Howitzer.

I hoped that's what Taras and Nestor were doing while I was taking Dahlia's hand and sprinting for the exit ramp. I weighed other flight possibilities and all of them left us exposed longer. The best plan B had been to get to the next street and jack a car. I couldn't come up with a timing count on that that didn't allow the boys time to catch up with us. Heading into a maze, we'd have cover and a few seconds to think of something else. You'd have done it differently? Well, I was improvising as fast as I could.

With Dahlia puffing at my side, we charged along the sidewalk, past the yellow curb and up the exit ramp incline. A surprised attendant in his little lighted booth jerked his head around but didn't have time to speak as we dashed right then up a parking row.

I got the cell free and thumbed redial.

"Talk to me, Arch."

"Found my car. Working on getting in. Valets had the key."

"Expedite."

Dahlia and I ducked into a space between a couple of SUVs that could have accommodated the Saints defense and sank down onto cold and gritty pavement, panting. Over our puffs, I could hear quick shouts somewhere behind us, then staccato speech that sounded like Belarus street slang.

"Should we go?" Dahlia asked in a whisper?

"Wait a while. We're needles in a haystack at the moment."

I tried listening for footsteps but couldn't pick up anything, and voices had silenced. Nestor and Taras had decided I didn't need to track their whereabouts any more than I wanted them knowing mine.

"My parents hired you to look for me?" Dahlia asked. I realized she trembled in spite of the night's heat.

"Something like that. It's better to keep quiet right now."

"Are they okay?"

"Other than the debilitating depression."

The longer we sat, I could smell oil and antifreeze along with remnants of exhaust and a faint, acrid waft of urine. Plenty of smells. Still no sound.

The absence of sound or any sign tightened my insides. They

could be creeping up on us, or moving up the ramp beside this level. I looked through the space to our side, but I saw only tires and axels.

I needed a look. My intellect told me it was better to sit still, but that squeeze in my gut kept telling me I needed to look over the top of the car. I patted Dahlia's arm and motioned her to sit tight, then twisted and rose on the balls of my feet, looking through the rear windows of the SUV. They were tinted to keep out Crescent City sunlight, but they made the garage look like midnight. I thought I saw a smudge moving down at the mouth of this level. I couldn't tell if it headed our way.

I thumbed the phone.

"How are you?"

"Rolling," Archie said.

"We're on Level 2. We'll be watching."

I inched back along the SUV and looked around the rear taillight. Taras stood at the mouth of this level with his back to us. He focused somewhere to his right, motioning with a handgun. The shattered windows must not have caught the attention of the cops.

I twisted around, wincing as grit sounded under the soles of my shoes.

I nodded toward the space near the SUV's hood that opened to the next level ramp. The concrete angled upward, but there wasn't much of a barrier. Dahlia moved that way, and I gave her a boost to squeeze through the space. After a glance back, I followed and we crawled between an Accord and a silver sedan.

"Keep moving," I whispered. I wasn't sure where Nestor might be, but running to meet Arch seemed worth the risk. We trotted up the incline and jagged to the right toward the next rise.

Headlights hit the wall near the end of that ramp. I pulled Dahlia back an inch and watched then breathed easy when I saw the front fenders of Arch's car round the corner.

I waved an arm. He screeched down our way and slowed as we dashed in front of him, grabbing for handles on the passenger side. I put Dahlia in the back seat and ordered her to buckle then dived into the front.

"She going to stay with us?"

"She's worried this has gone on so long they'll kill her for real. Let's roll. Let's head for the entrance."

He stomped the gas, wheeled past the pillar that marked the ramp's corner and shot down the ramp we'd just climbed, wind whistling through the hole in his window.

"Down," he shouted.

Spider webs appeared on the windshield as one of the boys fired. The slugs sighed into the back seat, inches from where Dahlia's torso had been before she'd rolled into the floorboard upon his command.

"Get us outta here," I shouted.

"You got it."

Tires screeched, the odor of burned rubber entered through the window hole, and we were through a couple of turns that pointed the car toward the entrance.

Happily, no one was trying to pull inside at the moment. Another astonished gate attendant peered through a booth window with wide eyes, and we ignored him as the car shot through the narrow entryway, the grill ripping a gate arm away as we exited into the night.

CHAPTER 20

The Holsts looked like they'd had a bad time at airport security. They'd thrown some of the previous day's clothes back on, stuffed things into suitcases and hustled out of their house. Sleeves were rolled up. Shirttails not quite tucked right and items stuck through the cracks of their bags.

They hadn't flown anywhere. We'd all converged after a drive to a spot just north of New Orleans. In a parking lot at a deserted office complex in Mandeville, an awkward bit of hugging and sobbing transpired. They looked at Dahlia not quite the way they would have looked at a ghost. She reacted to them with the silence and stiffness of a kid forced to greet an aunt and uncle she didn't really remember and certainly didn't want to be hugged by.

I'd called Rose from the Pontchartrain Expressway following a series of turns and twists and minutes of sitting against a curb with the lights off here or there to make sure no one picked up our trail, cop or otherwise. Putting twenty-five miles of water between us and Alexeeva didn't mean much, but it had a soothing effect.

"You're gonna want the Holsts out of their house," I'd told Rose. "Ten minutes ago. Got me?"

"Talk to you soon," she said without hesitation.

By 2 a.m. we'd settled into the common area of a little blue and white guest cottage in the town's historic area, piled on padded sofas, sipping beers and soft drinks. I was relieved when Arch mentioned he'd put modified plates on the car as a matter of course. That helped everyone if they muscled security footage out of the garage.

"We stumbled into it," I said when questioning began. I wished they could just cut us a check and let us be on our way. I wanted to be on the road long before anyone got around to checking the club's security footage. I'd be a blur, but that didn't stop me from looking over my shoulder.

More than the money, at the moment, I wanted to detach from the family reunion, let them have their privacy and avoid questions and discussion. They'd already asked a couple of times about Dagney. Was she alive? Did Dahlia know where she was?

"Where's he kept you?" Grace wanted to know as Dahlia worked on a club sandwich.

"I've stayed a few places."

She was generally tight lipped, but she talked about some kind of ex-stripper den mother and a house off the quarter, promising she hadn't been molested. She hadn't seen Dagney there.

They were going to want her found, and that sounded like a job for the cops or a big agency, not an addendum for me. I detached Rose from the crowd and guided her out to the porch. Arch could thank me later for leaving him behind to watch the bonding experience.

Outside, the air wanted to attach itself, and mosquitos dive-bombed in spite of the haint blue porch ceiling, but it gave us some privacy.

"Have you heard anything about my kid yet?"

I wanted to facilitate a family reunion of my own.

Her head tipped down for several seconds as if the porch planks had a really interesting stain or a hidden message in the wood grain.

"We don't know a specific location," she said.

"Fill me in."

"It still looks like Florida, but they're off the grid. More effectively than you usually see."

"Some money would be nice, we pinpoint something. I could snatch Juli myself, and head for somewhere in the Caribbean they don't send you back from too readily."

"I can't suborn illegal activity, but I could check on the spots with good schools."

That highlighted the absurdity of the idea a bit. I'd be limiting my daughter's options even as I sought to keep her safe. Though she would be considerably better off there than at a shooting gallery or even fetching Sandra's mom lemonades or more likely Long Island Iced Teas.

There was a bright side. If I could avoid notice regarding The Runnel and dodge going back to David Wade, Sandra and Finn would eventually get picked up for possession or some crime aimed at funding their next fix. That would make me look like Father of the Year in family court. It'd almost tip things in my favor.

"Are the Holsts going to pay or are we going to have to renegotiate?"

"That hasn't come up yet."

"A live daughter's got to be worth at least as much as a dead gangster."

"Maybe you should approach them now while the elation's high."

"Maybe we should give them a little time and approach in the morning. I hope you got separate cottages. I don't want to have to see Arch in his skivvies.

In my cottage, I dreamed again of Juli on a sunny beach. She ran. I'm not sure my dream applied that slow motion effect you'd see in a movie or on a home video camera, but I remembered it that way. She jogged across white sand, splashed in waves and then Sandra and a man with no face intercepted her, and I was pulled back somehow, drawn away, watching them grow smaller and smaller as they stood waving, Julianna with a big and joyous smile.

CHAPTER 21

In the morning, with soft sunlight streaming through the oaks and the wind tickling banana plants along the property line, I felt like I'd awakened in some subtropical middle American Dream neighborhood.

I sat on the porch sipping coffee maker output and looking across at the pastel cottages with white paint gleaming around the windows and at the corners. I tried to slough off the dregs of dream that were darker than the coffee.

The Holsts were probably enjoying a flashback to a previous world, waking up with their child in the house, waking with part of the bleak emptiness inside filled, waking to a world on its side but not upside down.

I was anxious to get moving. We couldn't sit here for long. They'd start thinking not about what they had but what was still missing, and I didn't need to be in the vicinity at all when the authorities came. The FBI needed to be involved, and I wanted to be long gone.

I was nearing the bottom of my second cup when Rose came drifting across the grassy expanse between cottages. Barefoot, wearing a simple white cotton dress, she fit into the fantasy scenario, breeze toying with the skirt and the wavy hemline below her knees. I had an extra chair, but she stopped on the steps and leaned against the railing, and I felt like we were in a Tennessee Williams play for a moment.

"I don't guess you have a check in a pocket somewhere."

She curled her lips inward and shook her head a couple of tics.

"They want to talk to you."

"Really a thank you note would do."

Her head moved from side to side again.

"They don't want to pay?" I asked.

"It's not about welching, but they have two daughters." Emphasis on the two.

"I was only supposed to kill one guy."

"Remember, I don't know what arrangements you had with the Holsts, but they'd like to talk with you about amending the details."

"Right, Special Counsel."

"This should be more in the line you're comfortable with," Adam said.

He looked a little less like a lost tourist. He'd had time to splash water on his face, and I had a sense he'd found a few minutes to rehearse.

"If we'd hired you to investigate up front—"

"We might not be where we are," I said. "If you had investigators on Alexeeva's trail, and she stayed below radar, this is nothing but a supreme bit of luck. They weren't looking for a live girl, and that helped, but neither was I."

"He figured we'd stopped looking. If Dahlia is still alive, Dagney could still be alive, and—"

"And you need an agency and an agency's resources. Not me and my makeshift crew."

"You know what we lay awake all night thinking about," Adam said. "What he might have her doing. What she might be forced to do."

"Doesn't look like he did that to Dahlia, thank God."

"He might have had plans. Something to twist the knife in you, so to speak."

"Dagney was younger. So beautiful. God, I'm asking where he might have sent her."

No one wanted to say the word trafficking. I'd sniffed nothing to indicate Alexeeva's business interests veered in that direction, but it would be no surprise if he diversified. The only comfort came in the fact that didn't seem to be his use of Dahlia, the one I'd just found.

For her to have been invisible at the height of inquiries meant he'd kept her under wraps somewhere for a while, though, maybe even out of the country. He'd have had her somewhere not connected to him, somewhere that couldn't be associated with him.

It was pretty bold to let her work on the street now. Maybe he used the younger sibling for intimidation and control. There'd been hints he'd threatened her parents if she failed to cooperate.

The terrified version of Juli in a dank chamber flashed into my mind. I had to look over at an abstract painting on the wall to stop that flow of thought, but it gave me a hint of how Holst must be feeling now.

"I can't just leave her to a life this man controls," he was saying.

"All the more reason to pump your cash into a well-organized and focused investigation. You need the kind of agency that won't hire me right now. I can give you the names of guys that can handle it. Ex-cops just like me...."

"We pumped money into big agencies. Nothing."

"There's more to go on. They can talk to Dahlia. They'll have databases, teams for surveillance. He's guilty of kidnapping and she can testify to that."

"He'll deny it and lawyer up, and she's just a kid. They'll twist what she says."

He was right about that.

"You could have him picked up and Dagney's location could still be leveraged in a plea deal."

"You know he's got his trail covered, and he's clearly got friends. He's developed more friendships and protectors over the past few years. She's a runaway with a fanciful story who wandered into his club. He won't give Dagney up for, I don't know, spite."

He had thought it through in the night. Alexeeva's story would have even more nuance, and he had a twisted sense of everything. That was becoming clear.

"I had dealings with a businessman a while back, a man originally from Russia," Adam said. "This was at a time it really looked like there might be legitimate deals to be made with Alexeeva, when I was still considering whether to work with him. I should have listened. This man warned me even if Alexeeva wanted to work toward respectability, he had had dealings with people he believed were dark and heavy handed, and he said possibly worse. I didn't press him. I think he was trying to warn me that Alexeeva played long games and kept a lot of balls in the air for later use. He really is the devil. We weren't making that up."

"Who was that businessman?"

"Gregory Vitalievich, currency dealer. Respected and above board. If he's right and Alexeeva has some weird, long game going, then he's still got Dagney or access to her, and he has some scheme to maximize our pain."

"Again, all the more reason to hire a big firm or go straight to the cops."

"Rose mentioned something about the new developments in your situation."

Of course she had. They were her client. I wasn't.

"We'll pay you the full fee we offered, whatever information you turn up about Dagney. You don't have to put her in our hands, but we have to know."

"We looking at half otherwise?"

He looked at me for a moment, solemn and silent. "Yes. We'll honor the agreement. We'll make a payment that brings you up to half for what you've accomplished. That's half if you walk away. I'm sorry, but that's the only card I have."

Half wouldn't take me as far toward Juli as *all*. I turned over possibilities in my mind. Was there some way I could make the gig look like gainful employment? Probably not, though given the first assignment, I'd found a little high ground with this proposition.

The bottom line: more cash would be better.

How much more dangerous would Alexeeva be in this situation? I'd already risked getting on his radar. Digging deeper wouldn't go without notice.

"Expenses could mount up," I said. "More so than before. We may need to dangle a carrot in front of him to dig deeper. That's a dangerous game."

"What's this carrot related to?"

"I don't have a plan yet, but I picked up an inkling he had an interest in a Ponzi scheme. It's something he's trying to get a slice of."

"Just run the big costs by me."

"I still need to think about it."

"Take a walk by the lake, Mr. Reardon. Get some fresh air. Give it some thought. Think about what we all have to gain or lose."

"If anything, he's going to be more dangerous," I repeated to Arch. "He's going to be alert now and pick up on any sniffing around."

"A given," Arch said. He'd joined me for my walk. "You know the obvious response for me here is 'not my circus.'"

"I'd understand that. You've never had any dealings with him, right? Head back to your compound, grow your beard back and you have only the ATF to worry about."

"They're going to be reviewing whatever security video they have. It's not going to be clear, but you're not completely unknown. If the court would allow it, leaving the state might not be a bad idea for you in case you're recognizable."

"Since I can't?"

"Maybe keeping tabs on him's the best option, watching until he makes a wrong move. Getting paid for what you need to do anyway isn't a bad idea."

"If he's still got the other girl and he's been playing a mind game with the Holsts, he's going to put her even deeper under wraps. I don't think he's going to just let her waltz through his club like Dahlia."

"Why did he still have these girls? Or why did he have the one you found? It's kind of insane, dangerous, and in his world not very objective oriented. I hate to say it, but in his world, their highest purpose isn't running numbers or whatever she was doing."

"Agreed. We've been talking about that. Maybe Mr. Holst is right. Maybe there's a reveal coming on the older daughter. Fate worse than death to drive them further toward insanity and grief."

"Jesus. What a mind fucker he is."

"Maybe there's a way to leverage him if we're going to get anywhere," I said. "Maybe there's something we can do, play a long game of our own."

"You keep saying `we.'"

"I took a writing correspondence course in prison. It's the editorial we."

"Yeah, maybe you should start a blog. Document his activity" He raised his hands. "You really gotta think about it. I gotta think about it. Kenneth and I can take care of ourselves, but this guy's a dangerous character to piss off."

"So I've noticed."

The sun had climbed higher and, despite a breeze off the lake, was starting to warm the morning air. It reminded me the world did not stay cool for long. Then I thought of Juli, and the world was not filled with breezes and sunlight any longer, and the bucolic paradise seemed false and sour.

PART 2
THE SEARCH

CHAPTER 22

I asked Adam Holst if the business acquaintance he'd mentioned would be willing to talk to me. We all decided it might be a good idea for me to get his perspective on twisted goals, and I had a little more freedom in talking to people for an investigation than in planning an assassination.

I'd almost decided to move ahead. I could still get into trouble, as far as licensure and handling things that should be turned over to the cops, but I had more moral high ground and fewer concerns about leaving a trail even though I needed to stay off Alexeeva's radar.

I claimed the meeting would help me decide, but I'd pretty much made up my mind. There wasn't time to waste on any front.

We also decided it would be a good idea for the Holsts to stay off the grid, so it was through Rose, I got a meeting with Gregory Vitalievich at Meridian Investments.

The offices were in a gray stone building a few blocks from Broad. I had slipped back into my suit, and I made sure my shirt was tucked in well as I waited in the lobby until the AC cooled away my perspiration from the walk from the parking garage. Then I took the elevator up to face a receptionist with dark hair, an Irish Channel accent and an interest in appointments and intentions.

I told them, in a matter-of-fact fashion, that Rose Cantor had sent me. It was about possible security work for Mr. Vitalievich. Word hadn't filtered out here. She informed me that Mr. Vitalievich was very busy, but she buzzed something that brought forth a woman of about fifty in a smart gray suit that matched the iron streaks in her hair. They conferred in hushed voices a while, and then the grey-suited woman disappeared.

When she returned, she said Mr. Vitalievich would make a few minutes for me.

He proved to be a tall man with hair color about the same as that of what I'd decided must be his executive assistant. His three-piece suit, the jacket of which was on a wooden hanger on an elegant hook behind him, was a shade darker, nearing charcoal grey with a subtle window pane check.

"Would you like a drink, Mr. Reardon?"

I declined with a gesture.

"I suppose this little talk was arranged to allow you a bit of background for whatever you're undertaking."

"I suppose that would be right."

"A memory of mine might at least be of general use to you. I issued a warning some time back about a business deal, a warning of treading with caution if it involved a certain individual."

He'd worked hard on his English and his accent, and he was choosing words carefully.

"I see," I said.

"Meridian is a successful business and a scrupulously legal one, Mr. Reardon. We deal in international investments and currency transactions. Those are looked on with some scrutiny these days."

"Makes it hard on the terrorists?"

"That's what it's intended to do. Doesn't help common criminals nor honest businessmen either. Makes all of us adhere to regulations and fill out more forms. My partner and I came to the U.S. to be successful and most important of all to be honest. Some choose a different path and pursue less than legitimate avenues."

"So sometime early on while you were being scrupulous and everything, you got a call from the thieves in law back home?"

His face lost a little color with the mention of the old-school name.

"Not in-laws of mine. Tendrils of old ways reach forward," he said.

"So, the old friend wanted to infiltrate your business?"

"Never a friend. Never friendly, but essentially yes."

He decided to pour himself a drink. He took a swallow before sitting down again. "We can drop the delicate dancing, and I will trust you, Mr. Reardon."

"I need to trust you can be discreet as well. In the future."

"Of course. Officially, this conversation was solely about a security job for you that didn't work out."

That would certainly be believable.

"When the individual you're dealing with, Mr. Alexeeva, was a younger man, he worked with a mentor, you might call him, someone who was a bit more heavy-handed. He had ties to true members of the *Vory-v-Zakone*, the thieves in law you spoke of."

"Who was that?"

"Filipp Popkov. Have you heard of him?"

"Rings a bell, mostly from the papers, not any of my personal work. Leather jacket, gold-chain, tattoos."

"That would be him. He was prosecuted and deported on a number of charges from your federal agents. He's long passed away now, but when he was here, he wanted to use our firm. He had money...."

"I can get a general picture. He needed laundry services."

Vitalievich nodded.

"My children were young. He sent pictures of them playing at their school, getting into the car that took them to school. He showed he could find them anywhere."

"Threat of abduction?"

"Absolutely. We hired extra security and were frantic until he was arrested for something else, dealings with someone else, but he knew how to strike terror."

"So, other than being this guy's pupil, did Alexeeva have a direct role?"

"He was a messenger, a very subtle messenger. He never voiced an outright threat. He never touched the photographs. He didn't do anything but chat with us, caught us in the lobby of a Midtown hotel after a meeting. And he started to speak not of the Vory but of the Volkhvy. He said it was because we came from the same background and wasn't the Volkhvy's history interesting."

"I don't remember Volkhvy coming up in any FBI bulletins."

"You've had crimes in New Orleans tinged with voodoo, no? Was that actually discussed much?"

"You use what helps a case. If you get too far into hoo doo the jury rolls its collective eyes."

"So, you that's why you haven't heard of the Volkhvy. They were part of a pre-Christian order in my homeland, priests, sorcerers maybe you'd call them. It might all sound like superstition."

"Did Alexeeva suggest this Popkov would call on a wizard to curse you or something if you didn't pony up some funds?"

"There's no real magic implied, but there is a certain, let's say, subset of individuals, who have adopted the verbiage to make themselves seem more fearsome. He alluded to a line of *volkhv* priests or sorcerers carrying traditions forward. The church, as it tried to make inroads into Russian in the tenth or eleventh century, struggled with the Volkhvy," he said. "Persecuted them in some cases. People were slow to stop consulting them for predictions and guidance, and they'd quickly turn back to a *volkhv* priest at any sign of crop trouble or other difficulties."

"So just an extra tint of menace?"

"Essentially. If you dig a bit, and we did, you can find reference to *volkhv* being consulted well into the nineteenth century, and like with any superstitions there are sad stories, old women practitioners burned upon blame for illness outbreaks and the like. But Alexeeva noted that someone who had a line on something ancient like the strength of the *volkhv* might wield dark power."

"Intimidation?"

"I thought about that. He said sometimes the Volkhvy could see grim things in a person's future. Of course, grim predictions could be made real."

"Without it actually being claimed as a threat."

"Something like that. An added little chill, icing on the threat cake? Also an indication of his philosophy, I suppose. It says deep down nothing is really over or buried."

"Maybe so, maybe a suggestion of subtle and insidious power and secret knowledge. He said many things had been handed down, things not recorded in history books but passed forward in families. He mentioned that the Volkhvy had been called on in the old days to deal with many problems in the old world. They would pinpoint people whose grim spirits supposedly caused problems, crop failures and the like. They would pinpoint these people and kill them."

"That's cheerful and upbeat," I said. "Maybe I will have that drink."

He rose and poured a generous splash into a tumbler.

"He implied then that much more can be done in the present to deal with an individual who is a source of difficulties."

"How'd he avoid the sweep that got his teacher?"

"He was smart then. He was already always thinking ahead. Maybe he just stepped away in time and looked clean. I wouldn't rule out his having turned in his mentor, or provided details that law enforcement utilized and in turn looked on him favorably. He's always several steps ahead, Mr. Reardon. And I think he developed a taste for striking terror the way his mentor taught him. Playing twisted games like the one you're involved in with the Holsts."

All the criminals in the world, and I had to find the one who was taking things to the next level.

CHAPTER 23

On that cheery note, I knew I'd better get my act together, make some amends and put a plan in place, The Putting Things Right and In Order Tour. First stop while I waited on Arch, a liaison with Crystal. She greeted my call with words she wouldn't have used in a girlfriend experience.

Once she calmed down, we set up a meeting. She showed up in faded jeans with rips at the knees and a loose-fitting blouse color coordinated with her baseball cap. Her hair was pulled into a ponytail that bounced through a small opening in the cap's back, and she hadn't bothered with makeup. Incognito.

She joined me on a bench in Jackson Square, and we watched tourists drift past.

"Didn't expect the evening to turn out the way it did," I said. "It was a reconnaissance mission, and Arch and I wouldn't have made it through the door without hot girls. I had to act when the opportunity presented itself."

"In degree of hazard, my job ranks somewhere right below ice road trucker anyway," she said. "I know how to take care of myself. Your conscience is clear."

"I've actually got a ways to go to achieve that," I said.

"Well, if you'd filled me in, I could have done more. I started out as an actress." Her eyebrows arched up, anger still boiling in her eyes. "Nice of you to settle up. Did you want anything else?"

"Couple of things. My work's not finished. I'd like you to keep an eye out for this girl. Sister of the one we found at the club."

I passed a photo of Dagney over to her. She'd be ten now, so we'd had a portrait aged by computer.

"I don't think I attract the same clientele."

"God willing that's not the situation. We're not sure what she might be doing, but every set of eyes around town might help. I can't put her on a milk carton or Facebook given the circumstances. The photo's not for you to pass around. It's to help you to be on the lookout."

"Aren't you a cop? Can't you squeeze this guy, or get some current cops to squeeze him? Kidnapping's kind of serious, no?"

I'd explained some generalities on the phone, after the swearing.

"He can say Dahlia, the one we grabbed the other night, just wandered into his club and that he knows nothing. The old phone call to the parents was a bad joke. He's not from around here. Doesn't understand our culture. Headache for him, maybe, but with influential friends, he'd walk. Then he'd hide her even deeper, if he hasn't already shipped her to the Ukraine or an Emirate. We need to try and ferret her out before we go the professional route and the Missing Children Information Clearinghouse."

I'd thought of the clearinghouse for Juli as well, but I couldn't do that yet. Not given either set of circumstances.

"I'll keep my eye out at parties. What else?"

Time for the real reason. I kicked back a shot and smiled.

"I might need you in a slightly modified professional capacity. Especially since you're an actress. I'm not sure yet."

"Working with this guy?"

"No, the road to this guy, but you'd be in less danger."

"Hazard pay's going to need to kick in anyway. I'm not sure I need the stress. I asked around about this guy once I found out who he was. He's not just a club owner."

"I'd kinda picked up on that myself."

"If I'd known, I would have told you to fuck off the other night."

"Your friend okay?"

"Yeah, I don't think we were made. There are a lot of ladies who date in this town."

"I'd heard that too."

"This work, it's to help the kid?"

"Yeah."

"How's the one you found? "

"Jury's still out on that."

"How's your client feel about having a call girl on retainer?"

"I don't think they're checking my budget by line item."

"So, who do I have to blow?"

"It may not come to blows. I'm working on it. I might need you to be friendly to a shady businessman. Again, not the club owner."

"That's all in a day's work. So, okay, on retainer?"

I slipped her an envelope with some of the Holts' money. "For the other night too. There's some in there for your friend also. Buy yourselves something pretty."

"Like body armor?"

"Your choice."

CHAPTER 24

I asked Arch about setting up a computer. He told me I needed his friend Jael. "They'd be a big help."

"There's more than one?"

"Don't pull at the thread. Just use the name Jael and accept the help."

The meeting was set up in a coffee shop. It was not quite as cookie-cutter as a Starbucks. The tables were dark brown and a little worn around the edges, showing cigarette burns left over from days you could smoke inside, but the aroma now came from strong brews and chicory.

As I entered and looked around, I saw a wave from a small Asian in black jeans and a long-sleeved tee that matched the obsidian lenses of round workman's shades, the kind John Lennon or steampunks always wore. The haircut had taken off most of the growth on the sides, leaving a straight copse of black on top. I sensed I was being studied too, and the obsidian lenses made me feel even more like I was getting a cold stare.

I had made an effort toward incognito with my jaunty charcoal gray hat they'd called a Trilby in the vintage shop where I'd bought it. With cultivated stubble, I thought I looked like I might fit in a jazz combo and definitely looked different than I had at the club. Here we were, just a couple of hipsters out for lattes.

"So, you're good with computers and research," I said as I settled into a facing seat.

I apparently couldn't have broken the ice with anything more boring.

"Hashtag puh-leeze. That's what you were told isn't it?"

"It came up."

"Whatever you need is probably easy eno…." The dark lenses bored into me, or it felt like it. "What?"

I'd been studying the curves beneath the tee and jeans, mostly out of curiosity.

"Nothing."

"Did Arch tell you I was trans or something?"

"I was just told to go with the pronouns provided."

"I'm bigender. Do you know what that is?"

"I witnessed a lot in prison, but the term's not one I picked up."

"I'm probably not what you saw there. I'm just not tied to gender, so don't ask what I was born as."

"It's not really an issue. Internet, research, that's all neutral. I'll write up an equal opportunity policy if you like."

"Whatever."

A few questions arose about what access I had to email and data, and I fumbled a bit. A guy had come by to set up a router for me, but I was as unclear on some of the language in the questions that followed as I was on gender terms.

"Jesus, you better just let me check out your setup."

This coffee shop was not far from my new place of residence, so I suggested we walk there and take a look.

After the lenses glared at me, I assured them I understood there was no implied invitation and that I had no designs on what might reside beneath the jeans and tee.

"Okay, God knows what kind of vulnerabilities you have." A little sneer formed. "With your computer."

With a little cash to flash around—also from the Holsts—I'd moved to a spot the real estate website called new construction. Advanced payments always make landlords happy, and they ask fewer questions.

The place was in a house that looked pretty much like the houses on either side, frame structures refurbished by the same firm with fresh pale blue paint and white trim. My rooms had a side entrance with a little white railing on the steps. The paved street in front was a little spotty and rugged, and a vacant lot a few paces down was unkempt and littered, in some cases with things I didn't want to know about, but I could skip to the Quarter from there. All in all, the location was not bad for what I needed.

And the spot should make me at least marginally harder to find for a while, especially since I hadn't closed out the guest house. It was already listed on too many documents for the courts as my official residence.

I'd spent a little time sitting on a new futon wondering where I could find an orange crate to add to the ensemble. I plopped back onto the futon while Jael found the new router and gave it an outside inspection. "You're going to want a VPN if your work is like Arch's."

"Let's go with not quite."

"Let's go with it's nobody's fucking business regardless."

"Good way of putting it."

I produced my new laptop for analysis and downloads.

Fingers danced across keys, some prices were explained, and in a while, I was set up with what I was promised offered a degree of anonymity in whatever I was browsing. I was given to understand quite a few items of interest might be out there in the cloud somewhere.

After a brief tutorial on using a virtual private network, I got a lecture about the world and the grid in general as well as mentions of Jael's "meddling fucking parents."

"What else do you need?" Jael asked. I detected the mental itemizing of the work so far.

"I can do some here, but on the research front, whatever you can find on a guy named Ryan Moates."

"Spell it."

I did, and it seemed to process and imprint somewhere behind the lenses.

"I'll spend a little time with it. Won't take long. Anything else?"

"That's it for now."

Jael had my email. I provided my burner number and got a handshake.

I'd earned a few points for not prying it seemed. I kept that in mind and didn't analyze the bounce of the ass in the departure with too much scrutiny.

Arch called while I was picking up lunch at a little kitchen in the Quarter. I guess my call for a recommendation had put me at the front of his thoughts.

I pressed the burner to my ear with my shoulder as I accepted a foam take-out plate with a poor boy roast beef sandwich and dirty rice.

"Jael work out okay?"

"We found a way to work together," I said.

"The work will be solid."

"I'm secure in the knowledge that I have a VPN now."

"Word up's you can hire a hit man on the dark web."

"Well, that's interesting," I said.

There was a bit of silence.

"Speaking of that, I'm not scared of this guy," he said. "What are you paying?"

"What do you get for guiding a group of businessmen?"

He named a figure.

"We'll up that. Hazard pay," I said recalling the conversation with Crystal.

"I'll squirrel it away for Kenny."

"I'm in the process of doing some ground work. I'll give you a call when I'm in need of your services."

"I can't always be at your beck, you know."

"I'll try to plan ahead."

"You know my uncle's a...you know my uncle. That's him. I'm not like him. Not as bad as he was."

"I know."

"Okay, I'll help you get the little girl back then."

CHAPTER 25

You've heard a lot about New Orleans cuisine and great places to eat if you come to the Quarter. Cops and reporters have many choices of watering holes and restaurants, some with music, and other forms of entertainment you've also heard about.

Some feature Creole specialties, some Cajun trending toward blackened. Still others offer Italian and Irish specialties, and some focus on local standards like fried shrimp poor boy sandwiches or muffulettas or andouille sausage. I've already mentioned poor boys.

Most of *Big Crescent* magazine's online operation had moved out to offices in Metairie, part of cost-cutting moves, but the writers had to venture into the city now and then to write about the music and other matters.

When the guy I was looking for drew an assignment that took him to the *Vieux Carre*, I learned, he had lunch not in a gumbo hole-in-the-wall nor a great sandwich shop, but in a health-friendly restaurant just off Canal. The place was in a little freestanding building under a shady oak, adjacent to a shop that sold even more healthy foods you could take home, and it offered lectures and yoga classes.

Gluten free, vegan, all the things you think of when you think New Orleans cooking—hashtag: sarcasm—were on the menu in the spot. That meant I had to eat it too to get close to the guy. A chalk board featuring the specials including the veggie smoothie blend of the day hung over the order counter where various bean sprouts and bean and corn salad mixes that would have caused a prison riot at David Wade were on display under glass. I chose a chicken sandwich with avocado slices along with a flavored tea in order to blend in. Best meal I could put together under the circumstances.

The guy I was looking for was seated on a barstool near a front window. Wisps of white curled up from a cup of soup in front of him on the wooden counter. Interesting meal choice given his lumberjack's beard and curled mustache.

An iPad in a black case was propped in front of him. Gah, I should have asked the Holsts for one of those too. He seemed to be watching a stream of sports scores as he nibbled a wrap bulging with carrots and other chopped fiber specialties.

He wasn't the society writer from the magazine. He was on more of a city beat.

Once upon a time, he'd worked for the *Picayune*. Yeah, that's the name of the local newspaper if I haven't mentioned it or you haven't picked up on that.

His job now seemed to include a little society and a little business with a dash of music. Once he'd been charged with keeping tabs on business and various and sundry things that came out of city hall, affecting everyday life and lifestyle, nothing particularly interesting unless strip club regulations came up.

Jael had fairly quickly directed me to some of his older articles on Nola.com, and I read about Moates as well as Alexeeva, who had earned occasional mentions in stories about the city council and its subcommittees such as the transportation committee. So here I was to interrupt the meal and pastime of Jeffrey R. Kirkland. Blue checked shirt, dress casual. Skinny guy, vegan dining will do that. Looked pretty much like the photo that ran at the bottom of his online articles along with his email address and Twitter handle. The feed used the same photo. He tended to tweet news headlines, general interest oddities from the wire services with his stories mixed in, and a sports mention now and then, not selfies or anything convenient like where he ate. That had been a little harder to nail down.

Happily, I was here now, and the stool next to him stood empty, so I slid into place in my own incognito hipster regalia. I peeled paper back over the gluten-free bread. From what I'd heard about it, I probably needed to eat quickly before it grew a beard just like Jeffrey's.

"Pelicans fan?" I asked after my first bite, trying for a casual glance toward the screen.

"I'm kind of a general NBA fan," he said. "But I have some affection for them, just not quite the fervor I feel for the Saints."

Who dat?

He mentioned some players who hadn't been around before I went into the can, but then I remembered when the team had still been Hornets. I just nodded as if I respected their stats and said something about needing to get out to more games.

"You look familiar," I said.

He turned fully toward me for the first time, pausing from a bite, taking me in to see if he recognized me. I saw recognition flicker, then caution and skepticism.

"I work for the *Big Crescent*," he said. "My picture's on my stories. I read the news as well as the sports. Your picture's been in the paper a few times."

And me, all incognito and everything. Hopefully this was because he was more attuned to the news than others.

"A few," I said.

"You need something, Mr. Reardon?"

"A job with health insurance like everybody."

Yeah, I was paraphrasing Chandler. Like I said, I went to a good high school. I also read a lot while I was inside. It passed some hours, helped with tutoring others.

Back of my mind, I was prepping for a job when I got out, though deep down, I kind of knew how the interviews would go.

"You looking for your own column? I'm not sure we have an opening," he said. "You want to give me an exclusive on your life after the incarceration, we might have something to talk about. You haven't talked to anybody."

"There any interest in what I have to say?"

"We could figure that out."

"Let's say that's not on the table yet, but I'll think about it. At the moment, as much anonymity as I can manage is preferable."

"Everyone's not a trained observer like I am, so you may be all right. Think about it, and I'll think about whatever it is you're about to ask." He turned back to his scores.

I led with Alexeeva and his expression changed again. Something flickered in his eyes, and his eyebrows danced upward. He'd heard things on the city beat.

"Interesting character," he said. "What are you involved with? Or should I say, do you know what you're involved with?"

"I'm getting an impression."

"Aren't there cops you could talk to about this?"

"Cops are pretty tight-lipped with me just now."

Kirkland was nodding to what I'd said about tight-lipped. "The bio he's currently putting forward is that, he's a self-made man who's worked his way up and is shaking the correct hands. Rumor level, that which can't be proved without fear of lawsuit, that which I wouldn't put in print, it gets a little more ominous."

"I'll stipulate to some of that, but what have you heard?"

He flashed a grim smile and shook his head. "I think I'm going to get back to my sports news, Mr. Reardon. My email address is on the website if you change your mind about providing an interview."

"We could edge that further up the 'I'll Think About It' category if I had a taste of your skills."

He pushed his iPad away again.

"What are you needing to know, Mr. Reardon?"

"Any idea why Alexeeva would be courting a guy like Ryan Moates?" I asked.

"Business in this town's complex," he said, not turning back just yet. "Maybe Alexeeva sees Moates as somebody who can help him in areas other than those where he's already accessed and made friends. He has a few friends. Or so I've heard."

"None to put into print?"

"Not at the moment, but I'll say Mr. Alexeeva clearly wants more. Servicing the carriage trade's not all it once was with Uber and Lyft."

"He's got a club. But I suppose that's not really a way to earn a fortune."

He confirmed with a little tic of his expression and a slight tilt of his head.

"Maybe Alexeeva sees a financial wheeler-dealer like Moates

as someone who can help him connect to more of the right people."

"What do you really know about Moates?" I asked. "Way it used to be, you guys usually know more than you say in print. I've provided deep background a time or two in my career. What's not on the official record you can let me know about?"

"You know some rumors if you're sniffing around. I'm not going to say it out loud because I can't prove it." He smiled. "I will say that while I was still at the *Picayune,* I talked to people who used him as a financial advisor, before he launched this deal he's got going now. A lot of times he couldn't really talk them through where their money was as far as funds and annuities and the like. They were able to get out with their savings and an autographed copy of his self-published book on finance, but they kind of felt lucky."

"This doesn't really come as a surprise."

"What are you looking for? He's a guy that started with nothing, and he looked at the great houses on St. Charles and upper crust and wanted that. Was willing to cut a few corners."

I'd known guys like him. I'd arrested guys like that whose shoes had to be Testoni, coats had to be Burberry, and umbrellas had to be Ghurka. It's hard to maintain that lifestyle. Often lifestyle wins over ethics and legality.

Somewhere in that mix there'd be leverage.

"Let me throw you one bone," Kirkland said. "Not the kind of dirt I deal in, in print, but for you, maybe it's of use."

"The bone got a name?"

"As a matter of fact, yes. You were a cop long enough. You can take it and run with it. Holton King."

CHAPTER 26

Being a cop means knowing who to ask.

Rose turned up the details on Holton King. I thought it must be another businessman, but that proved incorrect. *She* had an MBA and a little town home on a street called Common. The importance of the gender difference, in this instance anyway, became apparent when we learned she and Moates were having an affair. So that was the kind of dirt Kirkland had been talking about.

They were both married. She and her husband also had a house in the country and attended the trendy Baptist church in a community nearby.

Arch and I visited the Common address around 4 p.m. the following Tuesday. She'd left the office early. We'd noticed that was a habit on Tuesday.

After a few rehearsals, we had put on our suits and neckties. Arch's military demeanor was apparent, and with the cop air I couldn't have shrugged off if I'd wanted to, we seemed pretty crisp. That was a good thing. It would encourage assumptions.

Slipping on sun shades, we approached Ms. King's door, and Arch gave it the fist. She answered after a flutter at the peep hole and probably assumed we looked official. Wrapped in a silky blue floral robe, looking surprised and flushed, her red hair tangled, she creaked the door open a few inches and peeped out.

"Can I help you?"

"Holton King? Holton Marie King?" Arch asked. "We need to have a word with you."

"I'm sorry. What is this about?"

"Ryan Moates."

She either figured we were private investigators working for his wife or her husband or that we were officers from the Securities and Exchange Commission. Either way, she let us in, working with the belt on her robe and not asking to see the fake credentials Jael had whipped up.

If assumptions failed, we were prepared to impersonate federal officers. What's one more ding on the rap sheet?

A few seconds after we crossed the threshold, a guy about 28 with curly dark hair came into the room wearing tight workout pants and nothing else. His naked arms and torso rippled with muscles. Apparently, Moates wasn't the only guy on her dance card.

"What's going on?" he asked.

"Sir, I'm going to ask you to step over there," Arch said, slipping right into the mold.

"Who the fuck are you guys?"

He took a step forward.

"Sir, please don't resist."

"Let them talk, Owen."

Owen?

Arch kept his shades aimed Owen's way and his muscles and posture tense until the body builder relaxed and then lifted his hands in surrender.

"You want him here for this?" I asked.

"Owen."

He threw up his hands again and moved back into the bedroom.

"May we sit?"

We moved into a small living room with cream colored furnishings and settled into arm chairs. With the AC churning, the air was almost cool enough to make the suits bearable.

I watched the folds of the robe part over firm knees as she settled on a sofa behind a small coffee table.

"What do you want to tell us about the Eternal Fund?" I asked.

"Want to tell you?"

"You have an opportunity here," I said. "Limited window.

Goes away when warrants are served."

The flush had been on the wane. It left her face completely now. In fact, any trace of blood departed.

"What do you think you know?"

"People aren't dying fast enough for your friend, Ryan Moates."

From what we could tell, thanks to Rose and Jael, people weren't dying at all in most of his Eternal Funds investment opportunity, and they needed to. It was a life settlements investment opportunity sold in little private meetings for Ruffin and Whitehead's very wealthy clients and maybe advisors who weren't sharp or at least were more interested in Testoni shoes than ethics.

It involved purchasing paid-up life insurance policies from the elderly. They received more than they could cash a policy in for but less than the full pay out. The investor became the beneficiary and received a bigger payday when the party died. The term's viatical transaction. It's a workable and legal—if ghoulish—idea in theory.

In practice, Ryan had run into trouble and started funneling cash from new investors into dividends for longer-term investors who'd come to expect those. Classic Ponzi, as rose had first mentioned. With the hint from Alexeeva's interest, what Rose and Jael had learned was what a lot of investors had no idea about. Just like those who'd been told their money was in good hands with Madoff. Those who quietly suspected couldn't get anyone to listen. Anyone but me, via my proxies.

Moates was clearly siphoning some off for himself, part of it possibly going to keep Holton King in this town house where afternoon tussles with a boy toy were included. More had to be channeled into his lifestyle. I wondered if Owen had paid for his own sweat pants.

Clearly Alexeeva wondered that too and if there might be potential in the Eternal Fund with just a little finesse applied.

In the back of my mind, when I'd first asked, I'd wondered if Moates's business might be something to get me in an isolated place with Alexeeva for just long enough, even if there were risks of a trail associated. Now I needed something I might harness not just for a private meeting but to locate Dagney. Even a few spread sheets might offer a basic carrot, but things were a little more complicated. And nerve-wracking in contemplation.

Intimidating Holton King was not a proud moment, but I told myself dealing with me would go a little easier on her than if Taras and Nestor paid her a visit. That would happen eventually. Moats had spilled blood in the water and that attracts sharks. The task the Holsts had given me was at once more preferable and harder than popping Alexeeva in a parking lot would have been.

When Holton hesitated after my statement, Arch threw out a reference to obstructing justice. Improv, but it got her attention again.

"What do you want from me?" she asked.

"Financial records, something that shows us a clear trail."

She buried her face in her hands. Thinking, breathing through her mouth.

"All right, you guys are upsetting the lady."

Owen had returned.

"Do I need to call your lawyer, Hollie?"

So that's what she went by.

Arch was already moving in his direction.

"Sir, you were asked to step out of the room."

"You can't just come in here...."

"Do you want to be charged with interfering with an investigation? Sir?" Arch really made good use of that menacing "sir." A real cop couldn't have done it better. If I'd had my Trilby on, I would have tipped it to him.

Owen stepped forward anyway, looking like a moving stone wall. Pectorals and biceps bulged as he clenched and unclenched fists at his side.

Arch planted his feet the way he'd talked to me about and kept his demeanor calm and firm. "Sir." With even more menace. *Damn.*

I wasn't worried about the brute force. The bodybuilder might be able to best Arch at the bench press, but strength didn't mean he matched Arch's hand-to-hand combat skills. We hadn't come for that, however. A beat down would pretty much torpedo our little scenario. Unless we could convincingly let Owen go with a warning since we had no real lockup to haul him off to for assaulting an officer.

I braced, ready to bark a warning of my own in my best authoritarian cop style, but I didn't have to.

"Owen, you're not helping," Hollie aka Holton said. "Why don't you head out?"

Owen stared and breathed a while and kept his chest bowed, needing to posture and process events. Cogs turned somewhere behind dull eyes, and he gave up on sweaty tussles for the afternoon.

I breathed easier as his muscles relaxed. Arch maintained his stance and the palpable intimidation level as the body builder stepped back into the little center hallway. Off to look for a shirt.

"I could probably get you something in a couple of days," Hollie said.

She'd been multi-tasking in her head during the floor show, thinking things over while she watched. She'd worried this day might come and concluded her position was tenuous at best. She looked at me with an expression grim and serious.

I'd hoped for something on the premises or something she could access and download, but willingness gave us a start.

"Why don't you get things together and sit tight?" I said.

I slipped a business card from my pocket. Jael's work wouldn't go to waste after all. A bit of effort had gone into the mocked up and realistic looking federal logo and an assumed name. John Overholt. It was real if she checked with the SEC switchboard, though it wouldn't hold up if she asked to be transferred. The number went to a burner held by Jael who'd answer appropriately and take a message.

My hope was Holton aka Hollie would just wait to be contacted and pray that she wouldn't be. A little stewing always helps with a snitch or criminal informant, and I wanted a little time on deep background.

PART 3
THE GAME

CHAPTER 27

"They're not in Casselberry, Florida, anymore," Rose said. She'd come over to the new place after I returned from the chat with Hollie King.

She sat on my steps as I leaned on the white railing since there was only the futon inside. I wished I could offer her an iced tea but I hadn't stocked the pantry nor bought a kettle.

My stomach sank a little.

"No forwarding?"

"Finn takes odd jobs when he's between longer term gigs. He's a little hard to trace even with tips from your cop friend."

"Maybe I should go look for myself."

"Leaving the state might not look good. You don't want to trigger the prosecution to think about a do-over."

"My current activities could do that too."

"At the moment you're working private security for a family. You're employed." She held up a hand. "I don't want to know about any technicalities. Start looking like you're a flight risk, you could find yourself back in the accommodations of the state, and Finn's still living with your family. Find the missing daughter. Get the Holst's payout. Fight in court. They'll turn up."

"Your focus is on your clients. Will info turn up before Juli's hurt?"

"My advice is wrap this up fast."

"I'm working on it. This is not a typical missing person case."

"Do you think cozying up to Moates is going work?"

Despite the "no technicalities" request, Rose felt a little freer to talk about current activities.

"I've got to find some way get Alexeeva to tip the hand on

Dagney. His interest in Moates's Eternal Fund may be the best carrot I've got, and it may blur his vision just a bit in spite of recent events. He's got a reason for eying this account. Maybe it's an intense one. Moates may need him too for a cash infusion."

"Ponzi schemes don't usually last forever, but Moates is light on his feet, and I predict he'd be quick to come out swinging at anyone who bothers him," Rose said. "He gets in much trouble, he'll start challenging warrants."

"I'm working to avoid some of that."

"Given what you're turning up about Alexeeva's propensity for long games, I don't know if he wants something in his back pocket or if he has immediate plans for Moates."

"Let's hope for immediate, but regardless of the goal, if I can get them in a dance, it gives me a way to sniff around Alexeeva's operations with an eye toward finding his hidey holes."

"So, get the conversations going, see what happens? Be careful."

"Always."

CHAPTER 28

When the burner rang the next day, I thought it was probably the Holsts calling for a progress report. I was wondering how I'd spin an account of shaking down Hollie King and Owen into assurances that I was gathering valuable intel, so I was a little slow to answer.

I discovered instead Grace had word that their counselor had decided, under prodding, that Dahlia was ready to talk to me about information I might need. They thought that I might be able to elicit information she wasn't willing to share with others.

I had been spending the day scrolling information Jael had been churning up. It could certainly wait, so I agreed to meet mid-afternoon. They'd arranged to have the counselor come to them.

They had just moved to a new location, a borrowed apartment, because they'd grown afraid they were being watched at the local BnB where they'd spent several days.

Grace greeted me at the apartment door. She looked a little less emaciated than our last encounter, as if one daughter's return had fed her a touch of new energy. She wasn't fully restored, but her eyes were slightly less lost and sunken, her skin tone a little less ashen.

"How are you, Mr. Reardon?"

"Okay," I said.

She showed me into a living room where a TV played an old movie, and Adam waited with a woman with straight, chin-length brown hair. She wore a simple and professional blue dress. Her arms and face were almost pale.

She wasn't exuberant about seeing me but offered her hand in a cordial fashion with a polite smile.

"I'm Andrea Sims."

"Pleased," I said as a preamble to awkward silence.

Finally, after a bit of that, she put her hands together and the corners of her mouth ticked up in a polite and well-practiced smile.

"I don't suppose there's been time to fill you in on me," she said. Her accent was soft and Southern, not a New Orleans accent. I couldn't place where she was from.

"I'm a licensed professional counselor. I have specialized training in working with survivors of trauma, abuse, and betrayal, and I also work with patients experiencing anxiety and depression as well as behavioral issues. The Holsts have authorized me to talk to you about Dahlia, and they've filled me in about your...circumstances."

I gave a nod.

"You should know we're skirting the edge of reporting requirements, even with patient confidentiality protections. I understand there's some concern over tipping your hand in your investigation."

"That would be right."

"You're going to find Dahlia lacks specifics. Since her sister is now classified as missing, I don't have true knowledge of a child abuse or child endangerment situation or even knowledge she's alive. Police have an open file on her and the culprit you suspect has already been investigated. My wiggle room is limited, but I'm giving you as much leeway as possible."

"Understood. We don't have a direct tie to anyone on this, just a location where I found her, and the original phone calls, Mr. Holst's word against the third party."

Mostly true.

She nodded.

"I also want you to know I have a family. My first child just turned a year old, so I can empathize with your personal situation as well as the Holsts."

"How are things going with Dahlia?"

"We're making progress, building trust. I want to be careful that you don't dredge up things she's just learning to cope with or trigger a re-experiencing of trauma or open the door again to intrusive thoughts."

"Has she been harmed?"

"Emotionally, yes. Has she been physically or sexually abused? No. That may come as a surprise, but she apparently was treated with a hands-off approach. The separation, the sense of loss and trust are severe, though." She nodded toward the Holsts. "The family wants the missing girl back, but they want this daughter back as well from an emotional prison. We're trying to get her there."

"You understand the culprit we're dealing with and the potential danger of reprisal?"

"Well, we've tried to minimize danger with this location. I'm sure you're good at making sure you're not followed."

"Not as good as I once thought, but I'm pretty confident about today."

"Great, other than that, I'm counting on you to keep me out of it."

"It's probably best if you don't give me your business card. So, what can I ask and what are the trigger warnings?"

From the flash in her eyes, she didn't like the way I said trigger.

"It would be better if you didn't press too hard about things she's experienced. She's having bad dreams, and she's perpetually afraid someone's coming for her. We can summarize what we know up front and let you focus on information that might help you in locating Dagney."

"Okay."

"She hasn't seen her sister in years. They were separated right after they were taken. If she's had direct contact with the gentleman you have reason to suspect, she doesn't remember it. She simply had a message for someone at the club and slipped in to deliver it."

"Of course he'd be careful. Where's she been kept?"

"Dahlia, here and there. I'm told you think she might have been out of the country for a while. She doesn't know. Lately, she's been moved a bit, usually apartments it seems. A lot of couches. I think they moved her to wherever they needed her. It seems she's been used mostly as a messenger."

"Street kid no one would pay a lot of attention to."

"Exactly. Goes even to the attire you found her in and what she's mentioned so far."

"No indication of prostitution?"

"No. We don't know about her sister of course."

"Can we get started?"

"Let's try this."

She led me back to a bedroom where she tapped on the door. "It's Andrea."

A sullen voice sounded a "come in" on the other side, and we walked in to Dahlia in jeans and a new tee shirt with a band that might have been popular, but I wasn't sure. Arms folded, leaning against pillows, she looked weary and closed off. She was tapping keys on a gaming device. New magazines someone had thought might appeal to a teen rested beside her, and a plate with wadded fast food packages and a few remaining fries sat on a bedside table.

"You remember Mr. Reardon," Andrea said.

"My white knight returns."

A white rattan chair sat in a corner. I nodded toward it and ticked an eyebrow up at Andrea. She nodded, so I pulled it over to the edge of the bed.

"Can I talk to you a bit?"

"The brain wizard here must have okayed it, so I'm sure there's no stopping you."

Andrea took a seat at the foot of the bed and folded her hands on her lap.

"It's to help your sister."

"If she's alive. You may be looking for a corpse. They always told me, I did anything wrong, anything went wrong, she was dead. You might get us all killed doin' it."

"You been threatened?" I asked.

"You could say that."

"This is territory that gets upsetting," Andrea said.

"Ya think?" Dahlia asked.

"Andrea tells me you've been moved around a bit. You remember any addresses?"

"Think you're going to find a landlord without a fuzzy memory?"

"I can try."

"In the Quarter sometimes, then out and about. All over. I was in Westwego then 9th Ward a while. And Algiers. You ever been there?"

"It wasn't my district. I went once to pick up a guy on a warrant. He had a lot of friends on his block. Got interesting, but that's another story."

"Nobody bothered the people I was with. I don't think anybody would spill much to you."

"So, you've been working pretty much as a messenger? Go between?"

She shrugged. "Something like that. Sometimes they'd just have me take pictures with a phone. One they'd had made special for me. Couldn't call home."

"You get much of a sense of what you were passing messages about?"

She folded her arms and pressed them into herself, taking an interest in her feet. "I was told not to ask questions. I'd go to rooms where a bunch of guys were working on computers."

"If you can remember anything...."

"One time they were kind of excited about some black guys. One of them getting a sentence."

"Drug dealer?"

"Yeah."

"Hank Carner," I said.

That recognition clicked, and she dropped the snark just a second.

"That sounds familiar."

"Drug trafficker. Got a federal life sentence. Opened the door for some other entrepreneurs to step in." The news had reached me up in David Wade about a year and a half earlier. He'd been a target of the feds for a long time. I'd worked cases that had ties to Carner. Gunplay and death were usually ancillary to drug trafficking.

He'd been nabbed not in a gun battle and not in a sting set to snare him. He'd taken a meeting with a guy in Texas that authorities there had under surveillance, passed the wrong suitcase at the wrong time, ill-advisedly handling it himself.

"So, they were excited by that? News he was caught?"

"Yeah," she closed her eyes tight as if fighting to recall. "Kinda that they thought they knew who'd be stepping up."

"Interesting. What else did you do?"

"Sometimes I was shuffling flash drives," she said. "No idea what were on those."

"If these guys couldn't move data online without getting it noticed they wouldn't be very good," I said. "That can't be all you did."

She ticked her head in an "all right" acknowledgement in conjunction with a roll of the eyes.

"They'd send me over to guys who had places they wanted me to look around or post me to watch since I wouldn't be noticed. Punk kid having a smoke."

"What are we talking here?"

"Lots of places. Businesses sometimes. Warehouses. Places at the port."

"You took pictures there?"

"Yeah, but they even had drones out there at times."

"They mention cargo theft?"

She shrugged. "Didn't share with me."

"You were never asked to entertain clients?"

Andrea took a step toward me but didn't interrupt.

"Nah."

"Why not?"

"Never said."

"Never came up?"

Andrea put a hand on my shoulder at that point.

"Maybe I wasn't pretty enough, though you know what they say about...."

"Were you ever used to calm other young people down?"

She shook her head.

"Never any heart to hearts?"

A no.

"Never just asked to show up and look well fed in front of other kids your own age?"

Andrea's grip tightened.

A shrug from Dahlia. "That might have happened and I didn't realize it. Shit."

Andrea released her grip a little but didn't let go.

"You've been shown his picture. You never saw Alexeeva before the other night?"

She looked down a bit and shook her head, letting just a bit of the façade slip.

"If I ever saw him, I don't remember it."

"You weren't told to look for him at the club?"

"I was told to watch for a skinny guy to come out. I just got tired waiting."

What a happy accident for me.

"Hear the name Ryan Moates?"

"Sorry."

I looked up at Andrea, who still hovered near my shoulder.

"You haven't seen your sister in all this time?"

"No?"

"No one mentioned her to you?"

"No. She never came up. I stopped asking. I just got desensitized to all of it, I guess. I'm sure Andrea here has a term for it."

"Well thanks," I said.

I let Andrea lead me back to the living room. The Holsts' eyes looked deep and sunken with glimmers of hope in and around the haggard exhaustion.

"Did you learn anything?" Adam asked.

His wife put a hand on his forearm then clutched the fabric of his shirt.

"Nothing specific. There were some things I could glean. Alexeeva's interested in who has money, possibly even money shipped in."

"Nothing about Dagney's whereabouts?" Grace asked. The glimmer glowed a little brighter.

I hated to throw water on it, but I shook my head. "Dahlia doesn't know. This did sort of give me a line on some things, maybe something that will help one of the avenues we're pursuing, but their purpose with her was mundane."

I wished I could give them more, almost as much as I wished I had more definitive information about Juli. I could project my unease to the heights they were experiencing. Sleep if it came couldn't provide any rest. The tight feeling in the stomach could never relax. The thoughts never stopped and the dreams were bad.

How could you rest, put your head on a comfortable pillow, close your eyes in peace if a loved one was out there somewhere being tortured? What right did you have to rest? To comfort? To respite?

I wished I had more, thought about mentioning more, but I didn't want to over promise.

I said: "I'll keep working."

CHAPTER 29

If I was picking up anything from Dahlia's account of her experiences, it was that Alexeeva was interested most in keeping an eye on people who had illegal money or who might be amassing interesting amounts of it. That further pointed at why he'd be interested in Moates and the Eternal Fund.

So, when Holton or Hollie showed up for her next assignation with Owen, Crystal had drawn him away. She found me at the door to the town house instead.

I was back in my suit, all shaved and proper, standing just under the eaves for the shade so I stayed crisp and didn't break a sweat. I still wasn't the sight she wanted to see. She'd hoped I'd gone away.

"I was wondering when you'd show up again."

A couple of days after our past visit, she'd left a nondescript message in the in-box we'd set up for the business card I'd left, just as she'd promised. I'd been too busy to get back to her right away, but letting her stew hadn't seemed like a bad idea.

She made no move to open the door, though she maintained a stern air. She wore a severe gray pants suit this afternoon, armor for tough meetings, I guessed. You could have chipped ice with the stiletto heels.

"Can we sit down and talk?"

She drew in a breath suggesting the demeanor was built on foundational Jell-O. I ticked my head toward the door. She didn't let the demeanor do more than flicker, but she took out a key, unlocked, and we stepped inside. The living room was cool and a little dim with just the light from the windows. I had to hand it to Owen. He kept the place neat, and he was saving energy while he was away.

I offered up a silent prayer for the AC while she flicked a switch that awakened lamps in the living room and gestured toward an armchair. She dropped with her handbag onto the sofa, crossing her legs and leaning forward.

"Have anything for me, Mrs. King? May I call you Hollie?"

"I'd rather you not call me at all."

I had put that one right over the plate for her, but she could have given me other suggestions or told me I could talk to her attorney. She was in the game, playing things cautious. Dirty hands lead to that.

"But I was in the neighborhood."

"You waited a while to show up again," she said.

"I knew complying with my requests might take a little while."

My other distractions had been beneficial. She knew the approach we'd made had to be a little unorthodox and had probably hoped it would go away. Now, here I was to drill a hole in the bottom of that boat.

"You made demands," she said. "Without any offers."

"You know I can't promise any deals that would hold up. You need the prosecutor in the room for that. Do you want that?"

"Should I call for my lawyer?"

"Last thing we want is to get you officially on the books. This goes well, you need to be able to parachute out. Not that you're not a great catch, Hollie, but we're trolling for other fish."

She hesitated. She wasn't stupid. She wasn't involved in the kind of crime stupid people pull. That would be me.

I'd hoped to offer a good reason for cooperation keeping her from getting cautious enough to demand something in writing. Cooperation needed to seem more desirable than the wise move.

"I'm not the one you're after?"

A bit of hope appealed to her.

"Not you. Not Moates, though I assume you have some data for me."

She touched her handbag, and when she noticed my warning expression she slowed. I didn't really expect a polite little handgun, but I was prepared for that contingency.

"It's okay," she said. She slipped a hand in and slipped out a shiny silver flash drive. I could slip that into my new laptop the way all the kids at the coffee shop were doing it.

"What's on it?"

"I've got some spread sheets. Accountants can connect the dots from what's here."

"Show the living are paying up the dead?"

"Something like that."

"Great." I reached over and let her place it in my palm.

"I'll hold onto this. Call it insurance. I'd like you to sell Mr. Moates on a meeting with Valentine Alexeeva."

"That's not going to happen. He's been trying to court Ryan for months. Ryan's not interested in whatever he wants to peddle. He's a climber looking for the next rung, but he's also dangerous. Ryan doesn't want to be involved with someone like that."

"We're well aware of Mr. Alexeeva and his aspirations. You help us get close to him, I might forget where I got this spread sheet."

"Ryan's going to want to know why this is happening, and there's not really anything in this for him."

I looked around the town house, nothing exquisite, but not a shack either. You could live comfortably here. *I* could live comfortably here. It was better than my new construction.

"I can't believe you don't have a bit of experience in influencing Mr. Moates' behavior," I said. "You got to keep Owen after all. I'm sure that took some persuasion."

Her cheeks colored a bit at that but she didn't break eye contact, defiant but not quite ready to mutiny. She might have legal high ground, but pushback would draw attention and media coverage to the end-of-life investments. Glass houses.

"I'll see what I can do," she said.

"I'll be in touch."

CHAPTER 30

I knew there'd be a bit of a wait.

The next morning, I got up early and went for a jog, keeping the burner phone with the number I'd given Holton in my pocket and keeping an eye over my shoulder as always. I realized I had too many things that might be gaining on me.

The jog was the first real exercise since I'd been out. My legs were stiff, and I got winded pretty easily, but it was good to breeze through the streets, taking in the smells, good and bad—the occasional waft of food cooking from the restaurants, rot from the garbage bins. There's little variation in smells in a cell. Even the worst odors that struck me served as reminder I was no longer incarcerated.

The flurry of imagery wasn't bad either. Shop windows stuffed with crap for the tourists, street performances, artists displaying canvasses, even the flashes of pastel colors on the buildings that deluged me with peach, orange, sea green made me feel free.

After I tired myself and sweated, I sat on a bench for a while across from a refurbished Creole cottage where a guy in an elaborate band uniform stood on an orange crate, frozen holding a saxophone to his lips. He'd propped a sign beside his open red-lined instrument case. It read: Sax Machine. Tip to Activate.

Whenever a passerby dropped in coins or bills, he'd burst into movement, blowing a jazz tune, fingers dancing on keys, knees bending, body swaying. If no more coins fell, he'd wind down. I could identify. I felt a little like a wind-up man myself, not really acting of my own volition at the moment.

After I'd cooled off, I stopped at a smoothie juice bar where the flavors and mixes were displayed on huge chalk boards behind a counter with large blenders awaiting handfuls of strawberries and other victims. I wound up with something bright, icy and orange in a clear plastic cup which I carried out to a round table in front of the shop.

Jael came along as I drew sweet crystals through the straw, tugging out a laptop while settling across from me.

"I'm really just tapping into what you could get yourself." The expression was sullen again.

"But I enjoy the pleasure of your company," I said, looking at the screen to see what I might learn from the Jefferson and Orleans Parish assessors.

I wanted at least an idea of Alexeeva's acknowledged property holdings.

Sequestering a missing child on his own land might not be the best idea, but if he owned a property with a convenient dungeon, that might be worth checking out while Hollie and Ryan Moates simmered.

My smoothie's level sank gradually as I got the hang of scrolling on Jael's computer touchpad, and once we'd noted a primary residence and a few other bits of land, we branched from Orleans to Saint Tammany Parish to scan the North Shore area. The property values were high up there. It was the kind of place Alexeeva would want to have a home. And sure enough, a $1.2 million spot on the lakefront.

I had a friend who moved to California once upon a time. When he'd come back to Louisiana for visits, he claimed people would take him out to dinner in L.A. just to hear stories about how low property values were in the Bayou State. A million and change would get you a mansion the same amount wouldn't even make a down payment on elsewhere. Had to be a pretty nice spread. A few more taps on the screen, and Jael offered an overview of the area. Looked pretty isolated, tucked behind a gate and wall. Who was to say what might be located on the grounds or what he used it for?

If it wasn't isolated enough for concealing a prisoner, it might have other uses. I made a note of it.

Then we moved on to another request.

"I haven't found your ex," Jael said. "I have turned up some things of interest."

That included the fact Sandra had a Facebook page after all, under her maiden name. I'd searched earlier myself, but I'd always felt inept and had run across only an empty account in the name of Sandra Reardon with a faceless silhouette as a profile picture. This time the algorithm worked somehow in my favor.

Her page hadn't been updated in a while. Or at least if it had, her privacy settings were ratcheted down so tightly I couldn't see much more than a profile picture and that she'd changed her cover photo to a shot of pilsners arranged on a shelf, shiny and pristine and sending off dancing needles of light. In the profile picture, Sandra looked about the same, but a small stranger stood by her side.

Juli was taller than I'd seen her last, of course. Her hair fell to her shoulders in a tangle of blonde waves. It was darker than I remembered, and her smile was slightly askew. She was caught in one of those moments of trying to figure out how to smile correctly for a photo, showing teeth, not quite getting the upturn at the corners of the mouth.

Her features had taken more shape, gained definition that had been lost in doughy cheeks in the snapshot in my head, and her eyes showed sparks of understanding and experience that had before been fresh wonder.

I choked even though that wasn't what I'd come for. A backwash of rueful sorrow overwhelmed the rush of elation at discovery. Moments and years had been lost, and the eyes looked at me and accused.

I stared back for a while, wishing I had bourbon to splash into my drink, but I composed myself as I realized Jael had reached over to pat the back of my hand. The sunglass lenses ticked up just slightly as eyebrows twitched upward in a hint of a sympathetic ripple. That caught me before weeping set in and got me back on task.

As I scrolled down, the Facebook page let me see a few older profile pictures, just tight frames of Sandra smiling, separated by occasional picture-and-script bromides like "use your mistakes as stepping stones." If I had the skills, I could probably use Jasso's pontifications to create epigram images of my own.

Since Sandra's "friends" button offered a view of nothing due apparently to privacy settings, the saccharine-message images came in handy in another way. Comments from friends showed up there. That at least gave me people who'd been in somewhat recent contact.

I remembered a couple of the names and zeroed in on one who'd been a fairly close chum from when we'd been dating: Teri Beal. She'd drifted away after a while once we were married, but I seemed to recall occasional messages between the two. She was worth a check, especially since her profile at least suggested she worked at a restaurant in the Quarter called Armantine. That wasn't too far away, on Dauphine. I could squeeze that in. I thanked Jael who shifted back to stoic with a nod. I felt I was wearing them down.

I went by around three, aiming for a time the staff might be on hand and gearing up for the dinner hours without being in full siege mode. I found a door in back with a buzzer for staff entry and pressed it. When I got an answer, I asked for Teri. I looked non-threatening enough when someone came to the door that I was told to wait. Just a couple of minutes passed before she stepped out wearing a white kitchen uniform jacket with a meat thermometer in a small pocket on a sleeve short enough to reveal tattoos on her forearm. Her reddish hair was cut shorter than I remembered, and she wore a little black hat over most of it. Without much makeup and a little flushed from the kitchen, she looked a bit older but still familiar. She recognized me too after a second or so of looking at me with a cocked eyebrow, and curiosity melted into a deflated "Oh, boy."

"I haven't heard from her in a while, and she wouldn't want me telling you if I had," she said.

"Nice to see you too, Teri."

"Si, this is my job, come on, don't make a...."

"I just came to talk. Do you know if she's okay?"

"She had quite a ride. It was tough on her after you went in."

"This guy Finn."

Her eyes widened at that. I couldn't be sure if it was surprise or a bit of her own concern seeping through.

"She was looking for an anchor."

"He's that stable?"

"Look, I didn't know him well."

"Where'd she meet him?"

"I don't know. A club, I think. Someone bumped into her and she dropped some glasses and he was close by, was nice while everyone else was clapping."

"I'm worried about Juli. Did you have any sense…?"

She took my arm and guided me back through the exit, letting it close so that we had the privacy of the street. At least there wasn't much foot traffic at the moment.

"I don't know anything, but I can tell you the guy always made me kind of nervous. I wasn't around him much, but there was a sense something was simmering there."

She really had a way of helping me feel better.

"Have you heard anything from her?"

"Not in the last couple of months. I got the occasional message after she went to Florida, but lately it's radio silence."

"Have you tried to call?"

"Yeah, her old number's not in service and she wasn't taking calls anyway. Sorry about that."

"Would have been too easy. I can't see much on Facebook. You were her friend there. Anything?"

"The last post was probably something at the beach with Finn."

I wanted to ask if he was anywhere near Juli, but that wasn't really productive.

"Can you check her page, see if there's anything that might give a hint? For the sake of my kid? I don't want to bother Sandra."

"I guess I could do that."

I offered my burner.

"Now?"

"You've got a couple of minutes before the dinner rush."

She sighed, gave me a look that said *seriously* with scare

quotes, but she leaned back against the pastel-colored wall and accepted.

The log in was clumsy for her, but eventually her thumbs proved up to the task. She got into her account, clicked a few times and offered over her view of Sandra's page.

I had to scroll past a string of birthday wishes to which Sandra hadn't responded and then I hit a couple of memes she'd re-posted from others about drinking. Sidesplitters like: I hate when people say you don't need alcohol to have fun. You don't need running shoes to run, but it fuckin' helps."

Jesus, what had I been missing on the inside without Facebook privileges?

Eventually, I scrolled past a timeline selfie of Sandra in a pink hoodie, showing a few more lines in her features than I remembered, some put there by the ordeal I'd created, I'm sure.

I found the beach pic mentioned a little further down. Sandra in a bikini and beach jacket beside Finn, tall, thin and shirtless in jams. I'd checked before to see if he had a Facebook page, but I hadn't found anything, but now, here he was. His eyes were kind of sunken and he didn't have much of an expression, though the one eyelid that folded slightly downward made him look threatening. They posed in similar fashion in another pic at an outside party. I couldn't read much in his appearance, but my gut tightened at the sight of him. Somehow putting a face with the name made it easier to visualize the terrible things that had been haunting me.

"I need to go," Teri said. "Things are not getting done while I'm out here. That needs to be logged off before I go."

"I won't post mean things about your friends."

"Come on, Si. I can't trust that. You could try posing as me to reach Sandi."

"Will you send her a message? I just want to know Juli's all right. You can call me if you hear anything or give her my email address."

Because I had one now.

She hesitated but nodded and took the phone to key in a quick message, accepting my email and phone numbers as I dictated it. She turned the screen toward me so I could see what she'd entered. Then she let me watch her send it. The process was a little awkward, but it worked.

I should have had Jael set up keystroke tracking ahead of time, but I hadn't been thinking that far ahead.

I left Teri with my number written down at least. I didn't really expect her to call, but I was glad I'd made the effort. I felt like I'd done something.

That sense of satisfaction got me thorough a couple of hours.

CHAPTER 31

Alexeeva's spread on the lakeshore was in a community called Eden Isle sandwiched between I-10 and Pontchartrain Drive. I'd worked my way out from checking out holdings in the city that the old agency reports had included. This one was newer and Jael had pinpointed it.

The Eden name had been challenged by Katrina as she'd beaten, battered and dumped water on the area, but money had poured in, and elegance and grandeur had been restored. The address I sought wasn't on the shore proper. A network of canals stretched in from Pontchartrain and snaked around forming little peninsulas as the real estate folks called them. Alexeeva's place sat on a little jut of land bordered by wrought iron fencing protecting the drive from the street.

He could have done worse. The house was a white columned colonial with a fountain in front and a guest house. I could see it from the road even though it faced the end of the peninsula which was almost parallel to the street. It must have felt like having an island.

If life settled down, I wondered if I might have a shot as a realtor. I could wear a suit and pitch the notion of a dream home while discussing spacious living areas and spots great for entertaining. "That? No, it's not mold; it's just a discoloration. Paint'll take care of it."

Later, after I had Juli safe.

I cruised along a couple of streets after doing a U-turn at the end of the drive in front of Alexeeva's. I figured I had a few passes before someone phoned the sheriff's department about a suspicious character. I'd had the car washed, and I was dressed nice in a Lacoste shirt and creased khakis. I could be a guy in the market for a million six.

Eventually I ran across a little park area with a pavilion and pulled to a stop. A man with silver hair, wearing a track suit worth a month's rent, sat in a motorized wheelchair. A Filipino man in a golf shirt and khakis sat beside the chair on a little wooden bench.

I walked over and said hello. The attendant said hello back and introduced himself as Danilo when I approached.

Phlegm rattled a bit in the old man's throat. Then he coughed and spat a wad that arched into the grass. It wasn't an aggressive move. His expression didn't change. He was present, but he wasn't really with us. He stared into nothingness, hands resting, motionless on the wheelchair arms. The middle finger on each hand was circled by wide, ornate gold rings. The pattern was braided rope, I decided. I wasn't sure what it tied him to. If they were supposed to be a magical ward they'd failed. Whatever voodoo curse he was under, it wasn't letting go. It was a curse even privilege couldn't break.

Danilo had to be bored. I told him I was looking for a summer place and that I was curious about the house at the end of the peninsula but wasn't ready to call a realtor and hear a pitch on a house that didn't even have a sign up.

He allowed the owner threw elaborate parties from time to time but wasn't there much. Maybe he'd sell even if it wasn't on the market. The small talk came easy. I channeled the old days in interrogation rooms when putting guys at ease would often lull them into telling you what they'd done: mugged a tourist, slashed their own grandmother, whatever.

"I've known quite a few people that have worked there," he said. "The man's tough to work for."

"Picky?"

"That, but strange too."

"How so?"

He looked at his silent charge, who must have had his moments but seemed like much less of a challenge in comparison.

"He plays games, gives 'em bonuses based on how they compete against each other."

"In what, the home version of *Jeopardy*?"

"Races to finish cleaning different rooms first. He shrugged, fun ones, I guess. but weird little mind games too."

"How so?"

"I heard he had a gardener once. Figured out the guy was kind of a sad sack and not too bright. He told the man he had a cousin in Belarus who needed to come to this country, but she needed a husband. Green card woes, all that. Showed him a picture of a pretty girl, got him convinced she was interested in him. Wanted to come South for the sun and warm weather."

"What'd he do? Tell him she needed money for a passport and garner his wages to help her come to the U.S.?"

He shrugged. "Probably wasn't paying the guy much anyway so savings would have been nothing to him. I think it was somehow for the fun of it. Strung him along, conveying messages from her, acting as the go between, sending back poems the gardener wrote to her, passing back the usual from her, come-ons. Poor guy fell for this made-up cousin. Talked about how she was coming to America to see him and all that. He made plans. Then she got sick. Had to wait on tests, finally word came it was bad, then he got the reveal. Not real, and he was fired. Tore the guy up. The feelings are real, you know."

I'd heard of catfishing. That was one thing I didn't feel bad about missing out on.

"Why'd the boss go to all that trouble?"

"Gardner probably didn't trim the hedges the way Mr. Alexeeva liked it. The man's just that way."

"Hell of a way to fire a guy," I said and offered the gardener a moment of silence. "What's the place like inside?"

"All of the places out here are nice. Big, grand, has a couple of sun decks by the water and fairly easy access to the lake. You looking to buy, not a bad choice you got the bucks."

This guy could have been a realtor. Maybe he was thinking about future options. He looked back to the old man. This gig wouldn't last forever.

"This gentleman's place is pretty nice also," he said.

"It going up for sale soon?"

He lifted his shoulders. "Hard to say. Docs say his heart's strong. Head's the challenge."

I looked back in the direction of the Alexeeva estate even though we couldn't see it from here. "How many people does the place we're talking about house?"

"How many people you need to accommodate? I think he lets people stay at the guest house from time to time. Under the roof, assorted family. A few servants. Occasionally there are big, private soirees. Special staff for those, I've heard."

"I have kids. Is the place all right for kids?"

"There'd definitely be room. I think I've seen kids there, sunning on the docks."

That made me a little uneasy but also hopeful.

Pulling the picture of Dagney at the moment would set off too many alarms. I wasn't sure who he'd tell, but he'd find someone who'd whisper to someone until it got back to Alexeeva. If I'd wanted someone to get a warrant, I might get close enough if Danilo said he recognized the girl, but a search of the house that failed to produce her would have the same effect we were already worried about, a move by Alexeeva to hide her deeper or ship her off through some pipeline that produced the results everyone was terrified about.

I talked a while longer and then said a goodbye, leaving Danilo to watch the old man stare and spit. There could be worse ways to await the reaper than sitting in sunshine, but he didn't know it.

CHAPTER 32

I opened the Google search on my phone like Jael had shown me and tried key words to check old news. I'd noticed something when I'd been reading assiduously in tech and financial journals in preparation for seeking a legitimate job, and it had popped back up in my thoughts.

It was the sort of move that bubbled up every now and then, but it had made me wonder about some of Alexeeva's motivations and how I'd been thinking about them.

The articles I found now in the online journals sounded the same as they had for some time, possibly since 9-11. Things trickled down to cops at my level were half rumor, products of a game of telephone, twisted and embellished.

My search skills weren't fine-tuned enough to see if the most recent activities had progressed past discussion because you needed to scan not headlines but deeper records of congressional activity. Too many other things were in the way that summer.

I dialed Rose.

"Any truth to the headlines that the government might crack down on shell companies?" I asked.

"That would be pretty sane. A lot of people are probably twisting their Congressman's arm to go the other way, but there have been some moves to encourage more disclosure. Wealthy people with a reason not to want it, even if it helped thwart criminals and terrorists, might make some calls."

"You think the criminals and the terrorists are sweating?"

"Possibly."

"Enough to be looking for other avenues?"

"Possibly. Hypothetically. You get all this from the chat with the girl?"

"Indirectly," I said. "Alexeeva keeps his eyes on a lot of things, and he likes to fuck with people."

"Obviously."

"Dahlia's been kept on the move, but I get the sense from what she told me that he likes to keep an eye on a lot of things. A lot business. Legit and otherwise."

"Clever. As you note, Alexeeva seems to be always looking ahead."

"And maybe he's doing that with the viaticals. Thinking ahead. If shell companies go away, other people are going to need ways to maintain anonymity when moving money."

"A situation that's already a Ponzi scheme would be perfect for cash flow," Rose said.

"He's probably got a lot more things like this brewing. This is just the one we've caught wind of."

"His business is not the shallow racket it might appear. It runs deep. Does that help you?"

"Gives me some things to think about for the discussion with Hollie King and Ryan Moates. If we know what Alexeeva wants, helps us plan an ask."

"Where do you think he's got the girl?"

"If she's not in Dubai, somewhere safe from law enforcement and everywhere else."

"Why not just do something more immediately?"

"Let the wound partially heal then rip open the scar tissue? 'Surprise, Mom and Dad. We turned one kid into a street hustler, and we turned the other one out.'"

"Possibly."

"It's amazing the Holsts are able to hold it together as well as they have. New revelations about the youngest girl would end them, showing them that while they mourned, the girls were being destroyed."

"You offered a reprieve from part of that. Plus hope."

"Maybe he'd like to seize an opportunity to maximize impact."

"I guess we just have to hope he's that patient and devious."

"From one story I just heard, he is, and if I'm thinking the way he and his ilk think at all, she's the pretty one. That's not really a plus for her well-being."

CHAPTER 33

"So, about that meeting."

"I'm in a meeting," Hollie said. "Can I call you back?"

"Why don't you tell them you need a bathroom break, or something more delicate if you like?"

"Give me a few seconds."

I sipped my morning smoothie and leaned back in my bistro chair. I was really starting to cultivate the hipster flare, though I wasn't sure how in the moment it was.

The strawberry achenes slid across my tongue along with the coolness and flavor, and I let it all rest in the back of my throat for a moment as it melted. I swallowed when Holton returned to the connection.

"I spoke to Mr. Moates. He's willing to cooperate in a meeting with Mr. Alexeeva if he can get guarantees of immunity."

"We're not to a point of guarantees," I said. "That'll come after we evaluate the worth of the information that comes out of a connection with Alexeeva."

"I don't know that he's willing...."

"Is he aware of how much we know? The spreadsheets aside? It's his hat that needs to be in hand, not ours."

"Jesus, this is insane."

"Welcome to the world of economic crime. When you step in, it can get complicated." I made it a little more emphatic. "Tell Mr. Moates we'd like to meet tomorrow afternoon."

I didn't really want to wait that long, but I needed to seem reasonable and not desperate. You had to leave a little play in the line, so to speak.

Trying too hard might send them to lawyers who'd make

phone calls and figure out there was no investigation. I could hear her shuffling about in whatever hallway she'd stepped into, probably fighting to control herself.

"Okay," she said. "Three?"

"Three. Your apartment."

She rang off without further complaint or discussion. She probably had knots in her stomach that rivaled mine. Except I'd put hers there. I wasn't particularly proud of that even if she and Moates were up to their armpits in an act of fraud and misdirection. I was reminded of one of Sandra's inspirational quotes about wallowing in various symbolic cesspools. Didn't make me feel better nor untangle any of my knots.

I phoned Arch after that to check his availability. I wanted the intimidation factor high for the meeting with Moates. He promised he'd be shaved and in full Fed mode. Then I called Crystal and asked her about her acting skills. She said she could do pencil skirt, hair in a bun and stern expression and be a dominatrix secretary. I asked about a different persona, and she said she could swing that too, later. We discussed appearances and motivation a bit, and I thanked her.

It seemed I might just have a workable plan. It'd be shaky, but anything short of kidnap and torture of Alexeeva was going to be shaky, and the literature states torture is often ineffective. I'd seen the threat of punches and even occasionally actual punches scare details out of twitchy junkies, but Alexeeva was made of stronger stuff. He'd snicker if I threatened his kneecaps with a chainsaw and count the loss of a limb or his testicles as a cost of doing business.

Moates might think of himself as a player and a steely dealmaker, but he'd melt and defecate a lot quicker, and we might have a shot at convincing Alexeeva what we wanted was his idea. It'd be a long shot, but occasionally the wind and conditions are just right and help a long shot at least strike somewhere on the target.

I hoped that was where we were headed.

So, 3 p.m. the next day rolled around, and I knocked on Hollie's apartment door with my entourage at my back. We were all crisp and stiff and thankful again for the air conditioning. Arch had used a little too much Brylcreem to tame Kenneth's hair. He looked like a '50s ad for the stuff. Also, clean shaven, Kenny's round face looked a little pale and like a bowling ball, but as long as he managed his expression, he looked intimidating enough, especially with his size.

Crystal's severe look took intimidating to new levels, a navy blue suit with a crisp and buttoned jacket, a skirt that stretched past her knees and sharp black heels. She accessorized it with a riding crop for some customers but not today. With her hair in a tight bun and wire-rimmed glasses, she looked like she could do a mean job of cross examination.

Arch and I maintained the persona's we'd used before and led the way in when the door opened.

I'd been braced for a lawyer to be on hand and see through the whole façade, but they hadn't opted for that yet. Thank God for arrogance and denial. Those had helped me get a lot of confessions signed through the years.

I had a plan for a show of legal documents and deal making, but that would get complicated and Rose couldn't be a direct party to any of it. For the moment, if anyone asked, Crystal was an assistant attorney in the U.S. Attorney's office, someone Moates' attorney might not expect to know.

Happily, Moates was hoping that he could talk his way through this. It had worked for Madoff up until his sons ratted him out, and that had been in a much bigger league.

Only Owen stood by for support, hovering near the counter that divided the small kitchen from the living area wearing slacks and a sports coat that emphasized his broad shoulders. He glared too. Kenny locked on his gaze and stared back, and that took care of that. It established some sort of posturing vapor lock and kept both of them busy.

Hollie took a seat on the sofa beside Ryan Moates. I'd seen him in photos accompanying the articles I'd reviewed. He was a solid guy, though not as solid as Owen. Dark hair with loose curls that had a sheen to them. They spilled down almost to his collar in the back. He had to pay a good bit for the look at one salon or another. It masked some thinning patches on top. He paid a good bit for the suit, too, a light beige bespoke over a shirt of a pale check that complemented an azure tie.

He was of a variety of Southern businessman with all of the Crescent City tics. He sat with one arm resting on the back of the sofa. One ankle rested atop his knee. Affected casual, but there was a hard look in his grey eyes. You didn't play the game he played without a degree of intestinal fortitude.

"Who's doing the talking?" he asked.

We were dispensing with introductions and niceties. He knew enough of who we were.

A small bistro table sat in a breakfast nook. I took a chair from there, turned it around and sat down straddling it and folding my arms over the back. I could affect casual too.

"That would be me," I said. "Overholt."

I'd give myself a smoothie as a reward for remembering the name on the card.

"What's the over-under?" he asked.

I let my eyes cock slightly toward Hollie. She'd folded hands to rest atop one thigh of her grey suit, not anxious for eye contact. As I read that, she hadn't told him about the spreadsheets.

"You've figured out there's a bigger fish."

Owen made a move that rustled the fabric on his jacket a bit. Kenny kept the stare on him and took one step forward. I didn't cast a glance back, counting on Arch to keep him in check unless he needed not to.

"And that you're off the books on this a little bit," Moates said. It was a statement.

"Not exactly, but we're being informal."

I turned back just a tic toward Crystal and gave her a go-ahead nod.

"Mr. Moates, we have evidence showing the flow of payouts...."

She'd memorized a spiel and the words rolled out in a crisp and efficient monotone that he interrupted by lifting the arm from the back of the sofa.

"I know what you have me by," he said. "What do you want?"

"We want you to have a conversation first and foremost with Valentine Alexeeva. We're interested, of course, in the source of the channels for the cash he's likely to be funneling and the potential violations up the food chain."

I dropped some words including oligarchs

"You think he's been wanting to talk to me to establish a money laundering option?"

"We think he already has one, and he needs a new outlet. Not to insult you, but given the size of your pie, we don't think he's interested in a slice."

"I get immunity for arranging the conversation?"

"I think you know that's not enough, and you're not going to be able to go on with business as usual after this is over," Crystal said.

I'd shared my perspective on the prosecutors I'd seen in operation, and she'd incorporated that into her disciplinarian persona. I just had to remind her not to make him lick her shoe.

"The conversation's going to be about when you see daylight again, and you'll want us saying complementary things to my boss," she said.

Good to leave it up to him to decide

He didn't break a sweat, but then he'd known the clock was ticking on his party and the whole lifestyle he cherished. Hopefully, the paranoia he'd internalized was helping with his suspension of disbelief. Sooner or later he'd figure out we weren't who we said we were, and we'd have to shift over to pure strong-arm intimidation with the leverage of the spreadsheets to keep him cooperative, but in the meantime a little buy-in was helpful.

"How stupid do you think I am?"

"How badly do you want to hold onto some assets for when you get out?" Crystal asked.

I could tell him stories about new construction on pock-marked side streets, but it would be out of character.

"So, we get Alexeeva in a room and let you listen? Then we talk deal? That's what you're selling?"

"That's a starting point with him. It gets you to a negotiations table with us."

He looked over at Hollie. Trust was no doubt shaky between them now. Owen had been handy but he'd also become a crack in any wall of resolve. She returned what must have been aimed as a reassuring upward curl of her lower lip with a slight flicker in her eyes, but nervousness removed any value in it.

"So, what do we do here?" Moates asked. "Call him up and ask him to tea?"

"We want to do it here," I said. "It's real, on the books as a rental of yours. It's an easy enough situation to control. We'll have Ms. Remnick on site." I gestured to Crystal using a name we'd agreed on. It fit in a world with an agent Overholt.

"Just a couple of us in the apartment, but we'll have others close by. Your job at this phase will just be to find out what Alexeeva's interest is, but don't commit to anything. In fact, it might be better if you play hard to get. We'll see where things go from there."

"What if this guy's dangerous?"

"We'll be here, and his style's not to shoot on sight or anything."

"What is his style?"

"You get on his bad side, slow psychological torture."

"That doesn't sound good."

"You're on his radar anyway," I said. "He's going to keep coming."

"How does psychological torture served up with no plea deal sound?" Nice adlib by Crystal, who kept her features grim. I'd see that the Holsts paid her a bonus.

Moates thought her remark over for a few seconds.

"You're really just asking me to hear the man out. A sit down."

I nodded.

"Sounds easy enough."

"Why don't we go ahead and make the call?" I asked.

He looked over at Holton again. "Do we have the contact information."

"I have a number that was left."

"Do it."

She looked toward me. "On my cell?"

"That'll do."

"Speaker on."

"No, that'll make him suspicious. We'll rig earphones. Just get him here."

I tried to convey with my intensity that we'd shoot him in the knee if things didn't go well.

CHAPTER 34

"I have Mr. Ryan Moates for Mr. Alexeeva."

Hollie did a good job of making her voice crisp, cool and professional. I watched her hands tremble since I sat beside her with one of two earbuds in my ear. None of the tremble reverberated into her voice.

"Can you wait one moment please?" It must be Taras. Very professional.

"Yes, certainly."

She widened her eyes as she looked at me, wondering if she was doing all right. We'd decided on a few cues to communicate outside the conversation. I nodded just to let her know the preliminaries were going fine. We weren't far enough in for a screwup.

She drummed fingers on her thigh and drew in a breath, which she held a while. Fortunately, she'd set it free before we heard a voice again.

"I'm sorry Mr. Alexeeva isn't available at the moment. Can I give a message from Mr. Moates?"

"We understand Mr. Alexeeva's been interested in a business conversation with Mr. Moates. I believe you placed a call to us. Mr. Moates is at a point where he might have a few moments in the near future. If we could set something up."

We hadn't written that out verbatim, but it was what we'd agreed on. Aloof but willing to listen, just like Alexeeva was being.

"Where can Mr. Alexeeva reach you?"

She gave him her cell, thanked him and rang off then sighed a bit with relief when he'd clicked off.

"He was the one that wanted the meeting. How long is he going to make us wait?"

"That's going to be indefinite," I said. "He may let you wonder a while. When he makes an offer, we need to steer him toward a meeting here or at the very least an environment we control."

"What if he won't agree to that?"

"Steer casually but harder. Or work it back to here and keep the emphasis on hard-to-get even while you're trying to reel him in."

I left her with instructions to call the burner as soon as they heard something and to strive for a little lead time but not too much. I needed Crystal available.

We packed up the entourage now and moved toward the apartment door. Kenny kept his gaze locked on Owen as we started for the exit, tearing it away only after a final warning glare.

Hollie followed me to the exit.

"How long do we have to hold this together?"

"As long as it takes," I said.

"I don't know if I can keep Ryan on board…."

"You're going to want to," I said. "It'll keep things a lot less complicated."

I slipped the thumb drive from my pocket and showed it to her in my palm.

"He tries to lawyer up, you won't be allies, you won't be friends. You'll need a separate attorney. You won't have rental payments coming on this pad any more. Bye, bye, Owen, but you're not that attached, right? I'm guessing there's more to lose."

I saw all of that register in her eyes. I felt like an asshole, more than I had the many times before I'd guided criminals to confessions or cooperation with nudges, intimidation, or false assurances. She hadn't knifed a tourist or beaten up a girlfriend over a bad day at work. She'd just bought into a slick guy's flash and promises. Big mistake.

I had young kids lives in the balance. I had to exploit that. At least a little longer, until we had Dagney in sight where we could grab her.

CHAPTER 35

I'd been waiting two days when the phone rang. I'd fought the boredom with what was becoming my morning exercise ritual followed by computer sessions, improving my knowledge of shell companies and matters related to Moates and Alexeeva's activities.

Teri, my wife's friend, interrupted all that the morning of the third day.

"She called me back," she said.

"You get a number?"

"She had caller ID blocked. I'm not going to lie to you, Si. She didn't sound exactly blissful."

"How about Julianna?"

"She said she's fine. She kept saying all was fine, but I got a feeling she was nervous. I wondered if she felt like Finn didn't want her talking to me or maybe anyone."

"Did she say where they were?"

"No. Sorry."

"Did you get to tell her I was looking for them?"

"I got that in, told her you might be able to help. She didn't ask that you do anything."

"I don't suppose you got to give her a number?"

"No. I offered."

"You didn't get anything to go on?" I asked. "A location?"

"Sorry."

"Great job, Teri."

"You wouldn't know anything if I hadn't tried to help. She just said she'd try to talk to you when she could. She didn't ask for a number or give me a chance to give it."

When the call ended, I sat feeling a dark quagmire open for me to wallow in. I didn't pass it up. I sat staring at the wall as my emotions folded in on themselves, pain clawing at self-pity. If I'd had a bottle, I would have climbed into that.

Since I didn't, I just lay on my side on my futon and let the pain rage until I dozed and dreamed horrible dreams.

In both battles, I had a waiting game.

I thought about continuing surveillance on Alexeeva to pass the time. I didn't expect another bit of luck like we'd had with Dahlia, but I prayed for one. I needed one, but as it turned out Alexeeva made Moates wait only three days before suggesting dinner at a Creole restaurant with a French name.

"His assistant was insistent that Sunday brunch was the only time he had available," Holton said.

"We'll take it," I said. It wasn't ideal, but we couldn't get choosy.

I was getting good enough with the phone to keep her talking while I Googled the location, one of the historic buildings not far from Jackson Square.

"That's not far from the apartment. You can invite them back afterwards for coffee."

"It's a nice place. It's not that noisy."

"It's not a controlled environment. Keep the negotiations going and get him where we want him."

"Isn't that just an extra layer of complication?"

She had no idea I wasn't really interested in recording a conversation. It seemed a reasonable question.

"It is, but we want him private and we don't want to have to mic you or Mr. Moates. The equipment's not as cool as on TV."

"We'll do what we can."

"That's all we've ever asked."

"Fuck you."

I thanked her and called Crystal then Arch. We had a showtime.

On *Yelp*, the restaurant had great reviews and pictures of shrimp and crab dishes in herb-flavored sauces that gleamed and looked so rich in photos you could almost smell them. They'd won recognition awards in local publications and served up signature drinks alongside favorites like shrimp and grits that had long rivaled Charleston's. I hated that I wasn't going to get to eat there. Since Arch and I had been at the club, we didn't need to take a chance on being recognized, remote though it was.

Kenny and an Amara looking unrecognizable with her hair wound into a tight bun and dressed in a slightly more conservative beige dress got that honor. Crystal coached her on keeping Kenny in line as well as having an eye on the Alexeeva table and having a phone near the proceedings. I really wanted them there more to keep up appearances and Moates in line than to conduct surveillance. Arch was on the ground outside, watching at a safe distance, but the fun wouldn't begin until they brought Alexeeva to the apartment.

On that Sunday morning, Crystal and I headed there first, and Owen let us in with a grunt. Moates had insisted he be on hand. Now he was the bodyguard.

Given how Arch and Kenny had handled him, I couldn't imagine he'd be much of a stumbling block to Nestor making any kind of offensive drive.

Crystal just gave him a curt nod and carried a small satchel past. Dressed in her power suit at the moment, she maintained the prosecutor persona with ease. If the change in hair color registered on him, he didn't show it.

"We'll set up in the bedroom," I said. "Can you keep quiet?"

"Sure."

He gave me a menacing glare.

I patted his shoulder.

"Good boy. Sorry I didn't bring any treats."

He didn't like it, but he'd been coached to behave. He didn't like it when I told him to leave us alone either, but he complied with that as well, picking up a magazine. I sat in the living room a while after he was out of the way in a guest bedroom then I headed down the hall to the master bedroom once Crystal called out to say she was ready.

Time for more waiting.

Amara called after we'd been sequestered for a while, making a show of selfies with her cell, one earbud in. The place had tiled floors, so the chatter was loud around her.

They'd managed a spot near a window just a few tables over from Moates and Holton, so I could see them over her shoulder silhouetted against the establishment's cream-colored walls near a large pillar.

She spoke to an imaginary friend as she panned gently.

"Can you believe this table, Susie? How great is that on Sunday morning? We were so lucky."

"Take it down a notch," I said softly. "You've established the scenario for anyone paying any attention."

"Gotcha," she said, a fraction of a decibel lower.

"Hold it as still as you can," I added. "I don't want a seizure or motion sickness."

Alexeeva was paired this morning with a blonde woman of about forty in a flowing white outfit, the first hint I'd picked up of a serious relationship for him or a relationship at all. Or maybe she was there for appearances, age appropriate to avoid calling too much attention.

In the jumpy view from the phone's lens, chat seemed casual at the moment, everyone nodding even occasionally smiling. At a glance it looked like two professional couples enjoying a casual meal and not the opening shot in a negotiation for fraud and financial conspiracy.

A view for me wasn't essential, but we'd wanted Hollie to know she was under scrutiny so we'd told her to note the couple fitting Kenny and Amara's description.

After a few seconds of that, suddenly the phone angled toward the ceiling then did a quick pan of the room, sweeping past street-facing windows and exposed brick, taking in a couple of waiters then some chandeliers. I thought I was going to get motion sickness after all.

Then Kenny's face filled the frame, broad cheeks as pale as chalk in the available light.

"You want me to get closer?" he asked. "Let you hear?"

"No, Kenny. You'll call attention to yourself. We don't need to hear."

But the earbud jack was in, and the buds weren't in his ears, so he didn't hear the admonishment. A few seconds later, and he was on his feet and the camera eye was doing *Blair Witch* sweeps of the room, the floor, the ceiling and surrounding tables. Someone was having shrimp and grits. The shrimp looked huge.

Why did Kenny pick now to get animated?

I tried a couple more times to halt his progress, but he couldn't hear me, so I just sat, hoping we'd avoid a train wreck.

"Can you have Arch reel him in?" Crystal asked from over my shoulder.

"That'd be a bigger show than Kenny rampaging through a restaurant," I said, shaking my head. "All this was just to keep Moates and Holton on the reservation." I was reminding myself as much as explaining it. "Without calling attention that might get noticed by Alexeeva's people if they're close," I added.

"I know."

On the screen, Kenny seemed to have stopped near one of the pillars and was angling the phone somewhere I presumed to be in the direction of the Alexeeva party. I heard hubbub and the usual rattle of silverware and ice cubes with voices in multiple languages mingling in the mix.

Then Holton and Moates came into view past a half moon of Kenny's face. Soup cups had been placed in front of them, and they nodded and returned conversation while dipping round spoons and swirling in oyster crackers. Neither of them appeared to have much of an appetite, but they were trying.

I didn't see signs of conflict in the conversation, just nods, and the occasional tick of an eyebrow or wrinkle of a lip. Still in chitchat mode. That was good to know at least.

"Kenny, can you hear me?" I asked.

He still didn't have the earbuds in. He must have wrapped them around the phone or something but left them plugged in.

I saw his broad cheek turn. He had a bit of a grin. It must have seemed like a game to him, one more variation on maneuvers at the compound. We'd established him with Moates, so his just being seen didn't matter that much. Moates would just figure it was more confirmation we were watching.

He just didn't need to look too off kilter.

"Kenny, one of his men may be watching the restaurant. Go back to your table."

But he still couldn't hear me, of course, while audio kept pouring to us, though we weren't going to get real conversation in a crowded restaurant. We didn't really need to. It would just be helpful to know if the gang was headed our way, the other reason for positioning Kenny and Amara.

"You didn't see this coming?" Crystal asked from behind me where she was changing.

"Good help." I threw up my hands. "He pulled off the stare-down so well I thought he'd be stoic or at least manageable."

The phone stabilized again, and I caught signs of head nods and then some hands raised with palms flattened. Maybe some of the resistance we'd suggested from Moates was being carried out.

My breathing quickened. I tried willing Kenny through the phone to go sit down. What we were attempting was delicate enough and unlikely to work. We didn't need boat rocking, and he seemed to be slipping a little further around the pillar. I saw Alexeeva shaking his head now. Debate and pushback were probably good if we could stop Godzilla from storming through Tokyo.

A hand brushed past the phone's eye reaching for Kenny. As if my willing it was working, Amara had approached. God bless the initiative. A bonus for her as well. With the Holst's money.

"Come on, Honey," she said. "Our food's going to be here in a second. Don't want it to get cold."

She kissed his cheek and began to guide him away from the pillar. We caught one more fleeting glimpse of the conversation before we got live point-of-view video of the trip back to Kenny and Amara's table.

I watched the jostle of the phone as Amara took her seat, and then her features came into frame. Pinched fingers inserted earbuds as she looked at the screen.

"I don't guess you caught any of the conversation," she said, keeping her voice low.

"Too much hubbub. Just keep an eye on them. Call if they

get up to head this way. Ms. King knows to give you a signal."

"Got you."

She clicked the phone off.

And we waited.

Plenty of time to worry, not just about this operation but about Juli and life in general. To think about where I'd gone wrong and to console myself with the thought that I was trying to fight something grim and evil. It was easy to think of Alexeeva that way, especially with the talk of his dark magic qualities. In a city tinged with voodoo and other whispers of things beyond recognition, it wasn't difficult to let those thoughts on the dance floor. Usually dark deeds and violence took the center spot, but sometimes you could contemplate even the darker possibilities.

Crystal moved to a mirror attached to a dark wood dresser behind me, working on her hair, crafting it into the new look. Her fingers worked with a deft ease, swirling and capturing locks to tie them with bits of ribbon.

"Looking okay?" she asked, catching the reflection of my gaze.

"Sure," I said. What did I know? She wasn't terribly tall without the heels, and she'd done interesting work with the makeup. It ought to work.

We didn't seek Owen's opinion.

As she painted her toenails and then applied a colorful Band-Aid to one knee, we talked about the weather and the humidity and about nothing memorable until the phone trilled again.

The party was moving our way.

CHAPTER 36

"This Scotch is not bad," Moates said. "It's called Dalmore." We could hear him through the closed bedroom door as footsteps shuffled in the entryway.

"It's not quite midday, but we work with the time we have."

At least we could tell how he'd lured Alexeeva back to the pad. The promise of a dram. Despite the hour.

It felt for a second as if palpable evil had entered the dwelling, was in the air and seeping through the door. It had to be my knowledge of what Alexeeva was capable of, stimulated in my subconscious, but the sensation was more like a cold spiritual wave, what it must be like in a séance where a dark spirit has been conjured.

I steeled myself and pressed my ear against the door, straining to discern sets of footfalls. I'd been okay at that once, and now given my prior knowledge of the parties I thought I could account for both couples with no extras. I wished I'd dragged Owen in here to keep an eye on him. After Kenny, I didn't want any freelancing. Noise needed to happen when we were ready. Not before.

The footsteps diminished to a single set after a few seconds, so everyone must be seated except Moates who must be stepping over to the cluster of bottles on the counter that served as the bar.

I couldn't hear a lid being unscrewed. My ear wasn't that good. I probably wouldn't hear ice if there was any. They probably wouldn't diminish the subtleties of the Scotch or forfeit the show of manliness.

After a while the footsteps moved again. Moates heading back to the sofa.

"...twelve-year-old..."

Still talking about the Scotch.

I could hear muffled voices for a while after that, snippets that didn't sound business related then conversations seemed to diverge with a little more shuffling of feet. I wondered if Alexeeva wanted his companion to be aware of much of his work. Had the camps divided so the men could negotiate?

I thought I heard "...upside..." from Moates followed by a raised language.

Then Moates moved toward the kitchen, still talking.

"Currently things are pretty simple. I don't see complicating them."

He was on script. Or script outline, improving, drawing on his expertise.

Alexeeva had proposed something somewhere along the way, and from what I could tell, Moates began pointing out real issues with infusions of cash into his viatical company or a trust. Something called dirty sheeting got a mention and other aspects of viatical fraud that had come under scrutiny. I needed to look up all the jargon. I knew street slang, but this was crime in circles other than I was used to.

Alexeeva had done his homework. He countered with a proposal related to healthy people attached to policies being sold. It shouldn't matter if money came through, should it? I wasn't clear exactly how it was supposed to work even with details Moates had briefed me on, not through a muffled door. It didn't really matter. I'd told Moates to build to an impasse, to resist proposals to a point of breaking off discussions. Finding a deal breaker shouldn't be impossible with the proposed wedding of two illegal enterprises.

Minutes ticked past, and verbal sparring went on. Moates was essentially a con man, and his natural inclinations seemed to take over. Alexeeva maintained a calm tone in counter proposals, perhaps the way he always negotiated.

I'd endured a number of stakeouts in my lifetime but none quite so surreal. Mostly they'd involved sitting in a car, watching and waiting and keeping an eye on doors or windows.

As Owen grew restless and shifted in his seat, making me

nervous, Alexeeva began to offer inducements to sweeten the deal. Cars? He could make that happen. What about property? We might be getting closer.

Moates feigned interest in a couple of the carrots dangled then changed his mind. Nothing was quite worth endangering what he described as a stable business that could withstand scrutiny. Dollar figures were touted and countered, but, while he might be jelly on the inside, contemplating rumors of bad ends and swampy graves for people who cross Alexeeva, Moates remained a stern negotiator, unwavering.

The sweetest of offers had been rejected by the time I turned to the spot where Crystal rested, getting into character and letting her hair attain realistic twists and tangles.

"Curtain going up," I said in a soft tone.

She pulled herself off the bed and blinked a few times. She hadn't actually been asleep, but she'd had her eyes closed and that made her react to the light. She slid off the bed and lifted the back of her hand toward her face.

"Save that," I said reaching for her arm. "Open them in the hall."

I guided her over to the door then stepped back as she opened it and began a barefooted pad along the narrow hall toward the kitchen.

I gently pressed the door back into the frame, letting it stay cracked just the tiniest fraction of an inch so that I had slightly better audio.

The back-and-forth between the men continued several seconds before she reached the end of the hall.

"Hey, Ryan," she said in a soft voice, keeping it contained in the front of her mouth with the lilt high, not quite letting it squeak.

Their conversation stopped mid-sentence. Both of the men would be turning, taking her in. In her interruption and appearance, she'd be as much a surprise to Moates as to Alexeeva. That was planned of course. His reaction would be natural as would the embarrassment.

She'd donned tight, sky blue shorts, the kind that stop at the very top of the thighs, and a pink bare-midriff blouse with a loose neckline that slipped off one shoulder. Her hair had been tied into pony tails with bits of pink ribbon.

She'd either look under aged at a glance or come across as affecting a young persona. Either should work to suggest a proclivity on Moates' part that could be exploited. There'd be no mistaking her for a daughter or youthful ward, at least not for anything above board.

"You don't come by on Sunday, Ry," she said. "Sorry, I'm all yucked out. I was sleeping."

Moates stammered.

"Is this friend?" Alexeeva asked.

The women had stopped talking in the living room. Hopefully, being on Alexeeva's arm, the woman wouldn't be too quick to dial child protective services.

I wasn't sure if they could see her, but she'd practiced turning one foot in and cocking a knee just slightly all while she bit one thumb and opened her eyes wide with a gaze that was both naïve and nervous at the same time, not wanting to displease Daddy. I'd found it both uncanny and unsettling. She looked much smaller than her actual size and much more vulnerable.

Moates probably was finding it surprising too, making his expressions natural, and Alexeeva, if there was a God, was making a mental note.

"Looks like this is business again," Crystal said. "Or is this...a friend for me to meet?"

Moates stammered, managed to try a few words, but didn't.

"Just getting some water," Crystal said.

I heard glass clink, then the tap come on.

Then she must've turned around because in another second was padding back up the hallway.

When she slipped back into the bedroom, her eyebrows went up in a "How'd I do?" query. I gave her performance two thumbs up. She closed the door behind her and slipped the lock in the handle inward.

Now we'd just have to wait and see if the seed we'd planted bore any fruit. Of course, I couldn't imagine that Moates believed we were with the SEC any longer.

CHAPTER 37

"What the ever-lovin' fuck was that about?" Moates demanded, momentarily dropping his posh veneer.

The post-brunch party had wound down quickly after Crystal debuted her nymphet character. Sounded from where we sat like polite excuses and a little small talk and then a departure.

Seconds after the last goodbye, Moates was banging on the door.

"Who the hell are you people?"

Crystal was sitting on the foot of the bed brushing her hair. She caught Owen's attention as he appeared over Moates' shoulder. She was still in her Vieux Carre Lolita outfit. She just stared down at her colorful toenails as Moates continued to pound.

I pulled the door open and planted my feet.

"That's really irrelevant. Doesn't change your role in this," I said. "We needed natural embarrassment...."

"I'm calling the...."

"No, you don't want to do that," I said.

He had a hand in his pocket, but he left the phone there, remembering he had legal vulnerabilities. Plus, I'd made the statement with enough force and menace to slow him down, and so far, he hadn't decided to call on his meat-necked asset, Owen, for a beat down. That was good. Having to shoot him would throw off the production schedule just when we might be getting somewhere.

"What are you trying to pull?" Moates demanded. "Trying to ruin me? Rumors start to get around town I have a thing for little girls...."

"How would they like it if information about how you've been channeling money from new investors into payouts for longer-term investors reached...?"

"You don't know anything."

I rattled off a few more facts and threw information about life expectancy evaluations on policy holders that looked shaky, and reminded him of the possibilities of mail and wire fraud in the mix, using the word conspiracy a couple of times. All of it served to deflate him anew. Looking like a pedophile still seemed worse, but some of the people he rubbed shoulders with, especially the politicians he'd been donating money to, wouldn't be happy with either revelation about his reputation.

"What's really going on?" he asked, leaning against the door frame.

I gave him a thumbnail, keeping in mind we were still speaking in front of Owen.

"So, you're dangling me to bring out something he might have?" Moates asked.

"We needed to show the currency that might interest you, and we needed it to look convincing."

"Fuck."

"It's any consolation, you did a great job. Now, he calls back with any offers you just need to string him along. You've been swindling retirees to finance your houses and boats." I rolled my eyes upward at our surroundings. "And fuck pads. This is just another cost of doing business."

"How do I know that guy's not going to cut my head off?"

"Probably wouldn't be your head. Not first anyway. He'd want you to give some thought to the other body parts you were losing."

He repeated the single word he'd said before.

"Keep processing it. If you'd like, we can get a laptop, and I can show you the details we have that we could drop into an email to the real SEC."

We had him by them, might as well give his balls a squeeze.

"You want...?"

That's all Owen got out before Moates lifted a hand to shut him up.

Hollie had come into the hallway now. She had to be furious at me and harboring as many questions as Moates, but calming the situation took precedence. She didn't want him turning on her.

She stood several paces behind him, silent, daring just to put a hand on his shoulder. He sloughed it off. He had to have suspicions about what I knew and where it came from. He'd process those at some point, and whatever they'd had, if there had been any affection or real emotion and not just the shared energy of risk and lust, was long gone.

I'd seen it before from street criminals in interview rooms, and it was the same. For the moment, Moates was just focused on all of his world that was crushing in around him. His game required nerves of steel, the kind of nerves Bernie Madoff maintained through the years, or maybe some sense of invulnerability like Jeffrey Epstein, but the knowledge that things had to eventually fall apart always nagged. Now it was here.

He'd processed dealing with the SEC and had factored in their protections, and he'd allowed himself a glimmer of hope that he might come out the other side with a deal. I could see in his ashen features that he'd lost that glimmer. He bowed his head and raised a paw to wipe some of the beads of sweat off his forehead then looked back at....

Who the fuck was this guy making his life so miserable?

I could see it in his now glassy brown eyes.

"I was a cop," I said. "I ran into a few legal problems of my own."

He'd figure it out eventually anyway. He'd be looking for leverage.

He found a new word. "Shit."

Hollie tried again. Her fingers closed over his shoulder and she steered him to the foot of the bed. He let his weight sink onto the mattress, which gave a slight sigh. His slacks tightened over his knees, and he leaned forward, resting a forearm on a thick thigh.

"How do we even get the right girl? What if he's got...?"

"We made my associate look as much like Dagney as possible.

Our best hope is he'll include her in any casting calls, but it needs to be his idea. We start asking, he knows it's tied to someone looking specifically for her. There may be a chance he wants to be done with her, so that could push things our way. No guarantees, but this is not an easy job."

It was insane, and it sounded futile as we went over it, but it was what we had.

"How am I going to know her? If he shows me pictures or something."

"We've got a computer aged photo of her. What she probably looks like today.

"I help you get this prize, how do we all walk away from this?"

"Couple of ways it can go," I said. "We get the girl, and he can't really say anything without facing a kidnap and trafficking charge or we get the girl and send up a flare to the authorities. You're a hero who helped rescue a friend's daughter who he thought was long lost."

That seemed as unlikely as everything else, but he kind of liked that notion. He was bilking retirees. We got out of this alive, Rose would see the copies of the spreadsheets she now had in a sealed envelope found their way into the right hands, but he didn't need to know that.

He already had a gift of duplicitous gab. We just needed to channel it for a while.

"Otherwise? If it doesn't work?"

"For you, go back to your life. See if he calls. If not, I've got to find another way to get Dagney free."

I could be duplicitous too.

He looked around the room at nothing in particular, trying to think.

"Just don't think about screwing me," I said. "Or calling someone about me. I sniff anything, information I have goes in, and your best-case scenario is the Feds and they'll want you worse than they want anything about me. You're headlines and the job promotions those bring in."

He gave a little nod to that.

"I said `best case.' Worst, I know people who can cause you

about as much pain as Alexeeva. You know what this city has to offer, and I worked those streets."

He processed the threat level.

"Let me share some wisdom a friend of mine on the inside said to me once." It had been Jasso, of course in his deep and lazy drawl. "Life's a fool's run on a crooked road. You have to find the best route you can."

I looked at Hollie now.

"Get him a glass of water. He looks like he's about to have a heart attack."

CHAPTER 38

Arch ran a finger across a blue stretch on the map on his tablet computer, tracing the Geoghegan Canal, a narrow passage stretching from the neighborhood where I'd viewed Alexeeva's house to Lake Ponchatrain. I'd driven alongside it to the gated peninsula.

"This would probably be ideal if he picks the summer place. You can't get a boat from the lake into the canals around a neighborhood for obvious reasons, but we get a boat right here," he tapped a spot on the map, "then get the girl to it, we just have a short run to the lake, and then that opens up a lot of possibilities. He's gotta launch another boat to chase us. Somewhere in town where we have to make a run in cars, you're a cop, you know what that entails."

"What kind of boat?"

"A little bit of a souped-up outboard rig and a skiff would look normal and be ready to get us out of there. Kenny and I could pose as fishermen. We hang out, two guys casting, blend right in."

They could look right for that, no question.

I'd driven back out to their place to go over the contingencies he'd been considering since we'd dropped the bait for Alexeeva, to carry over the fishing analogy.

We'd been considering a lot of his locations, anything we could connect to Alexeeva in property searches, his home, the garage, the club, and a couple of other businesses he held a stake in, including a hotel near Midtown that Yelp reviews didn't speak kindly about.

"If he's wanting to keep things classy, the Slidell house is the way to go," Arch said. "Although the hotel has a reputation for hourly rates under the table, Yelp says there are customer service issues."

"Clerks bad about calling the cops?"

"Nah, just about keeping you in clean towels."

I'd looked at shots of the exterior online. It wasn't a spot for wooing and compromising a seedy if upper-crust associate even if you already had a slot for cameras.

A lot of money could be moved through Moates' operation. It called for finesse.

If Alexeeva proposed a girl as an inducement as we hoped, he'd want somewhere private and a little more elegant. It wouldn't be that hard to prod him toward the Slidell spot. A few suggestions here or there should do it unless he had another mansion tucked away somewhere Jael and the earlier detective agencies had missed.

"I think we can get them there," I said. "I wish I had a better way of getting the right girl. I'm hoping in his mind she's something special and he's been saving her. He's always got a couple of things swirling, but if we get any chance to offer suggestions we'll angle more toward her look."

"You gonna let Moates ask if Alexeeva doesn't come through?"

"That'll look pretty suspicious. He needs to make the offer, and we're screwed if it's someone other than Dagney. I hate to think of any kid resigned to a fate tangled in his fingers, though."

"Feels pretty awful," Arch agreed.

"Maybe we could get him pulled in with any girl he puts forth, and my buddy on the force could leverage Dagney out of him, but it gets shaky at that point. Further self-incrimination's not how he rolls."

"Neither's letting go of an asset easily."

"Unless he sees it as one of his games," Arch said. "Even if he's suspicious, and he figures whoever got Dahlia is perpetrating this, maybe he thinks that person deserves to be jacked with a little."

"I'd like better odds. On the location, and the girl," I said.

"But if that's how we get her, I'll play."

"Or at least we might be able to let Hollie King steer him toward the Slidell house without looking too obvious. She can mention a desire for privacy at least."

We looked back at the tablet screen, and Arch ran a finger across the blue form of Lake Pontchartrain. "You get 'em out there, gives us all this to lose them in before we go back ashore."

"I'll do what I can," I said.

Maybe I needed to find a vodou bokor or something to tip things our way or counter Alexeeva's Russian magic.

Or at least to know Alexeeva better. I'd learned enough to devise the nudge, to try and manipulate a manipulator. Was there another push I could try to bring him out with an offering of Dagney?

I was back home and casting about for ideas when Sandra called. "Unknown" flashed on my screen, but I clicked it to accept and say hello. I probably wanted to talk to anyone who had the number.

"Terri got ahold of me, said you were looking for me."

I recognized her voice instantly. It was like I'd talked to her the day before over breakfast, and the feel of what had once been natural flooded over me. It was like meeting someone you dated once at a club or restaurant and sitting down for a drink. It feels for a while like it always did when you were out together. Time travel. You laugh like you once did, repeat reflexive gestures from before, and the things that caused you to part are submerged for a while and the good things resurface.

Then you remember when it's time to leave that you're headed in different directions, back toward different lives and that you've just been in the past for a while or a part of a timeline that turned out differently.

For a moment I felt like I was on the job and taking her call, a call from her checking what I wanted her to leave me to warm up for dinner or if I needed the checkbook. Or to tell me something the baby had done.

All things that had transpired in between were forgotten. It was like a moment from long ago. I knew better in a heartbeat. My brain reminded me and suctioned the pleasant feeling out of my gut.

I searched, found words though they were very basic.

"I wanted to know how you were doing," I said. "How Juli is."

Just a couple of moments of silence followed, a hesitation, though brief. I interpreted it as a bit of emotion, regret. Then she said: "We're fine. I don't think it's a good idea for you to see her right now."

"Just for a while? Are you in New Orleans?"

"That's not important."

"Is everything okay?"

"Fine. I wanted to tell you...."

"Sandy...I'm working on something. I'll get a payout. I can put something together. I can help you both out of whatever you're involved in."

"That's not what Juli needs right now. Don't bother on our account. Don't...."

Her voice tightened and she just stopped for another long silence.

"Just leave us alone. Maybe down the road, but now...."

"I'd like to see Juli. Years of her life are passing. I don't know what she looks like now. How tall she is. She was barely talking when I went in. She doesn't even know who I am."

"Some of that's a blessing for her," she said.

"Is there...are you having any problems?"

"I'm fine. I told you. Not your concern."

I thought about telling her what I knew about Finn Alders, his rap sheet, about his potential issues. I worried she'd think I was overstepping, prying into her life, stalking. Concern for Juli counterbalanced that worry for a second. Let Sandy be upset, at least she'd know, even if I revealed I'd been checking up. At least the warning would be on the table.

I changed my mind again because I knew Sandy, and I knew if I tried attacking her boyfriend, it would push her closer to him, make her defensive.

"Can I talk to Juli? Just for a minute? Put her on."

"Not right now. It'll get hopes up. Cause confusion. Maybe down the road, like I said."

"Look, I haven't been snooping, but the guy...."

Damn caution.

"I don't want to hear it. Leave us alone."

I felt my jaw tighten, and I fought to control my voice.

"What if he's putting Juli in danger?"

"He's not the one who threw us into a world of confusion. Leave us alone. Will you? Stop trying to find me."

And the connection broke. You don't get that dull buzz of a dial tone any more. I suppose some have never heard that result of a clipped connection. I think the absolute silence is worse, even more final and absolute. A void.

I was definitely not in the past. I was sitting on my futon. Alone, in the void, worse than I'd been a few seconds before when at least there'd been a thread of connection and a few seconds before that when hope had lived and I'd been working toward a purpose.

Was there a need to go on?

CHAPTER 39

Rose kept a crisp, pragmatic edge with an underpinning of impatience. Faced with the choice between finding a bottle or calling her, I'd chosen the latter then wondered if a bottle might have offered more comfort.

"It's one phone call," she said. "Take it from a lawyer. Life's a negotiation."

We'd agreed on a coffee bar. It sat in a corner on the ground floor of a building off Canal a short walk from my place. The menu featured a full line of fresh grinds with Vieux Carré appropriate names but no options to make one an Irish. Less temptation that way.

"You haven't even begun to wrangle," she said, sipping something caramel-colored and cold. "Remember, I'm not your lawyer on this, I'm not giving you legal advice, but you have negotiations in your future. An emphatic no isn't really an option for her."

She waited for me to agree, and I did.

"You get your act together," she paused for a protracted emphasis on that point. "You get your act together, you get into family court, you've got a shot. It's going to behoove you not to get caught in the middle of any illegal activity of course."

She paused again and gave that thought a second to submerge.

"Not that I want to hear about what you're up to on behalf of the Holsts to get my opinion."

We were back to that. The message was: "Whatever you're up to, don't get caught."

I re-focused on what I'd really wanted to ask and why I'd really called her.

"How's the search on your end going? For a location. For Finn?"

"You don't want to go stirring things up with him at this stage. Even if you could find him."

She gave me a hard stare, but I'd been a cop a long time, and I'd learned to tell when a lawyer was hiding something with aggression.

"What do you know?"

"We don't have a definitive address or anything."

But there was something.

I let the silence linger until she filled it.

"Sniffing along a paper trail, there's a possibility he's been back in New Orleans."

"Court appearance?"

"Something on a credit report, such that it is. You can imagine he doesn't have a great FICO score. Let us keep up that search. You go on with what you're doing. And again. I don't want to know."

I didn't want her to know that I'd spotted at least one tell.

"It's sealed away," I said. "Chinese wall, isn't that what you guys call it?"

"Good. Finish what you're doing, then think about arbitration. Giving up's not going to do your daughter any good or get her to safety any faster."

It had been there all along. Save one daughter, save your own.

Screwing up wasn't going to do her any good either, and we weren't that close to the goal.

CHAPTER 40

Two days later, I sat in Jackson Square watching artists create likenesses of tourists while mimes and street musicians annoyed or entertained. Mostly annoyed, I think.

"We need to dangle something in front of Alexeeva," I'd said a little earlier. "Even though anything we do from now on makes a shaky structure quiver a little more."

We were at Arch's house sipping Keurig brews from Starbuck's pods. Kenny, who had no coffee, had disassembled an assault rifle and sat cleaning the components. It might have been a set of Legos. Arch knew how to keep him occupied.

"What if Moates had another suitor with laundry needs?"

If Alexeeva really was courting someone with funds coming soon and the Eternal Fund looked like as good an option to him as it did to me, the last thing I'd want to hear was that someone else was interested.

"Who's at the door with a bouquet?" I asked.

"Weapons traffickers?"

It was almost literally staring me in the face, and I didn't need to call someone in the ATF for a credible story.

"Someone who's been moving weapons across the border to Mexico," Arch said.

"You know somebody?"

"Of somebody. That's not quite our thing."

That kind of made me happy.

"But maybe, say, a middle man who's been moving guns from Eastern Europe and through the U.S. to Mexico to get around their gun laws," Arch said. "Or just a guy doing straw purchases and sending guns across the border. You know, guy gets a guy to buy a gun for him. Guy gets another guy to buy a gun. Eventually guy has a bunch of guys making legal purchases. Adds up and there's cash to deal with."

"And some asshole in Mexico has a new arsenal of assault rifles. I've heard of that. Never investigated anything like it. Kind of reverse multi-level marketing. Maybe a ring of people doing that? To really have laundry needs."

By the time Hollie agreed to meet me on a bench in the Quarter, I had a set of notes for her, and I was ready with one more round of threats. I was aware you could only keep this up so long before cracks appeared.

"I know you want this to be over," I said. I had to present this as a lifeline. "It almost is. It can be."

She gave me an impolite suggestion.

"We're going to give Alexeeva a nudge. We're going to start a bidding war, hopefully encourage him to get serious about an inducement. Moats kind of liked the idea of a partner after your last conversation. Now he's in a courtship with someone else."

"I never asked for this."

"I know."

"I was stupid. Ryan offered a little excitement."

"I know."

"This is...."

"I know."

"What do I have to do?"

I outlined a call for her to make to Alexeeva's contact number. A guy running a scheme to route guns to Mexico from Southern sites using a network of seemingly legitimate buyers to supply him. Big payout with future repetition, money funneled through the Ponzi scheme. Big cash cuts for Moates.

Whatever could Alexeeva offer that would tip the scale?

"Moates likes the idea of a cash infusion now that it's come up and sought him out after things reached a stalemate in talks with Alexeeva. He liked the idea Alexeeva planted, but you're nervous about the guy. You've got to sell this to Alexeeva. You want to stabilize and disentangle yourself, and you think he's the best option."

"Is this going to work?"

I could see the strain around her eyes.

I'd looked into her life enough to have an idea of who she was. She'd come from a modest middle-class family in North Louisiana, one where the women didn't often earn degrees. She had and that had opened avenues that took her to places she hadn't expected.

She had married an average guy and grown bored, so she'd been playing games, a little glamour and the cash Moates could throw around afforded some escape, some excitement.

She'd known Moates was up to something shady, but the excitement had superseded wisdom. She learned more, but by then she was wrapped in the benefits. Then it had turned into something she'd never anticipated. She'd turned into something she'd never anticipated. I could read that because I understood that.

On the flip side, I'd sweated a lot of suspects on the periphery of crimes, leveraging and intimidating to gather facts, confessions or an angle on bigger fish. It had always been part of the territory and a means to an end, usually snaring someone violent and dangerous.

I'd felt empathy for some of them just like I did for Hollie King, drawn into bad decisions by circumstances and lack of guidance and a moral compass lacking a pull to true north. I'd tried to do what I could for the ones who were caught in the snare of those above them.

Hollie was like one of the scared kids in a way. She'd been poised to make better decisions, but there was just enough naiveté in the mix, the naiveté of those not usually involved in crime.

"Is it really going to be over soon?"

"I hope so," I said. "If this one doesn't do it, you walk away. I'll lose the spreadsheets and try another way for the girl." Wished to god I knew what that was.

I wasn't sure if I was lying about the spreadsheets. I had little pity for Moates, but she wouldn't be of much further help after this gambit good or bad. She wasn't much use to me as an emotional wreck either. Might as well dangle a carrot for her too.

"So, I call...."

"Tell him you're worried Moates is making a bad call on the ringleader of a gun ring. There's enough real activity of this sort, if he sniffs around at all, it'll look like a sign."

She gave me a nod. She was schooled in persuasive talking on business deals. I looked into her eyes and gave her arm a squeeze.

"You're scared that it's going to lead to something that falls apart and that he looks like the best of a bad situation. Can you sell that?"

"I think so," she said.

I walked her through gun ring details a few times, stressing that she should parcel out information on the gun traffickers in small doses and that anything related to Dagney would generate caution with Alexeeva. He'd lost Dahlia and knew there must be someone looking for her sister, but he also knew he needed to make use of his second prize soon or not at all, and he didn't strike me as someone who wanted to waste what he'd think of as an asset.

After a few rehearsals, Holton tugged out a cell. We could have spent a day or more rehearsing, but it needed to be a bit desperate and confused anyway, peppered with fragments of information that would loosely sound real to Alexeeva and his people. He might even find a real trafficker like we were imagining if he looked hard enough.

We agreed the sounds around her would add a sense of urgency and help mask false tones or mistakes on her part. She'd slipped out of the office after a meeting, desperate for an alternative and placed the called outside of Moates's view.

I waited for it to go to voice mail, but she got an answer and after a little bit of explaining, she was put through to Taras. That was almost best-case. He seemed to be the calmer and more pragmatic of the inner circle.

"This is Holton King," she said. "I'm glad I got you. I needed to talk to you. To see if we could...I'm sorry discussions broke off before."

Nice touch.

"It's good to hear from you, Mrs. King," he said. Calm and stable. Promising.

"Thanks. I called because I'm worried Ryan is about to make a bad decision. Your overtures got him interested in the secondary possibilities of his fund, and he's talking to this fucking idiot with a...."

"Business is not best discussed on the phone," he said. "I will say if you have an offer he thinks is more lucrative...."

"I realize I'm outdoors and it's noisy. I stepped right out of a meeting...."

She stared directly at me as she improvised, her eyes conveying the effort and desperation. I gave a nod and expression to suggestion she was doing fine, though my insides were in knots as tight as hers.

"This is something that at best is short-lived. Not the scale of Mr. Alexeeva's efforts and not the...."

"Why don't I send a car for you?"

I shook my head and mouthed PUBLIC PLACE.

She repeated that.

"Where are you now?"

"Walking. I can be at Jackson Square in a couple of minutes."

"No. It's hot out isn't it? Why don't you head down to Harrah's? It's not far from there."

Noisy and probably crowded no matter what time of day. Not a bad choice.

"How will you find me?"

"Wait near the front on the entrance near the fountain. I'll spot your lovely hair."

I nodded.

"Okay. It'll take me a few minutes to get there," Holton said. She clicked off.

"Do you want me to turn my phone on when he gets close, open a connection to you?"

"We're not going to try anything elaborate. It wouldn't work anyway with all the slots and other toys. He knows that. You know what you have to sell him on."

"Will you be close? You still worried about them recognizing you?"

"I've got my Trilby, and it'll be dim and distracting in there, and I can't do worse than Kenny. I don't think Taras will spot me if I'm nearby even if Alexeeva has somebody inside with a view of the security cameras, and I don't think that's likely. I won't be able to pick up any of the conversation. You have the scenario. You can do it. We'll connect up somewhere away from the casino after you've had the talk and see where things are."

I talked her through the bullet points again, the irony of the term not lost on me. Then I put her in a cab.

It was hot out.

I grabbed a different cab near the Cathedral and had the driver drop me at a streetcar stop across from the casino. I found a set of covered benches at an angle from the entrance and sat down, adjusting so that I could look Hollie's way.

In spite of the orders to get comfortable inside, she had a seat on a concrete lip at the edge of the small array of fountains that stretched between Harrah's signs outside the covered bus and limo drop-off area.

I was definitely too far to hear anything, and I felt pretty useless. He wasn't likely to try and harm her. I hoped she'd catch sight of me for moral support. Or maybe just to appreciate my jaunty chapeau. As minutes ticked past, I watched a few newer red streetcars rattle by. I'd grabbed a paper copy of the *Picayune* earlier, and I pretended to read it as tourists and locals alike filtered on and off the cars, some heading down toward the Riverwalk. No one really paid much attention to my not getting on.

Twenty minutes were gone before Taras appeared, and I'd begun to periodically tug my collar and shake my shirt for a makeshift breeze. Taras had come alone. He walked along the cobblestone walk from down near a Hilton a couple of blocks away. Someone must have dropped him off. I didn't spot any companions as he approached Holton's seat.

She stood and accepted his hand, and then he gently took her arm near the elbow, and they navigated across the entry drive to a set of doors.

I waited a few seconds to make sure no one followed, but

Taras really seemed to be alone. I gritted my teeth a while, waiting for a horde of Alexeeva minions to converge, but that never happened.

A busload of seniors pulled up shortly after, so I hopped a low railing behind my bench and hoofed it for the gaggle so I could mingle with them as they entered.

And amid giggling silver hairs, I stepped into the low-lighting of the artificial casino world: dinging slots, babbling voices, falling coins and the subdued, gold-tinged lighting that makes time ambiguous, especially under a tiled ceiling that affected a look of a starry sky.

The chilled air was like a cool drape settling over me, offering almost instant relief to the outside heat that'd I'd almost become numb to.

Despite the ambiguity of time, the place wasn't as it would be later. It was far less crowded, dappled with that daytime casino gaggle of polo shirts and comfortable cross-trainer sneakers, ladies in spandex with sweaters and hats, a few soccer moms carrying plastic coin cups as they padded between glowing banks of slots.

I generally fit in and reminded myself I could be less conspicuous than Kenny and that I'd worried overly about being identified from surveillance video. I scanned a while before I located Holton and Taras near a circle of machines under a cluster of artificial palms.

I took a seat at video poker game in a covered section across a tiled walkway, not at the best angle but that made me less conspicuous. I could glance back from time to time like I was looking for a drink waitress while I tried to remember what I'd read about algorithms, card selections, and payout schedules. Then I started pumping in coins, wishing I'd brought more. I'd soon lost enough to make me look like a guy who needed a shot.

When I chanced my looks back, I saw Taras standing beside Holton's fleur-de-lis decorated chair, their conversation looking relaxed but serious. She appeared to be confiding the issues or tastes we'd discussed. Her expression looked earnest as she talked, probably working in details about Moates' supposed proclivities along with his desire for an American girl with a clean and virginal demeanor he couldn't quite get from a call girl.

After she'd spoken a while, Taras nodded back a few times then raised a finger to draw over a drink waitress in a little black uniform, placed an order then put a hand on Holton's arm. Reassuring?

I hoped for that as I turned back to my screen. I appeared to be on the road to a royal flush if I could get a Jack of Diamonds. I made the appropriate taps to the screen and promptly lost. Nice to have a reminder that, despite getting this far, luck was not on my side. I was glad gambling had never held that much allure for me.

I pumped a few more coins in and begged a free drink from a waitress as a prop and looked Hollie's way as I delivered my order.

Her acting seemed to continue on the mark. The brow was wrinkled, the head tilts and nod expressive, and I read reassurance from Taras, or perhaps I projected my hopes onto his posture. He spoke for a while then, and she listened. I allowed myself a side-saddle perch on my chair as if waiting on a drink refresh, looking past them but angling my attention their way.

The casino light gave her red hair a metallic look as locks bobbed a bit with a final, affirmative. Then Taras reached over, gave her shoulder a squeeze along with a final smile, and he turned and headed back toward the entrance.

I waited for her turn. She spotted me and saw in my eyes even across the distance that she shouldn't approach. We'd talk later, outside the gaze of casino surveillance cameras. Who knew who Alexeeva knew?

She did nothing to acknowledge me and slid off her chair, shouldering her handbag and heading for the exit.

My drink arrived then. I took it off the tray myself with a smile and sipped a long, cool sip and let it burn a fiery path down my esophagus.

"He's going to see what he can do," she said on the phone a little while later.

I'd finished my drink and absorbed its calm.

I reassured her some more that it would be over soon. Then I had stepped back into sunlight and headed to the streetcar stop to hop a ride, heading nowhere in particular. I just knew the streetcar didn't have drink service, and I didn't need to risk a refill that would encourage another and another.

I sat by a window as we clacked along the route, making a journey that would ultimately be a circle if I sat long enough. That felt oddly symbolic. If I completed one circle, I'd have another circle to begin to try and make it around, having completed the one before that began with the death of my partner and my shooting of Leo Maier. So it would go. I just had to keep following Jasso's admonition and find the best path on that crooked road, my fool's run for which I'd formulated a grim and sordid scenario because it was a world that lent itself to that, where the darkest of supply and demands were identified and met. I didn't feel particularly proud in the moment because I'd found the imagination to devise it, even though it was the hand I'd been dealt.

CHAPTER 41

I had a feeling that someone had been in my place when I made it home. I guess the whispers of Alexeeva's magic worked on me as well.

The door didn't really have signs of tampering, though a snap gun might not have left a lot of signs, and I couldn't rule out the window latches. A good burglar can jar some varieties open with a few carefully placed nudges. I had one of the winning varieties.

My laptop was still stowed where I'd left it, and more importantly so was the handgun. So, I hadn't been burglarized. I couldn't find anything really out of place, but I had some sense someone had been in the place. Or I was incredibly paranoid and imagining things, not a bad way to be in my position.

In spite of that, I took the PSM out, checked the clip then went through the house with it pressed at my side. I would have cleared a dwelling as a cop with a little more speed. I crept here, slipping through doorways and opening closets with caution, hairs on my neck doing a samba.

Maybe the few things hanging in my bedroom closet were spaced differently. Maybe I'd left some papers arranged in a different order on the dresser, but I couldn't pinpoint a sure sign anyone had touched anything. Was Ronnie's wife's makeshift gumshoe, Culler, still sniffing around? He'd developed more finesse or found an assistant if so.

I thought of Slavic sorcery again. Could that have primed my brain for this experience? I checked the floor in front of the windows and didn't spot any shoe prints or dirt that seemed out of place, did one more sweep and vowed to keep my eyes open for signs of anything out of the ordinary, like a Metairie cop sniffing around. If we got close to Dagney, I didn't need a loose thread from my past throwing the whole process off.

Maybe I was in a game. It was a good reminder to keep looking over my shoulder.

CHAPTER 42

I'd never been much of a sailor, so Arch was at the commands when we took the runabout out for a test drive on a sunny afternoon a couple of days later. Seemed like a good idea, and I thought it might calm my nerves more than sitting and staring at my apartment walls was doing.

The boat was a glossy blue and white, about 20 feet from bow to stern and fairly cozy with a couple of bucket seats up front, a bench seat in the back, or aft as those of us who've read a nautical glossary say. A couple of spots on the bow awaited the adventurous.

Arch made the handling look easy enough as he cruised away from the launch area and headed toward open water, tipping his cap to a couple of fishermen as he cruised past without creating much of a wake. It looked like steering a car.

He eased the throttle forward as we rounded a bend and cruised out past a stretch of shoreline where people stood casting fishing lines from the bank.

We picked up speed as we gained a little distance from shore, and wind swept around us, making the afternoon heat insignificant, and the front of the boat bobbed a bit until he cut the throttle back a tad.

I put a hand on my floppy-brimmed hat and looked back at the whipping white lines of water stretching out behind us now, snaking and crisscrossing the lake's surface.

"What speed do we get up to?"

"Faster than they want you to go out here," he said. "And faster than we should need to. It's got a customized stern drive."

I nodded, figuring that must be good.

Arch made a few turns of the wheel to stabilize then shoved the throttle forward and put my stomach in my throat. He gave a laugh as I gripped an arm on the seat.

"We'll get her out of that channel on the fishing boat then transfer you and the girl to this for a run. If he turns out to have a fleet sequestered somewhere to follow us, we should be able to outrun it."

He eased the throttle and curved the boat a bit, slowing to an idle.

"You want to give it a try in case you need to take the girl and go while Kenny and I run interference?"

I checked my life jacket zipper then traded seats with him, maintaining balance well enough to appear respectable.

"You got a problem with the water?" he asked.

"Nah, just with people shooting at me across it." Plus, I had flashbacks of trawling for bodies. Somebody else did the steering in those days too.

"It'll be dark. Probably."

I took the seat at the wheel, tested my grip and gave it a few gentle turns then let him talk me through moving the throttle forward and keeping the bounce down with the bow.

After a while, I had a feel for the handling and was testing the speed in long, straight runs across the open lake, churning up minimal spray around us. We cruised out toward the causeway before I looped it back and guided the throttle down until we were at a stop.

"I think it'll do," I said. "How much is it setting the Holst's back?"

"Nothing if we get it back in one piece."

"In the unlikelihood that there are complications from this well-planned endeavor?"

"Forty grand ought to do it."

"I'll let you drive home."

"I was figuring you probably didn't know the way."

I looked around at the open water in all directions then spotted the causeway again.

"I could probably figure it out."

"We might want to work on probably," he said as he settled into the captain's chair.

"Yeah."

CHAPTER 43

"Friday night."

I was having a smoothie at my new favorite morning spot. I put a hand over one ear to drown out other voices so I could hear Hollie.

"We have a go?"

"A go. Alexeeva's offering it as sort of a sealing of the deal ceremony."

"Do we know it's Dagney Holst?"

"Ryan was shown a book of photos. Girls in evening gowns. Based on the computer-aged photo you gave him, he's pretty sure Dagney was in the mix, and he pointed her out as one of two, his list. The guy who did the showing promised either's a virgin."

We'd be rescuing someone either way, so there was that.

"Interesting to know the selling points work in these kinds of transactions. Are we going to the lake?"

"I thought that might make you happy. Yes, the lake. Apparently, there are little soirees for clients and...girls to meet."

It gave me a sick little feeling. I was surprised and not surprised it was a party. It gave me a hint of how Alexeeva seemed invulnerable and how he was rising in status. He'd have powerful men on his guest list, and after parties like this, they all owed him favors.

Forty-five minutes and a quick shower later, I met Hollie at the apartment to hear details.

Drinks at seven with some casual time, dinner then a movie in a den with a home theater and a sound system that promised to be impressive. No promise Alexeeva would actually be on hand.

Guests probably wouldn't make it to the end of the movie. They would be slipped away for secret meetings with girls encountered during the casual period.

I'd dealt with terrible people on the streets, but something about how casual it seemed dropped a grim veil over my spirit. Just part of doing business.

"Ryan's concerned about signing anything that will be binding later."

She'd settled on the sofa in a black pants suit that seemed appropriate. She held a drink even though it was early.

"Tell him to refuse to ink until after he's spent time with his new girlfriend. That's the deal. That's the bottom line. I don't know that this is a signature proposition anyway. It's, and I use the term loosely, a gentleman's agreement."

"Is this guy going to be arrested after you get the girl out?"

"I don't know."

"There'll be proof he's involved in trafficking, won't there?"

I'd hoped this would come up later.

"He's slippery, and I'm not law enforcement."

"We'll be vulnerable."

"It's good that you aren't the only ones at the party. We'll make it look like an assault by unknown rivals with Alexeeva as the target. Gives you cover."

She swallowed a gulp of whiskey, and her eyes looked unconvinced.

"I'll be honest, Ryan may want to think about relocating after this is over, but then that was going to need to happen anyway. Path he chose and you followed. I'm sure he's got a few cars and Rolex watches to sell."

"He's not going to like that. What about me? I've got...."

"Might not be a bad time to travel out of state either."

"Why should we move ahead with this? We're probably safer with the Feds."

"Does Ryan want to be in a lockup trusting prison guards for his safety? All the time. Even if they're conscientious about keeping a man who swindled retirees safe? The media's going to find an elderly couple living in a run-down travel trailer with a sick cat that they're sharing entrees with to spotlight the height of the fund's evil. This at least gives him a chance to run. A crackdown just gets him sent away longer than Madoff, and believe me in the best case they don't really lock you up in luxury accommodations."

"Maybe he could cut a better deal with Alexeeva on his own. There'd be an infusion of cash."

"Keep him afloat longer? Believe me on this, if there's a double cross, even if I get offed in the process, the info on the viaticles goes to the right people. Moates goes down and Alexeeva's still pissed at him, and South America's suddenly the best option. If he can get there."

I was telling a lot of truth. Rose had info to disperse if I died.

"Maybe he should just run now."

"Tell him to try it."

She didn't know how big my operation was. Neither did Moates. Best to make my path look like the easiest choice. For all they knew, I had a network of biker gangs and rednecks covering the whole Gulf Coast, and I implied that. Knowing Jasso, it was probably true. I just hadn't asked to tap into it. Nice company I was keeping.

"Are we a go?"

"I want this over."

I took her glass and allowed myself a sip.

"So do I."

CHAPTER 44

Arch and I scouted the neighborhood in a nondescript car with a real estate sticker on the door and plates that would stand the test if someone got nosey on the other end of the digital security cameras that were everywhere. He'd borrowed it somewhere. Maybe we did have a network I didn't want to know about beyond his quasi-legal hunting and fishing operation.

We passed my Filipino friend on a sidewalk near the pavilion, pushing his charge's wheelchair in a slow crawl, a morning constitutional. It wasn't apparent the old man knew where he was. We might have gleaned additional insights if we'd stopped and talked, but we couldn't really afford that kind of attention now.

We'd looked over the area on paper, but the cruise gave us a better sense of the landscape. The lots were large near the gated entrance to the Alexeeva compound with not many trees. They offered very little to conceal an approach. The network of canals around the area offered a few more possibilities, but what we were doing was brazen, slipping around local security and the Home Owner's Association.

"Can you get a boat where you need to?" I asked.

"We'll do it. We won't kill any security guards."

If it were easy, thieves would use the approach all the time. At least the audacity would help make it unexpected. We pinpointed spots that would be critical, spots where roads and canals dead ended, and we marked them on maps with GPS coordinates and talked through everything step by step.

It had all the earmarks of a real cluster fuck, especially

if Kenny went rogue again. Arch assured me he wouldn't freelance anymore and that we needed his muscle, but I remained concerned.

"Maybe we should just call in a police raid when we're sure the girl's on the premises," I said.

"They could trigger a siege if they're not careful," Arch said. "They won't be aiming just to slip in and get the girl out like we are. Shooting starts, anything can happen. Or they knock on the door and he tells them to get a warrant, pulls in some favors from the people who are there, and we don't know where it goes. And then he knows it's time to send her to the Middle East to be the girlfriend of a sultan."

"Shit. You make a good devil's advocate."

"This is just a messy situation."

"That it is."

I was realizing it would have been easier to shoot him, even as I remained thankful I hadn't had to do that.

On the road, we'd come to a dead end. We pulled over and got out like we were lost and surreptitiously snapped pictures of the surroundings to help keep them familiar when we were fumbling around in the dark.

"We a go?" Arch asked. "I've got other things I could be doing if this is going to fizzle."

I shook my head.

"Keep your calendar clear. We're a go."

A sit-down with Moates and Hollie wasn't the sort of cordial evening you'd want, but we needed it. They didn't need to know the intricacies of the water work, but we agreed on signals and contingencies and discussed how we'd get Hollie out if there was a problem. Moates we could probably evacuate with Dagney. He wanted the assurance his hide would be safe in moving forward.

I gave it. It calmed him even though it was a lie. I couldn't guarantee anything.

CHAPTER 45

The evening arrived and seemed promising at the outset.
I donned a dark suit, and at dusk, I drove Moates in a town car from the city up I-10. We cruised over a narrow portion of the eastern edge of Lake Ponchatrain as the sky gave itself over to night, and the headlights washing the road ahead became a constant view and repetitive the rest of the way to the other side. For a while it felt like we were on a treadmill going nowhere, the way I'd felt since I'd been released. At last the crossing ended, and we began a glide toward the house.

"Depending on how many people they have here, they're either going to take you to the second floor or to a guest house on the grounds." We moved through a turn toward Alexeeva's street.

"Why do I have to go in at all if you know where she is now?"

"We'd rather walk her out than shoot our way in and out or cause a siege. Bullets flying, someone gets hurt. You just worry about getting in place and signal if there's a problem."

He had a concealed pen light for signals. We weren't relying only on cells. I'd suggested a hiding place that would conceal it from all but a cavity search, but he'd been reluctant about that even when we offered Kenny to help. We settled on his breast pocket beside a Levenger's fountain pen. It was supposed to be a super-bright LED output.

"Suppose I'm on the wrong side of the house?" he'd asked. "You don't see it."

"Go to another window," I'd suggested.

I announced Moates at the front gate intercom when we

arrived, and after a second, the gate parted, and I eased the vehicle forward in a slow crawl that took us up the cobblestone drive toward a circle in front of the house. I noted one small guest house to my left just inside the gate where rows of palm trees paralleled the drive. A guy in a red vest at the end of the drive motioned me to follow another sedan into the circle then leaned in at my window where I repeated who I was delivering.

"Great, you can drop your passenger then pull over to the parking structure," he said after checking a guest list.

That was a white-roofed canopy to my right. Beyond it I could catch sight of one of the docks on the property. I knew from Jael's research another sun deck stretched out in back and that another free-standing building overlooked the pool.

My money was still on the guest house out front for Moates because he was a new potential partner, and it offered more privacy for a newcomer.

In spite of being out front, it wasn't as likely to be in line of sight from the areas people would be mingling, but I couldn't be sure. I focused for the next few seconds on getting to the front door where another vested attendant was opening doors for guests.

I tried not to think about the intricate network of canals Arch would need to navigate to get the boat in place while maintaining access to open water. Activity like we were engaging in wasn't really to be encouraged in a residential area. The canals were for residents.

"This is absurd," Moates said as we inched toward the door.

I couldn't argue with that, so I didn't speak.

"Any final words of advice?"

"I don't know. Break a leg?" I paused. "Be polite. Nervousness is okay since you're engaging in a new criminal enterprise, but not too nervous. You must've developed pretty good nerves with your fund and the way it works."

"It's like the frog in boiling water," Moates said. "You wade in and it's not so bad, and the heat rising gradually doesn't get your attention until suddenly everything's bubbling around you."

"The water in my pot was already hot when I got in," I said.

"But there's one quantum theory that says if you keep watching, it'll never boil."

"I don't think we can count on that," he said.

"Worth a try. Keep your eyes open."

We reached the entrance, and an attendant opened Moates' door with a professional smile pasted on. Time for the show to begin. I watched him slide out, and he strolled toward a brightly lit front door.

When the back door thunked closed, I did a slow crawl the rest of the way around the circle and back to the canopy. There I backed in with an attendant waving me a few directions. No scratching the paint on the other limos. I wondered if he knew what was going on inside and decided probably not.

Once I was in place, I could sit watching the front entrance, and I was ready to move if needed.

I unfolded a newspaper and rattled it a bit in case anyone was looking my way. It seemed like an appropriate prop. Looking over the top of the pages, I watched other guests arrive. It was a small soirée, so I only spotted a couple of local officials I recognized then a few other guys in nice suits before arrivals ceased.

Only a few had come with drivers, and, like me, the other chauffeurs seemed content to stay in their vehicles once they'd parked. I didn't have to get out and share a smoke or make conversation about sports I hadn't kept up with.

I'd been through the paper and was on a second trip, reading the things that hadn't caught my interest the first time, when movement at the gate demanded my attention. The bars flagged slowly open, and a couple of long, black Lincoln Navigators cruised up the drive, pulling to a stop near the house.

Girls with long hair, decked out in sequined dresses emerged, accompanied by women in dark evening attire. From what I could see, none of them were Dagney, but I stopped paying attention to the newspaper.

After a while, the gate opened again, and a white town car cruised forward and stopped at a sidewalk leading to the guest house.

I saw figures slide out. It was far enough away that I could see only outlines without distinctive features. A tall man, dark suit, exited first then held the back door open. I decided the other two were both female, one taller than the other. They headed up the front walk toward the guest house, the taller figure holding the other's arm. The man followed after slamming the back door. After a second, the car eased forward, heading on up the drive toward the canopy.

If it was Dagney, I couldn't confirm it. Yet it had to be, and the white car seemed like the kind of symbolic flourish Alexeeva might come up with. Was that proof enough? Did I move now or wait? If they took Moates over, that would prove it, but that would be after cigars and drinks and probably a handshake. Right now, if only one guard was in the guest house, that might make it an easier time.

Maybe there were more guards already inside. Alexeeva wasn't stupid. He had lost Dahlia and had probably launched an initiative to figure out what had happened. He had to be taking some extra care with Dagney, especially if he was making a game of things.

Adding Moates and his handler to the mix meant that much more complication, though. I felt some sense of obligation not to get him shot.

Time to break radio silence.

I dialed Arch's number.

"It looks like my uncle has a house guest," I said, feeling a little stupid talking in code. If we were being monitored it would be easy enough to interpret.

"Entertaining friends?"

"Only a couple, I think."

"Maybe we could drop in a little early. I'm in the neighborhood."

"Maybe not a bad idea."

I clicked off, tossed the newspaper into the passenger seat and popped my door handle, reaching for my other chauffer's prop, cigarettes. I put one in my mouth as I walked to the back of the car and looked out toward the strip of water behind the canopy.

A cobblestone walk stretched around the edge of the property, allowing for a scenic walk beside the water. As I lit the cigarette, I headed to the sidewalk, drawing a puff and trying not to cough as I stopped to look out at the water.

The parking attendants stood in a small cluster chatting. I saw a couple take notice of me but they turned back to the conversation after a glance. I drew another puff then stretched my hand out at my side and studied the wavering white reflected light on the black water for a while.

Then I went for a casual stroll along the walkway up the peninsula. No one noticed, and I scanned for security cameras. I didn't spot any posts or obvious camera bubbles, but some had to be there, and the guest house would definitely have open eyes. I wouldn't be free to snoop around and peek through cracks in curtains, and someone was probably eye-balling my stroll from somewhere I was missing, noting my gate matched that of the guy who'd snatched Dagney from the club, no doubt.

The prevailing wisdom on hostage extraction, at least the last time I'd attended a continuing education lecture had been go in later unless a situation demanded otherwise.

Gather intelligence, make an informed move.

You know, luxuries.

Surprise was generally considered a plus as well.

I walked on along the sidewalk, puffing and casually dialing again.

"Where are you?"

"Getting close."

I turned, trying to seem engrossed in the conversation I was having. If I was on camera, it shouldn't look like I was heading toward the house, looking for a view through the curtains.

"I have a little bad news," he said.

"You want to fill me in?"

Slivers of light slipped out around a couple of front windows, but I couldn't make out people or anything distinct. Intelligence was out unless I waited for Moates to go in, and there'd be more security at his back. Had we done enough to assure it was Dagney in there? If it wasn't, as I'd been worried all along, we'd drive her so far out of reach we'd achieve all the things we'd been trying to avoid. That was probably going to happen anyway. Dagney needed to be in the house, and this needed to work. It was up to fate at this point.

"We had a little trouble getting a bass boat into the right channels," Arch said. "Some private security guy was sniffing around."

"What'd you do?"

"We found an empty house with a dock within the channels and borrowed a boat there."

"Okay, theft, bad, but we can work with that. We'll be leaving it. There's more bad news?"

"It's a, uh, party boat."

"Like one of those floating decks with a canopy?"

"Sorta, yeah. Good news, though. It'll do thirty-five. That's faster than you think on the water. All we need to do is take it as far as the spot by the road where we can just transfer to the speed boat and get moving. We'll shoot off across the lake at ninety. Hard for them to set up road blocks or give chase."

"There are some kind of boats in a little boat house over here," I said, scanning. "They're on the opposite side of the peninsula to the guest house and they'll have to mobilize to get in those and get after you. You'll have a little lead, but you'll also have to go past that dock to take the shortest distance to the road."

I worked on the scenario in my head. The trip was around Alexeeva's peninsula. Then back up the channel on the side I'd come from. They'd have to connect to another channel that would stretch to the spot where a small strip of land could be crossed on foot to reach the speed boat. It waited in the spot Arch and I had surveyed. The channel there ran parallel to the roadway and would lead on to open water.

"They're not going to get above fifty in this canal system," Arch said. "Things should be all right."

"How close are you to the dock?"

"Look southwest."

I could see their silhouette chugging up the canal that ran behind the neighboring land strips, Kenny's massive form near the front gazing forward.

"You see the guest house?"

"Yeah."

"Get there. Let's move."

I headed across the grassy area beside the driveway, crossing the cobblestones and picking up speed as I neared the front door. I slid my arm to the small of my back and tugged out the PSM.

If anyone was awake at security cameras, they'd spotted that move, so there was really not much more need to be discreet. I hurried under the front door's overhang and tried the door. Locked, and it's not as easy to kick in or shoot in a door as it looks on TV, and given the hurricane activity of recent years, I suspected the sidelight windows were wind-resistant and that meant resistant to just about everything else as well. Read that as hard to smash.

I rang the bell.

The matron I'd seen at a distance answered, a fortyish blonde woman in a sleek black evening dress. The hospitality started at the entrance. She had a burgeoning smile, expecting to meet the man her charge would be entertaining this evening, a part of the overall experience.

I put the gun in her face and interrupted the uptick of her lips.

"Where's the girl?"

"Who the...?"

I shoved her aside.

A little sitting area spread just inside the door. A lug wrench in a sports shirt sat with an iPad between his hands, playing a video game. His weapon was nestled under his armpit.

I leveled the PSM toward his face.

"The girl."

He didn't have to speak. The commotion had traveled down the narrow hallway. She'd stepped slowly and awkwardly out of the master bedroom to see what was going on.

One problem solved. It was Dagney. I'd looked at enough pictures and at enough computer renderings to be sure. Careful and subtle makeup had been applied, dark eye liner, blush, a little heavy but I could still recognize her. She wore an all-white ensemble, a lacy negligée with a sheer, matching robe.

"Back door," I told her.

She didn't hesitate. She spun and ran that direction.

I got the lug wrench in the face with a hammer fist blow enhanced by the fact I held the PSM. His nose crunched inward and spurted blood which really caught his attention. His hands shot to his face and pressed in, attempting to staunch the flow. I kicked him in the sternum while he was busy and sent him sprawling onto the sofa.

Then I grabbed the matron's arm and pulled her in front of me. I wasn't sure if any gunmen that might be in the back would hesitate to shoot her, but she'd slow the slugs down. It was a shitty move on my part, but she was in a shitty line of work and I didn't really care what had led her to that point.

Dagney had cleared the hallway and was headed across a kitchen area. The house plans Jael had accessed were still accurate. The girl skittered to a stop there near a counter because an intact version of the guy bleeding on the sofa had stepped into view.

"Down," I ordered.

Dagney found the presence of mind to obey.

The matron caused just enough hesitation.

I squeezed the trigger, and the slider moved rapidly as the shell flew. Even with one arm, I'd managed to maintain a little accuracy as the refresher from Arch coupled with my old, trained reflex kicked in.

A red blossom bloomed near his collarbone. His hand shot up to it, pressing in, and he dropped to his knees. I abandoned the matron and thundered forward, swinging the barrel into his face in a backhanded blow.

As he went over a glossy breakfast table, I knelt, grabbed Dagney's arm, and we sprinted for the back door. She actually reached forward and fumbled open the dead bolt and popped the handle lock, and we were out on the back deck in an instant. No Stockholm syndrome here. I guess she sensed who the good guys were here.

Relief gushed over me when I saw Arch standing outside with a lightweight black rifle.

"Get her to the boat," he shouted.

He fired a couple of bursts in the air then. The guard inevitably headed our way would hesitate a second.

I didn't look back I half dragged the girl across the rough-hewn planks of the dock, and then Kenny reached forward and hoisted her easily up and over into the small barge's interior.

I followed with Arch a few steps behind.

"Keep watch," he shouted, scrambling on his knees to unravel the quick mooring he'd looped around one of the dock's support ties.

Then he headed for the craft's controls. I dropped near the bow with the PSM ready, though we'd be out of its range soon.

"Who are you?" Dagney asked.

Arch fired the motor and steered the craft away from the dock, building speed without hesitation once he had us pointed in the right direction.

I turned toward her. "Your parents sent me."

She wept. In seconds the eye liner melted onto her cheeks.

CHAPTER 46

We reached the end of the strip of land on which Alexeeva's mansion sat and the engines whirred with greater fervor as Arch opened the craft up with a little whoop.

As the water kicked up around us, I had to agree with Arch. Thirty-five, if that was what we were doing, felt faster than I'd imagined. I looked back toward the house. We rounded the end of the peninsula and began the trip up the other side.

So far no one was headed toward the dock with weapons ready.

I yanked out the cell and keyed Moates. Radio silence be damned at this point. He answered after a few rings.

"There's going to be some confusion in a few seconds," I said. "If it hasn't started already. Use it to get out while you can. The keys are over the town car's sun visor."

"Do you have the girl?"

"I do. Good luck. They'll figure out who's connected soon enough."

We shot on past the dock and forward, sloshing into the perpendicular channel that ran beside the roadway. If we hadn't been doing top speed, we started then as Arch opened to full throttle, and we bounced on the water. As we'd established, this craft wasn't built for speed, but he didn't let up now. The path was straight enough, and seconds might matter.

We moved past a couple of houses and a waterfront apartment complex, and then he slowed, angling toward shore alongside a vacant lot, a single strip of undeveloped land. I wasn't sure why, but I was thankful for it. Arch drove the boat's bow up into the soft sand at the lot's edge, as if he were trying to run it aground.

"Go," he shouted. "Get the girl and go. Kenny's waiting for you"

Without pause, I went over the front railing then spun back and grabbed Dagney under her arms, lifting her over.

We hurried through the ragged grass that dappled the lot, moving toward the roadway and the channel on the other side that would stretch out to the open lake. I lifted a silent prayer that Kenny would be waiting and not distracted, and as we rushed through shadows, I peered forward looking for a silhouette beyond the road.

Kenny was indeed in place. I lifted Dagney into my arms and rushed on across the blacktop roadway and onto a little outcropping where I jogged toward the waiting speedboat.

Like the party barge, the runabout was almost aground, but not quite. I sloshed into the water's edge and passed Dagney to Kenny then climbed over the side. The boat rocked and pitched with the movement of our weight, but I managed to get onto the deck.

After he'd lowered her onto the bench seat at the back of the boat, Kenny dropped into the driver's seat.

"You got this?" I asked.

He nodded. "Here we go," he said.

The motor turned over on the first try, and he yanked the wheel hard right and shoved the throttle forward with a shout of "Wheeeeee!" Interesting contrast to his otherwise ruthless professionalism.

I dropped into a spot beside Dagney and looked into her confused eyes. She wondered if she could believe me.

"We're from your parents," I said to reassure. "We're going to take you home."

She began to cry. That reminded me the suit coat I was wearing had a display handkerchief, so I pulled that out for her than slipped the jacket off and draped it around her shoulders since the wind slashed around us.

In a couple of minutes, we reached the end of the canal, and Kenny slowed to navigate a shallow area near a boat launch but then opened up again as we passed from the mouth of the canal into the lake alongside Maestri Bridge.

"Next stop Metairie," I said. "We'll figure it out from there."

He nodded, and we picked up speed in a smooth uptick that avoided the bounce Arch had warned me about. A spotlight on the bow sent gleaming white streaks across the water's surface, as if it were a line guiding the way.

I should have known it had all been too easy, but with adrenalin pumping and a sense of elation that we'd turned up Dagney at all, I was distracted.

The headlights appeared minutes into what should have been a straight shot across to wherever we wanted to off load. At first, I thought we were watching after-dark fishing boats or other pleasure excursions, but the lamps converged until we were looking at twin white eyes directly behind us.

It seemed impossible, but maybe someone had pinpointed us, and they were moving in.

They'd almost had to have been out here waiting for us or had boats outside the neighborhood canals.

Then it hit me.

"Dagney, did they bring you in on a boat?"

She nodded. "A yacht."

"The yacht had other boats escorting it?"

She nodded. "One of them took us over to where the car was waiting for us."

Kenny steered right in an effort to lose them, but the lights veered in the same direction.

They'd match us move for move, get on our tail. I squinted into the pod lights, picking out silhouettes of men behind the blazing light beams. They'd do more than get on our tail. I could see weapons. They were ready to blow us out of the water. I could see rifles cradled, heavy firepower, and I thought I could make out the bulky form of Nestor Zhirov.

I was glad I hadn't called the Holsts already and over promised.

CHAPTER 47

I felt my soul deflate, and about then Dagney's fingers dug into my arm. I glanced at her in the glow of the boat lights. She was terrified. If they sprayed weapon fire our way, we wouldn't come out well.

"I just thought they left," she said.

I leaned toward her, spoke close to the side of her face as Kenny eased the throttle back and pulled us into a perpendicular stop in front of the boats.

"This isn't over," I said. "Stay low."

I ducked with her to the floorboard, and Kenny charted a route through a passage under a draw span of the Maestri, jerking us out of the light beams and under the bridge. Water churned high and white around us, and the boat shuddered beneath us as we zoomed into the darkness.

We missed any obstructions. Kenny was good even at a high speed. I was glad I hadn't had to drive. Motors roared behind us, but no shots rang out. They didn't want to risk hitting Dagney. She was valuable cargo. That was good all around.

Kenny moved the throttle forward, and angled away from the bridge, charting a course somewhere generally south. The sound of engines behind us seemed to split, a zippy, slightly more shrill motor heading one way, the deeper and grumbling, the other.

"They're coming under too, and they're going to try to flank us," I said.

"On it," Kenny shouted, and we picked up more speed, getting a little of that undesirable bounce Arch had spoken of but propelling us still faster in spite of it. Again, I couldn't judge speed on the water, but it felt significantly faster than we'd managed on the party barge.

I scanned the south shore, looking at the scattered signs of light. Nothing stood out as a more obvious spot to make for. I didn't offer any suggestions. I wasn't processing any great options other than keep away at the moment. Or maybe cops. I yanked my phone out. Maybe it was time for the coast guard. With Dagney on board, the reasons not to call in official help were generally gone. The shrill motor cut in our way before I had a chance to key in 9-1-1, forcing Kenny to adjust his route to avoid a sideswipe.

"Wa' the hell?" Kenny shouted.

The gruff motor came in on the other side. They were trying to hem us in and perhaps control our trajectory.

I kept an arm around Dagney and flexed my fingers around the PSM.

"Get us out of this, Kenny."

"Workin' on it," he said.

I think he was having a good time. He went full throttle again and tried to tack left and get ahead of the shrill craft.

Wind ripped at us as he gained a little ground, but as I looked over at the running lights on the craft to our left, I saw they were almost keeping even. They had about the same horsepower.

I thought I saw three men on board, all with weapons. I wasn't confident I could do much more than draw responding fire if I blasted in their direction with the PSM at the distance. Before I could even entertain that thought much further, they started cutting toward us.

"They're coming to try and sideswipe us," I shouted.

If they tipped us, retrieving us from the drink would be easy enough. We wouldn't have a lot of options then, besides drowning.

"Giving it all we got," Kenny said.

Squinting against the wind, I scanned the shoreline. Most of it was lost in the darkness. We'd veered away from the highway and now faced the marshy Bayou Sauvage wildlife refuge. I hadn't been there since I was a kid. Things might get treacherous out there even if we could lose ourselves. I couldn't rule out gators well enough to suit myself.

Not far from the wildlife area, the outskirts of the city stretched, some neighborhoods speckling peninsulas not unlike the north side where we'd been. In land configuration at least if not housing costs. If we could go to ground somewhere near the proximity of other humans, we'd discourage gunplay. There might have been better possibilities for putting to shore, but they weren't coming to me at the moment. We'd been pushed into an area that wasn't as ideal as other spots might be. Had they wanted us to head that way?

Kenny cocked his head in my direction, inquiring.

"Keep going," I said. I looked at my phone. I wasn't getting much coverage. "They're right behind us. We need to call in a mayday."

"Need my hands," he said.

Kenny zigged and zagged a bit then put the throttle all the way forward again, getting us a little further away from the flanking crafts.

"There's a pass up there," he shouted, surprising me just a bit. He tapped the Garmin screen on his console.

"Get us close to a highway?"

"Yeah."

They'd already kept us from getting too close to I-10.

I slipped my arm from around Dagney and moved forward in the boat, keeping low to maintain balance and avoid being a target.

Chef Menteur Pass, which I could read on the screen, curled through the marshy area and ran under Highway 90 as it wended toward Lake Borgne which opened to the Gulf. The older Chef Menteur Highway crossed as well. Maybe there'd be people somewhere there, maybe even some bars or something public that was open. I tried for a cell signal again as we neared the mouth of the pass, but it wasn't happening.

This was supposed to have been an easier extraction than racing away in a car. It might have been for someone less organized than Alexeeva. Fate had dealt us a shitty hand, too.

I knelt at Kenny's side, tried to steady myself and stared at the radio. We were actually near New Orleans city limits, which at least technically stretched out here somewhere.

"Not the top-of-the-line unit, but there's a distress button," Kenny said, nodding toward a radio. "It'll send our location."

I squinted in the dim light from the console, spotted the red button and pressed it, producing some beeps.

"Call in the mayday now," Kenny said. "Coordinates are on the screen."

I grabbed the mic and babbled: "Mayday," remembering you were supposed to call it three times. I was waiting on the response when shots roared above the motor noise. I wasn't sure they'd been fired at us or just in the air above us, but I scrambled back to Dagney's side.

She'd learned to be silent in her time in captivity, and she held to that now. She had no idea who we really were or what we wanted. I tried to assuage the terror she must be feeling and suppressing, but there wasn't much hope of that.

"We'll have you home soon," I said. I hoped it was the home with her parents and not the one she'd come to know.

She just looked at me with wide, still child-like eyes. She'd been controlled and helpless for so long she didn't know what to convey.

"Stay low," I said, shifting to practical mode.

Kenny lowered the throttle as we moved into the mouth of the pass and our front light illuminated more brown water before us. Hopefully the Coast Guard would mobilize and any other boats in the area would relay the call as well, and they'd hone in on our passive signal.

We chugged up the first arm of water that stretched toward a curve around an outcropping on our right. According to Kenny's electronic map, we'd wend through a couple of curves before Highway 90 crossed over. We made it along the first open stretch at pretty good speed then slowed only slightly before rounding a curve and gliding forward.

That slow-down was what they'd been waiting for. The pursuing crafts that had been hanging on our wake shot past us, one on each side.

"Uh, oh," Kenny said.

The one on our right angled into our path, motor slashing a

white trench that buffeted us as we hit the waves off the wake.

Then the craft was in front of us, perpendicular. Their throttle cut, almost expertly, as another shot past us and joined it nose to nose.

In an instant, we were headed toward their side as more boats sounded behind us. How many did they have? We were about to be boxed in. It wouldn't do them any good if we rammed, but it wouldn't do us any good either. We'd be in the drink a long way from shore. They'd snatch the girl before anyone arrived.

I looked for a second toward a narrow bar of land off to our right, starboard in boating terms, a stretch covered in vegetation, dark in the night shadows, nothing more than a strip draped in blackness and wisps of mist. I could make out a few bits of a crumbling brick wall behind it. Then I remembered again there'd been a fort here, a guard post during 19th Century wars to keep enemies out of Lake Pontchartrain.

"They've got us on water, Kenny," I said. "What about over there?"

He glanced that way and saw what I was talking about. His head seemed to perk slightly.

"Fort Macomb," he said, almost with elation. "We could hide in there. It'd be cool."

I was thinking gators in the wildlife area might give us a better chance, but he jerked the craft that way and accelerated with almost the same expertise we'd seen from the other craft, and our boat jetted in the fort's direction before the boats behind us could pull aside.

PART 4
IN THE REALM OF CZERNOBOG

CHAPTER 48

"We may be screwed," Kenny said. Gold star for restating the obvious.

"No argument there. We have to hold out until the coast guard gets here." At least that would give me time to rehearse my statement for the police.

A dark and cold feeling clenched my ribcage.

If we hit shore, there were roadways and houses not too far away, but it would be a trek on foot with the girl. We might not draw enough attention before the guys on our tail started shooting individual motorists or nosey residents.

From what I'd seen of the guys on the boat, they looked impatient and could pretty easily finish us both and take the girl back as well in a flat-out battle. Suddenly, our best hope was that they'd toy with us first.

Maybe we could play to our strengths. Or toy with them.

"Keep going," I said.

Kenny guided the craft up the inlet, not sparing speed. The bow movement was less than ideal.

A brick wall stretched beside us, a wall overgrown with intense vegetation at its earth packed the top. It looked like a Chia pet. Below the brush, the wall was dappled with small arched cannon ports that looked like deep set, haunted eyes when our light swept that direction. If the old fort had stood against gunboats for so long, maybe we could hold off a few guys. Or, if they turned out to be, commandos.

Kenny angled toward a spot we could pull ashore. I moved to the bow, adjusted my footing to a steady position and waited for the hull to slide up on the bank. Then I stepped out and dragged the boat up onto land, tugging it in just enough to keep it from drifting away.

Then I crouched and checked the PSM at my spine where I'd tucked it. It snuggled securely in my waistband. With luck, it wouldn't discharge and blow off my coccyx.

Behind me, Kenny slid from his seat and crouched in the floorboard. He'd pulled a MAC-10, a machine pistol with a long suppressor, from a compartment. He cradled it in his arms. Knowing Kenny, he'd selected it because it looked cool, but if the way he'd handled the boat was any indication, he'd be helpful.

I stuffed extra ammo clips into my pockets, and Kenny grabbed a satchel from the compartment.

"Might have stuff you can use."

Tugging it open, he pulled out what looked at first like sticks of dynamite, which he offered me as examples. That seemed a little extreme, but I accepted, fearful of instability until I realized he'd handed me not dynamite but emergency flares. On a boat, what a concept.

I tucked them back into the bag, found a shoulder strap and slid it over my head then stepped onto the bit of shore we had found and rolled up my sleeves.

With the girl between us, we hustled up a narrow dirt road that led to the chain link fence.

"What else you know about this place?"

"It's really pre-Civil War," he said. "Designed when the U.S. needed to give gunners and cannons a covered position to fire from, so it's really a bunch of tunnels and cannon openings, embrasures."

If you picked one of his topics, Kenny truly was an encyclopedia. He and Arch had probably led businessmen on fishing tours this way.

"The outside walls are really all hallways or really tunnels. There'll be a structure inside at the center, ruins of barracks and what not. They use the place now in movies a lot and TV."

"That's great news."

"It was in *NCIS* and *True Detective*. Did you see that?"

"Must have missed it."

"It was on HBO. Good show."

"They didn't spring for the premium channels in lockup," I said. Might have been helpful to have seen the place.

Motors roared behind us. I looked skyward, hoping for a Coast Guard helicopter, but nothing was in sight. So, it was the fort.

From what I could tell the structure was roughly a triangle constructed in its day to fit the available ground. We reached the gate at the end of the dirt path. It didn't seem formidable.

"Place is closed. No state money to make it safe," Kenny said.

Unstable bricks didn't seem that threatening at the moment.

The gate had already been bent a few times for explorers wanting a look in spite of potential hazards. I curled my fingers around the edge and twisted it against the chain and padlock, and we made a space that let Dagney slide through. I followed with Kenny's help, keeping up the pull and twist.

We had to bend it with a bit more effort to try and accommodate Kenny's size, and I heard shouts from somewhere behind us. They were coming.

"Go on," he said. "I'll be along."

He abandoned his efforts to get through and headed into brush along the roadside, shoulders slumping downward.

"Just get to cover," I said. "Stay safe."

"I will."

I almost barked instructions for him not to try any heroics, but he'd disappeared, and we needed to move. With my hand around Dagney's wrist, I led the way on toward the fort's nearest wall. I released her arm and yanked out the lighted face of the burner and turned it forward, letting it chase shadows back a bit.

Jasso's old remark returned to me yet again.

Life's a fool's run on a crooked road. I'd found the truest iteration of his notion.

A heavy wooden door or maybe even an iron gate had probably once barred the arched passage, a sally port, but now only another chain-link gate had been erected across the opening. That hung from loose hinges. I bent that, and we slid through it easily and into the open archway.

The passage stretched on through the wall. I led Dagney forward with as much speed as she could manage. We needed to find an opening into the cannon passages. Let 'em try to find us in there.

I found the PSM and slid the weapon from my waistband. The grip didn't fill my palm. It felt a little like a toy to my hand that was more familiar with my old service weapon, especially in this moment when I didn't know what I might be facing.

In spite of that, I reminded myself the weapon should have the power Arch had claimed, and I recalled the test firings out at his compound. Then I gently slipped the de-cocking lever out of its safety position the way he'd showed me. It had worked on the lug wrench back at the guest house. We'd see what the rounds did in the dark against something other than a paper silhouette if I had to use it again.

Once inside the fort's perimeter, I scanned the area. It was overgrown with brush and grass, and rows of dead shrubs that looked like a crop of witch's brooms. The jagged and rectangular inner brick structure stood as Kenny had predicted across an expanse of grassy ground.

I pulled Dagney close then moved past the stone remnants that had once formed a small pool, maybe a watering hole.

Selecting an arched opening amid a row of archways on the main wall to my right, I did a quick check above to make sure no loose bricks were waiting to brain us then stepped forward. Grit and dead weeds scraped under my shoes on the brick floor as we entered. Keeping the steps short and cautious, I moved us on into shadow. I'd gone up a lot of halls and alleyways and into a lot of places chasing suspects or preparing to break up domestic situations or make collars.

Often, I'd worn a vest, reducing the risk. Given what had happened already tonight, I should have one on now, should have asked Arch to supply one. In the past, I'd always felt my throat clinch and my muscles tingle with a hot fire at nerve ends, sensations that had to be overridden even as I calculated the actions of sweaty and desperate men.

The ones who came after me here would be a little less nervous than the crooks I'd been after. They'd be thoughtful, canny, possibly trained soldiers. That didn't really make me any more comfortable. A cool and calculated shot would kill me just as dead as a twitchy junkie's erratic one. Then where would Juli be?

I found a spot in shadow just our side of the opening so that I could look out. In what moon and starlight the night offered, all that grass and the weeds were teased by wind that danced across the grounds. I saw no men yet. They'd have to clear the same gates we did, but they might even have bolt cutters. They'd be along.

I listened, trying to catch hints of voices or movement, but I picked up nothing. After letting a few heartbeats pass, I took a chance on poking my head out further. I still saw only the twitching brush. It was all over the ground and growing out the tops of the walls, vines spilling down like tangled hair.

I pulled back inside, telling myself we just needed to move a short distance up the passage and find a defensible place, a nook to wait things out. The Coast Guard would be drawn to the boat by the distress signal and coordinates, I told myself, though then they'd have to look further when they found it aground. Despite that, their presence ought to scare our pursuers.

A bit of outside light spilled in through archways ahead, giving me a view of the area stretching forward, piles of bricks, more archways. Beyond that, the passage branched into deeper shadows. It was like I was in the final act of the old black-and-white Bela Lugosi *Dracula*, looking for the count in his coffin in hidden chambers.

I took slow steps forward, keeping Dagney behind me. Working to control my breathing, I led her on through black shadow, heading for the front wall.

"You doing all right?" I asked in a low voice.

"I'm okay," she said.

"My name is Silas," I said. "I have a little girl. She's a little younger than you. I'm going to try to take as good of care of you as I would her. You understand?"

She nodded.

"This will be over soon," I said.

I'd comforted Juli after nightmares, wiping tears, but she'd been much younger. I didn't really have training for this or know what a child comprehended.

"If men come, we need to be really quiet," I said.

"I know."

I hoped she could see my smile and nod.

"Let's go a little further, then we'll rest," I said.

"All right."

I took her wrist again, and we inched along, keeping to the shadows.

Finally, I heard the voices I'd expected outside, orders being barked. They'd found their way inside the walls. They'd risk coming in the passage. They didn't know where we were or when I'd start shooting, so they'd fan out and do a systematic search. Some would go into the barracks. I'd figured they'd think that was the first place we'd head.

Some would search the outer walls. I'd only have a few to deal with at a time, but they might even have night vision goggles.

Who was I kidding?

They probably had night vision goggles.

I guided Dagney on with a little more speed until we found a narrow rectangular chamber in a spot in deep shadow near what would have to be the front wall. They would have called it a magazine and stored gunpowder there. We crouched and remained quiet, and seconds ticked past as we listened.

Men or anything else might lurk our way along either right or left, but this was a pretty good spot. Not a tomb, I told myself.

My mind chose then to remind me this was an area with open walls near water in Louisiana. Rats and large nutria—twenty-pound rodents with long and curved front teeth—might have sought shelter here. Gators? Snakes wouldn't be out of the question, though they wouldn't like the cold stone in the absence of sunlight. Still, if they sheltered here, I imagined water moccasins, pit vipers, black and invisible. Hopefully Dagney wouldn't come up with these possibilities. I patted her shoulder to reassure and keep her quiet.

Meanwhile, I held my breath and listened and realized I should have let Arch get me night-vision goggles of my own.

Kenny's MAC-1O might have been nice too. Walking into a spit of rapid fire would make the bad guys think twice.

Who'd have imagined this might be a scenario? Had I ever thought it was a good idea? Things had been happening fast on the water.

I heard only that deafening nothingness that permeates the world when all else is removed, that impossible-to-define absence that seems to bar anything.

Had they entered the tunnels near us or were they waiting in the yard? Waiting on me to get antsy and make a move.

I kept telling myself time was on our side, but I had to survive a while. The thought was agonizing of what would happen to Dagney if they killed me. I didn't want to come this close and fail. Not her. Not Juli—my larger concern.

Another horrible idea crept into my mind. Could Alexeeva call in favors that held the Coast Guard and other responders at bay?

Time was on our side and on the enemy's as well. Time and silence let every wrong scenario play in the screening room of my mind. Could they reach the coordinates of the initial distress call and think we'd gone down? How long would it take for them to rethink that?

Getting crazy or claustrophobic would be a mistake, but my heart hammered. Every nerve ending tingled. My throat tightened. I remembered I hated walk-in closets. Then I forced myself to keep thinking. The first weapon in my arsenal would continue to be avoiding panic. If I could stay strategic, I'd extend our options all the way up to futile.

I pressed my back to a wall and let the cool stone pull my temperature down in spite of the humidity. Then I checked left and right again, up and down the passage. At the moment no one was close.

Someone might lurk nearby, might be comfortably ensconced near one of the openings, cooled by the night air, tingling as well but bolstered by the advantage of numbers and the possibility that I might grow impatient and make a mistake.

I listened.

No coughs.

No sounds of movement.

No pebbles of mortar nor brick shards kicked about by accident.

No grinding of grit under a boot sole.

These guys weren't making mistakes.

Of course, they were professional. Alexeeva had probably recruited right out of Russian special forces. What were they called? Spetsnaz?

After seconds turned into a couple of minutes, I thought about moving, but we really had no advantage in that, no objective.

I flexed my fingers around the weapon handle and worked to control my breathing.

They were letting us stew.

I was about to chance a look around the corner, when they changed their approach.

"Hey, Mister?"

Heavily accented. It carried from a distance along the front wall's corridor with a slight echo effect.

I didn't react except to put a hand on Dagney's forearm to remind her to stay silent.

Footfalls sounded now, careful, slow steps from the direction the voice had come.

Had they eliminated other possibilities like the barracks and tunnels in the other walls? Were they narrowing down our location? They'd have to be. They may already have an idea. This place wasn't that large.

Where the hell was the Coast Guard?

They might be to a point of flushing us out. The one speaking might want us to move, maybe trying to flush us toward where others waited.

I flipped the camera on on my phone and inched it around a corner, angling so I could see the screen, dim though it was. I could get a bit of a look up the passage, a bit of light spilling in through gun ports, a patchwork of shadow. Arches seemed to curve shadows, those shadows merging, melding into blackness just beyond some moonbeams. If someone waited in the shadows a short distance away, it was beyond my view.

How long had passed since the distress signal? Long enough for the Coast Guard to mobilize. They'd have to be figuring out where our boat had been. Tracing the signal.

Should we sit still?

I slipped the satchel Kenny had given me off my shoulder and gently unzipped it, taking out a couple of flares.

The voice sounded again, grim and heavily accented.

"Do not shoot."

I remained still, pressed against the wall to my side and chanced a look in the direction of the voice. A tall and lean man with a needle face inched forward.

He wore black tactical gear, a tight tactical helmet and a vest with a row of pocketed clips right below his breast bone. Those looked like they fit the nasty looking rifle on a strap over his right shoulder.

"We know you, Mr. Silas Reardon."

So, someone had been in my apartment.

Maybe it had been Culler, the guy working for my partner's widow, and he'd turned up something with Alexeeva's name which he or Joy had turned over to him just to jack me up.

Somehow, they'd gotten wind and they'd been prepared tonight in case this was the night. Over prepared.

"What do you want?" I asked, admitting nothing.

He laughed.

"The girl, of course." He let that sit for a second. "And it is important for you not to win."

"Sets a bad precedent?"

"Something like that."

I pressed back into the stonework as far as I could. Dagney stared at me wide-eyed, aware of the danger, more than aware of how sinister the man was.

He slipped a black metal tactical knife from somewhere on his left side and let me see it wave about a bit then tossed it from hand to hand.

He just laughed on top of that, and not a laugh of real emotion. Of course, that's who you'd find for a mission like this, some sociopath without empathy. He stepped forward, deft, moving in and out of shadow with dance moves.

I let the coolness from the stones seep into me again and glanced in the other direction. Of course, he was keeping me busy as men moved our way, guns ready but hoping to take Dagney without her getting hurt.

The knife wielder would be in body armor, and the helmet protected his head. The same was probably true about the guys behind us.

What else did I need to think about otherwise in the stone cavern?

Ricochets.

Cave-ins.

Noise.

A miss.

Any outcomes seemed negative. I'd have to go with fighting chance despite the downside.

"It's a little damp in here," the knife wielder said. "The girl. She might catch cold, but I am not hurting her."

He crouched on the balls of his feet, comfortable but ready for any move I made.

What could I do with this? He was well trained. He'd maintain tremendous self-control, but he had to have adrenaline coursing just like I did. How could I get him on his feet?

Toss a flare? Hmm.

I eased back into the magazine, keeping the move as silent as I could. Then I turned on my phone for a little light, held up one of the flare's I'd pulled out in front of Dagney and cracked the top off, showing her the striking motion. She nodded that she understood when I arched my eyebrows, so I motioned left in the direction of the group of men.

She nodded again, and I looked back in the bag.

"Mr. Reardon?"

The usual. Fishing line. More flares. WD-40. No handy butane lighter to go with it, but getting all James Bond with a homemade flame thrower would probably get me killed before it startled my bad guy. A compressed canister air horn, the same. It would require fumbling to sound it while I needed to be in a shooting stance.

Then my fingers brushed what might just work, at least for

a quick surprise in these close quarters. I'd have to calculate, be very strategic with everything else and move fast, but it might just be exotic enough to elicit a move.

Kenny's fucking whistle. That shrill, spine chilling, ear splitting device. I recalled the odd, discordant note it had played out at their compound, the way it had startled me in the dark. Then I calculated my best options.

Anything shy of watching the guy's knife coming for my throat had to be dubbed an upside, so I did a few mental calculations, bowed my head, meditated and decided it was time to go ahead.

I flexed my legs, sliding my back up the bricks behind me until I was in a standing position. Then I drew in a deep breath, put the whistle in my teeth, and held back the exhale. I didn't want to play a tune too early.

I spent a few seconds getting my left foot in position, an almost uncomfortably wide stance, the way Arch had shown me. Stretch now for ideal balance later. I recalled the man's height, closed my eyes and formed a mental picture.

Then I moved, pivoted with a single outward, sweeping step around the corner that put me in a balanced position. The PSM was comfortable in one palm, cupped in the other hand.

Whee-ahhha-reeeeeeeeee!

My deep breath produced a shrill and nearly deafening burst from the whistle.

The soldier straightened, moving his knife up but acting disoriented.

Dagney struck the flare in the same second. It worked on the first try because she ground it hard, determined to do as told here.

I was already squeezing the trigger, the PSM barrel level to my best calculation of where the guy's chest would be.

Dagney hurled the flare back along the passage behind me. If they were in night vision gear that'd be a nice surprise, and I got the benefit of the glow.

I didn't get a hail of bullets in my back, so I had to count it as a win. They were well trained, careful not to squeeze triggers on impulse.

The guy with the knife jerked backwards, struck somewhere. Then he jerked again, because I didn't fire just once. If you're firing to stop someone you keep at it.

He flailed backwards.

His knife fell. Clattered. His hand grabbed for the rifle on its strap, but he didn't find it before his fall began. I ducked back into the magazine.

Slugs bit into the bricks where I'd been. They'd overcome the flare.

As the roar of all the blasting echoed around us, I felt dust and stone slivers bite at my cheek, but I still didn't feel any lead. I pulled to the back wall at my right anyway, flattening myself, putting an arm around Dagney.

As echoes died, I didn't hear any more from the knife guy. Arch's soft armor-piercing shells might just have performed as advertised. At the very least maybe he'd felt enough sting of the steel tips along with the impact to be nicely stunned.

I chanced a peek out and to my left as I changed clips. The men there weren't rushing forward. They'd seen I could inflict harm and were regrouping.

I found Dagney's arm and yanked her from her spot, and we moved as I fired down the corridor. They were under orders not to hurt the girl. I prayed they would adhere to that.

"Is that man dead?" Dagney asked as we rushed past the knife wielder.

"Could be. I'm afraid he's just resting."

I kept the PSM trained on him and closed my fingers around his rifle, a short, rapid-fire Russian variety looking a lot like an AK-47. It featured a long, curved clip, and his friends had probably thought it looked as cool, but it also seemed pretty effective for making noise.

I had only seconds. The clips on his vest had been for a sidearm and were much shorter. I patted extra pockets on his legs and found a spare that would fit the rifle. Protracted rapid fire would deplete it quickly, and there was always the danger of jamming if you got too playful, but some rapid bursts might be helpful.

We scrambled forward then, on into a nook at the next

archway, and I wrapped an arm around her.

"Are you okay?" I asked, keeping my voice low.

"Yes?"

"Scared?"

"Yes."

"Sorry about that. I'm going to get you out of here," I said.

I guided her to the archway's edge, looking out into the expanse of weeds and dry brush. Off to my right, stone steps that looked reasonably stable led to the top of a wall. Tangles of brush had burst out of the earthen top, a jungle of living and dead shrubbery and vegetation that moved and danced in the breeze and spilled over the side.

If I could get her to the top, and if Kenny were still around, we could go over into the water. Seemed too risky since I didn't know where he was.

I watched for a second and thought I caught sight of movement in the brush.

"Did you notice how many men were back there?" I asked. "Two? Three? A crowd?"

"I think," she gave it seconds of quiet contemplation, "three."

A better move might be to another section of wall or the ruins of the barracks. Confuse them and buy a little more time. Really only a few minutes had passed since we'd sent the distress signal and bee-lined here.

The Coast Guard and perhaps others might be getting close. Shouldn't they already be here?

Maybe I just needed to shake things up.

"You see that center building?" I asked.

She nodded.

"We're going to run for it. I'm going to fire bursts from this rifle. That'll make them keep their heads down until we're close to the wall. Just get to the wall, don't go inside. One might be in there, and it's not a stable structure anyway."

She nodded.

"I understand," she said.

"On three."

I counted.

She sprinted.

I leaned out of the arched opening and squeezed the rifle's trigger, sending shells spewing. They wouldn't know where I was aiming. A quick burst, then I stopped squeezing.

And ran, following Dagney.

I swung the weapon high at my side and delivered another, ongoing burst back the way I'd come until I caught up with her.

Then I threw an arm around her and ushered her on into the barracks wall where we crouched in shadow near the jagged corner.

The noise of the rifle had served to keep everyone cautious.

I pushed Dagney past embrasures at the end of the building, paused when we reached a doorway that was missing bricks in several places but looked stable. I looked inside, glanced around and found the first jagged and crumbling chamber empty, so we moved in there and quickly pressed against an inside wall.

It wasn't the best position, but it was defensible.

They'd regroup in a second and pour everything they had into closing in on us since they knew where we were, and they knew their time was running out too.

With one clip for each weapon remaining I could only distract them with a run-and-gun for so long.

Staying cautious, I moved over to an embrasure and took a look out at the expanse of ground, at the brush and dry shrubs. The men emerged then, slowly. The three Dagney had counted, then another, moving forward with a mixture of commando caution and determination, half crouched.

I studied the overgrowth atop the wall again then turned my attention back to the men. They'd rush our way in a moment, counting on their protective gear and the fact I couldn't get all of them while I was moving, not even with rapid fire.

I needed a better plan.

"Hang on," I shouted. "I'll step out."

CHAPTER 49

"I want you to keep your head down," I said. "Understand?"
Dagney nodded.

I elicited promises of how careful she'd be and warned her several times of what to expect.

"I got it," she said.

"Great."

I slipped rolled bits of fabric into her ears. Then I gave her hands a squeeze around the PSM. She held it between both palms, the safety off. I left her standing under a patch of roof we'd decided must be reasonably sound.

Moving slowly, I kept back from openings in the wall so I wasn't readily visible through any embrasures or doorways and hoping they weren't bothering with heat sensitive viewers. I slipped out the opening at the end of the building.

"I'm over here," I said.

The men converged then. Still careful and cautious, but moving just a little closer together since I held the rifle loosely in an arm raised at my side, non-aggressive.

"I just don't want the girl hurt," I said.

They stopped about eight feet in front me, fanned out on the parade ground. Weapons leveled my way.

"I'll put this down," I said. "You've got us."

They stayed where they were, watching me crouch.

Then Dagney screamed. "Get them, Keeeennnnnnyyyyyy."

I rolled back through the passage I'd exited, ducking behind the stone wall.

I caught just a glimpse of the blaze of muzzle flare in the dark and their legs being ripped apart. Despite their training, I heard cries over the rapid spit from the MAC-10.

I lifted my head after the firing ceased in just a couple of seconds, raising just enough over an embrasure edge to peer into the yard.

The men lay on the ground, moving slightly but not concerned with weapons at the moment. They were focused on bleeding.

I watched dry shrubbery move beyond them, a large and bulky mass of switches, brush and grass inching cautiously forward. Kenny in a makeshift ghillie suit, not quite as nice as the one he'd worn the first day I met him but effective. They hadn't noticed him. They hadn't known to watch for Birnam Wood to come to Dunsinane.

He inched forward, the MAC-10's long black suppressor angled downward but ready, and when he neared them, he kicked weapons away, out of reach. No one resisted.

I stepped out slowly, looking around for more, but there were no more in evidence.

I kept my commandeered rifle ready, flexing a finger around the trigger but being careful not to send a burst.

"They're not moving," Kenny said. He lifted his weapon with a gesture. "Hollow points."

He was right. They'd be in agony.

I turned around, walked back into the citadel and found Dagney.

"In a little while you'll be home," I said.

As we stepped out, I heard a helicopter in the distance.

"I went back by the boat. I saw the bad guys shoot up the radio before they started in," Kenny said. "That's why I came in."

"That was a good thing."

He jerked his head skyward. "The coast guard lost GPS on us if they had it, but they're looking."

That explained a lot. They really did think we'd gone down.

"The boat traceable to us?" I asked.

Kenny shook his head.

"Let 'em keep looking," I said. "Let's get the hell out of here"

CHAPTER 50

A massive pelican swooped toward a squat, brown piling protruding from blue water in the inlet that ran beside my table. It was about 11 a.m., sunny, and a cool breeze drifted across the open-air deck at the waterfront restaurant. It was about like any seaside restaurant with nautical décor and faux thatch accents over the bar. I pushed the remnants of a fish sandwich around on my plate as excursion boats cruised past. As they called it on the Florida waterfront, Tuesday.

Arch, who'd made his way to a stashed Nissan Frontier with a dual cab, had picked us up when we reached a spot where I had cell coverage. We put Dagney in the back seat where she promptly dozed.

We found The Holsts staying in a long-term hotel in Metairie. It was actually not far from the causeway. I called from the lobby following an earlier, cryptic message suggesting I had Dagney and that she was safe. I didn't elaborate on the events at the fort.

They'd told me then where to find them.

I walked her through the lobby with an arm around her shoulders. We'd all cleaned up as much as possible at one of those mega gas-convenience stores where we could blend with a lot of weary travelers who buzzed about and didn't pay much attention to us. I'd bought her pizza and a pink rain jacket, one of those that you purchase flat and folded in a tight plastic bag… so I wouldn't stand out in quite the way I would walking a kid in an evening dress into a hotel.

The Holsts came out of the elevators in a cluster as we approached the doors, rushing at first, all hope and expectations. Recognition came after a brief pause.

Dagney remained stiff and a little uncertain after they swarmed her and the first hugs were executed. She looked at her mother's face then into the eyes of her sister and father.

Her gaze returned to her sister and some exchange of understanding passed silently between them, and then Dahlia stepped closer, touched her hair and that progressed into a tight hug with tears spilling from corners of tightly closed eyes.

When they parted, a bit of a smile crossed Dagney's features, still dappled with smeared makeup in spite of scrubbing at the quick stop. She remained a little confused, not sure how to respond or act.

Adam Holst turned to me and shook my hand, mouthed a thank you. His eyes were teary. Grace's cheeks were actually streaked with glistening streams. She embraced me.

Then, after a bit of an awkward exchange about talking to me later, they turned their attention back to their daughters. In a few seconds, the elevator doors sighed again, and the parents ushered the daughters inside.

There'd be a lot of therapy in their future, but the doors closed on a family drunk with relief.

I wondered if the couple would stay together. That's me. Ever the optimist.

At the waterfront, a little girl about Juli's age rushed to the deck railing and clapped as the pelican landed atop the piling. The bird stretched its wings to their full and impressive span for a few seconds before folding them into a casual position.

Once he felt comfortable, he peered down at the narrow inlet, probably scanning for fish but looking contemplative. I knew how he felt.

"Is he sleeping?" she asked.

"Resting his eyes," I said.

Taras had shown up on my doorstep two days after Dagney had been returned and the Holsts had moved to another new location.

I had the PSM at my spine again, ready for a quick draw I'd continued to practice. Nestor, the big one, would not be far behind him, but he showed no sign of aggression.

"Very impressive, Mr. Reardon," he said.

I didn't respond.

"We'd received word you might move on us in some way, but we didn't know when."

I remained silent.

"We had an interest in you anyway."

"I'd heard your boss liked a game."

"He has many interests as well. You know Mr. Maier's father was German, hence the name, but his mother was Russian. She wept for him."

Maier? They had had an eye out for the guy killed in the altercation that had sent me to jail? Or picked up on it when my name came up. Wheels within wheels.

"I did some time for that. You here to see that I pay more?"

"No. That might have been the case, but to Mr. Alexeeva, you have passed through the realm of Czernobog, the dark god. You have earned the right to step into the light."

"Sounds like quite an honor."

And I had something new to google.

"May I reach into my pocket?" he asked.

I nodded but kept my hand behind my back. He knew what was there.

He slipped out a large brown envelope.

"You have fought well. Played the game well. This is information that may be of use," he said.

Weird set of values and a strange sense of honor not to mention possibly odd remnants of Volkhvy practice. Or whatever aspects he chose to play with and craft to his needs. All of it was probably calculated to preserve and contribute to his own folklore.

Some days he lets opponents walk away....

I didn't look in the envelope until I'd watched Taras walk back to a car and leave.

It contained information about Sandra and Juli, not an exact location, but a lead.

I felt elated and chilled, probably his plan. I had a lead, but I got the message. If he wanted to find them, he could. And we'd seen what he could do. Was it supposed to mean he wasn't finished with me? Or that he was?

Rose had stepped in to help my attorney with the legal hassles of me leaving the state.

Alexeeva's info showed Finn had spent time in a rehab facility in Orlando. That had been overlooked or privacy rights had concealed it from general searches but not from Alexeeva's network apparently.

Finn had checked out, but he was probably still somewhere in that vicinity. I at least had a new starting point beyond the last known residence.

I felt as free as I had since my release, sitting on that deck with sea air sweeping in.

The Holsts had been generous following the reunion. I could run a while with the funds and mull over regrets.

Rose and I had talked later about tying Alexeeva to everything, but even with events starting at his Metairie house, the avenues for his deniability were high, his power significant, and my exposure was pretty severe and Arch, Kenny, Crystal, Amara and even Jael might be dragged into it.

Wounded men and a possible corpse had been left behind, questionably legal weapons had been used, and I had consorted with suspected criminals of a couple of stripes and racked up quite a few other things that wouldn't really dress up my resume.

Attorneys with polished oratorical skills would leave me on a witness stand looking like I'd been through a paper shredder.

Moates was a little less complicated. Rose arranged meetings with Hollie, her lawyer and the U.S. Attorney for the Eastern District of Louisiana plus an SEC representative in order to surrender information and tell what she knew about Moates' operation.

Moates and Hollie had made it out of Alexeeva's estate in the car we'd arrived in, taking advantage of the confusion surrounding the extraction. We'd discussed that scenario as one option for them since we'd feared we needed Arch available to help with Dagney.

I was glad they had not come to harm as part of our scheme. That was one bit of karmic destiny I'd escaped.

Rose and I had agreed it was the best way and that saving a few people their savings would have to be the victory. Plus, it would inconvenience Alexeeva in any money laundering possibilities he'd hoped for.

It gave Hollie a shot at a deal, the most decent thing to be done where she was concerned. Alexeeva might get to go on, but Moates was through bilking old people.

Hollie had actually mouthed a quiet thank you at one point. She'd wanted it to be over for a while and hadn't known how to disentangle herself.

Moates' troubles with the law might actually have the benefit of pacifying Alexeeva and any need he had for retribution. Or Moates might get a shank sometime down the road in medium security lockup. Maybe he'd saved enough for one of those prison consultants you hear about to help him get ready for the inside.

Maybe my karmic debt on that front was simply delayed.

Jael had shown me how to set a Google Alert to watch for a Moates indictment.

Everything was three weeks in the past now. I had no idea how events would go from here or when and if I might stop looking over my shoulder.

I finished lunch and walked down to the docks behind the restaurant to watch more boats for a while. The pelican was still on his perch and looking content at the moment.

They offer a lot of Bible studies in prisons. They want to give you hope even if there isn't any. Like any prisoner I attended to get out of my cell for a while.

I'd sat in one group or another at the detention center with a young, second-string minister from a megachurch in a city somewhere close enough for the drive. He had a divinity degree, and he wanted somewhere to use it since the senior pastor got all of the good speaking gigs.

He'd spent a few hours going over the 102nd Psalm one afternoon, the song of a man overwhelmed by his troubles, a song of despair, a lament. Great stuff for the incarcerated.

He'd drawn my attention back from a gaze out a window by pouring over a line in the text. I'm not sure what version he was reading from, but it stuck with me.

"I am like a pelican of the wilderness: I am like an owl of the desert. I watch, and am as a sparrow alone on the house top."

The loneliness and despair of that had imprinted, and the minister had gone on to blather about the plight of a water bird in a desolate landscape and the other appropriate metaphors in the passage.

I couldn't speak to where the pelican in my current view had been—maybe some fool's run of his own—but perhaps he had returned from a wilderness and rested here, happy to be where fish swam and the air was warm and moist with the smell of open water.

"Is he sad?" the little girl from the deck had asked.

"I think he's content at least," I'd said. "And he sees possibilities.".

ABOUT THE AUTHOR

Sidney Williams writes thrillers and dark fiction and has developed a body of work that includes traditionally published novels from Kensington Books and new works from Crossroad Press and short stories for a variety of magazines and anthologies. Horror great Graham Masterton once said: "Sidney Williams has the ability to conjure the genuine reek of hell."

Sidney teaches creative writing with a focus on horror, mystery and suspense plus short fiction and contemporary fiction.

Sidney's stories have appeared in publications including *Cemetery Dance, Hot Blood: Deadly After Dark, Under the Fang, Quoth the Raven, Cat Ladies of the Apocalypse* and *Love Among the Thorns.*

A native of Louisiana, he now resides in Virginia with his wife, Christine Rutherford.

He loves to hear from people online!

Visit Sidney at https://SidisAlive.com
Facebook: https://facebook.com/SidneyWilliamsBooks
Twitter: @Sidney_Williams

Curious about other Crossroad Press books?
Stop by our site:
http://www.crossroadpress.com
We offer quality writing
in digital, audio, and print formats.